THE SPIRIT IN QUESTION

This Large Print Book carries the
Seal of Approval of N.A.V.H.

A LILA MACLEAN ACADEMIC MYSTERY

THE SPIRIT IN QUESTION

CYNTHIA KUHN

THORNDIKE PRESS
A part of Gale, a Cengage Company

Farmington Hills, Mich • San Francisco • New York • Waterville, Maine
Meriden, Conn • Mason, Ohio • Chicago

GALE
A Cengage Company

LIBRARY OF CONGRESS CIP DATA ON FILE.
CATALOGUING IN PUBLICATION FOR THIS BOOK
IS AVAILABLE FROM THE LIBRARY OF CONGRESS

ISBN-13: 978-1-4328-5998-5 (hardcover)

Published in 2019 by arrangement with Henery Press, LLC

Printed in Mexico
1 2 3 4 5 6 7 23 22 21 20 19

For my family

ACKNOWLEDGMENTS

Heartfelt thanks to . . .

Everyone at Henery Press for your terrific work and general fabulousness! So grateful to have the chance to work with you.

The Hen House, Sisters in Crime, Malice Domestic, Mystery Writers of America, International Thriller Writers, and Rocky Mountain Fiction Writers. Very much appreciate the community and inspiration.

Readers and bloggers who have connected with Lila and/or introduced her around — you are wonderful.

Gretchen Archer, Mary Birk, Becky Clark, Annette Dashofy, Sybil Johnson, Leslie Karst, Julie Mulhern, Gigi Pandian, Keenan Powell, Renée Ruderman, Angela M. Sanders, Meredith Schorr, Craig Svonkin,

Wendy Tyson, Kathleen Valenti, and James Ziskin for assorted kindnesses; Ann Perramond, Mariella Krause, and Dotty Guerrera for thoughtful manuscript readings; and Chicks on the Case — Ellen Byron, Marla Cooper, Vickie Fee, Kellye Garrett, and Lisa Q. Mathews — for sharing wisdom and laughs on the regular.

The Guerreras, Crichtons, Kuhns, Rowes, Peterkas, West-Repperts, Hundertmarks, Abneys, and Welshes — for your amazing support; to Mom, Dad, and Wen for your loveliness and generosity on so many levels; and to Kenneth, Griffin, and Sawyer for absolutely everything, including being your beautiful selves and my sunshine. xoxo

CHAPTER 1

"Commence the murder!" Everything went dark, a shot rang out, and something crashed to the ground.

I held my breath, unable to move.

"No!" the man next to me yelled, disgusted. "The effect's all wrong. Let's reset."

So we reset. For the twelfth time.

I honestly couldn't tell the difference among any of them.

But the director Jean Claude Lestronge could. And that's all that mattered. He was an intimidating man who had achieved a level of celebrity most of us couldn't even imagine—globally recognized for his directing work, both on stage and screen. In many ways, he reminded me of a bear, with his large build and his dark, shaggy hair. Plus, when he was displeased, he roared.

"Are you sure you don't want to let them run through the whole scene?" I ventured. "Maybe we could come back to this later."

9

He turned to me, his thick eyebrows raised almost to the top of his head. "Did I ask for your opinion, Lila?"

"No," I admitted. It was my first time working as a dramatic consultant, but so far, my contributions had been comprised of offering opinions that he ignored and telling him that his own decisions were brilliant.

While the crew scurried about, preparing for our next attempt to perform up to Jean Claude's standards, I gazed around the Stonedale Opera House. Built in 1878, it was definitely showing its age. The ceilings still soared, but the gilded paint on the beams was chipped and the red velvet seats were downright tattered. On either side of a center aisle, the house rows angled sharply toward the wooden stage, which had several candle boxes set into the floor. Electricity was used nowadays — though every time a stagehand turned on the main lights by lifting the large metal lever protruding from the box, sparks shot out.

My thoughts were interrupted by the director's loud voice. He was barking at everyone as he settled on the arm of the chair next to me. The table that had been placed in front of the first row lurched slightly when he slammed his clipboard down on top of it.

"Show me murder!" He thundered as though he were presiding over a gladiator event, and the theater went black again. A shot rang out, this time accompanied by a larger burst of light, and a loud thud was heard.

"Finally," he said. He mumbled something else, but I ignored it. He was always muttering things under his breath. I'd often catch random syllables that I suspected belonged to French swear words — I'd studied the language in school, and one does acquire a certain amount of vocabulary not printed in textbooks but whispered from student to student.

The lights came up, the actors professed surprise, then broke into a rousing chorus of "Once the Body Drops, You've Got a Story."

I watched as they performed the high-energy clog dance, more in unison than they'd appeared the previous week. Jean Claude sat through the entire number without stopping them, which was a first. Maybe he was realizing that it should be cut.

In fact, the whole play should be cut.

It was a disaster, from start to finish.

Puzzled: The Musical was the brainchild of

Tolliver Ingersoll, a Stonedale University professor who once had a play produced off-off-off-off-Broadway and had somehow transformed that success into a tenure-track job at the same school where I taught English. From what I'd heard, the Theater department was less than enthusiastic about his work, but since he was a campus fixture, they had no choice but to every so often allow him to put on one of his plays. The local small theaters were more excited about his writing, as they were made up of younger folks who found his incomprehensible plotlines to be great fun.

This particular show was a misguided blend of just about every mystery trope, character, and author you could imagine. Sherlock Holmes sang a duet with Agatha Christie, femme fatales and hardboiled detectives performed a square dance at another point, and there were murders, thefts, and cons happening left and right while the protagonist was hot on the trail of some MacGuffin. To make matters worse, Tolliver had even named his main character, Oliver Zingerzoll, after himself.

Although I could not make head nor tail of the story, the songs were quite catchy. My particular favorite was "Waiter, I Believe I Ordered the Red Herring," in which all the diners in an elegant restaurant simultaneously leaped from their tables to do a spirited swing dance.

Off to the side of the stage, I could see the playwright scribbling furiously on his script. The first thing Jean Claude had done was to reduce Tolliver's ability to comment throughout the rehearsals. He'd seen to it that Tolliver was set up at a little table in the wings rather than out front with Jean Claude, and that he did not possess one of the headsets used by the crew members. Tolliver was told that they didn't want him to be distracted by the cues as he watched his masterpiece. It was done with such finesse, though, that he appeared to embrace his special seating arrangements.

Finally, the number came to a halt and Jean Claude decided it was time for us to stop. He called out directions to the cast and crew, and I saw more than one look of relief.

As I gathered up my coat, he said, "Do you have time to go over a few things?" By which he meant "listen to me rant about how terrible everything is and take notes because I'm too important to write them down myself."

"Of course." I sat back down and prepared to transcribe onto the script with the pen he handed me.

An hour later, the script ran mad with red ink as if it were bleeding, and my hand was cramped. He had deleted a good fifty minutes from the three-hour play — which was an improvement, in my opinion — and the cast members had their work cut out for them.

After he turned on the so-called "ghost light" left burning at center stage either for safety or paranormal reasons, depending on which tradition you subscribed to, we gathered up our things and chatted as we moved up the aisle into the lobby. When I pushed open the glass door to leave the theater, the sound was overwhelming.

We were walking right into an angry mob.

I stood perfectly still, taking it all in. A white-haired woman was on the highest stone step. She was leading a chant, shouting through a megaphone in one gloved hand and spinning her other arm energetically to encourage the others to join in. Her considerable frame was stuffed into a tailored blue suit topped by a rope of pearls around her neck, and the curved feather on her large hat shook with every gesture as if longing to take flight. Next to her, a round man with a white beard held up his cell phone, videotaping the event. Trade out his golf shirt and khakis for a Santa suit and he could have easily scored a holiday gig at any department store.

There was chanting — it sounded like "Save Old Stone!" — and ten people were marching in a circle in front of the Opera House, waving hand-lettered signs. The protestors seemed to be people of a certain age, not college students. Their signs had slogans like "Heck no, the play must go!" and "You're in OUR house!"

I looked at Jean Claude. His normally ruddy face was even redder, and his bristling eyebrows were drawn together.

"*Mon Dieu.* What is this?" He gestured for me to follow him and walked up to the circle of protesters.

"Excuse me," he said. The words were polite but the tone was gruff.

The marchers didn't stop; in fact, they moved faster.

"LET US THROUGH!" His fierce bellow stopped them in their tracks.

At that, the woman with the megaphone addressed the small crowd. "Look everyone, it's Professor Lestronge. Let's see what he has to say about what's happening here." She stepped down and rushed over to him.

Jean Claude scowled at her. "What is the meaning of this?"

15

"That's what I'd like to know," she said angrily, still speaking through the megaphone. "Why is this play happening?"

He glanced at me, and I lifted my shoulders. No idea what she meant.

"Who are you?" he asked.

"I am Mrs. Clara Worthingham, president of the Stonedale Historical Society, and this is my husband and vice president Mr. Braxton Worthingham —" she gestured to the man who held the phone, then paused as the crowd cheered "— and we are here to preserve our beautiful theater from destruction."

"Destruction?" Jean Claude threw his hands into the air. "We are simply staging a play."

"Exactly. But we are the guardians of this treasured piece of history." Clara put her hand to her breast melodramatically. I wondered if she had had some acting lessons herself at some point. "Like many of the small-town theaters calling themselves 'opera houses' in the 19th century, it has hosted not only opera but all manner of performing acts, everything from Greek tragedy to vaudeville to contemporary drama, featuring both amateur troupes and professional companies. It is a *sacred* site."

The crowd shouted in support.

"You should not be here. You did not ask our permission," she hissed.

The crowd applauded even louder.

She took a step closer until she was within touching distance of Jean Claude and raised the megaphone to speak again.

His hand shot out, and he pushed the megaphone down. Her mouth fell open.

"Please, Madame, it is too loud. Let us speak like human beings." He had taken stock of the situation, apparently; his energy was down about a hundred notches, and he sounded like a fair-minded person. "I don't know what permission is needed from your group. I've never heard of you. The university, who owns this building, scheduled the production."

"The university," she said, drawing herself up, "does not have the right to do that. Productions are not to be staged at this location. We have an agreement."

He nodded. "Again, I don't know about this, but I will call the chancellor. May I have your information to follow up?" He held out the script and handed her the pen that was stuck behind his ear. She refused to take it, but handed him a business card, which he shoved at me. It was good white stock with elegant black lettering that announced her presidency and, beneath that, the words *Etiquette Expert.*

"I appreciate your willingness to listen," she said. "But at this point, we are determined to stop the production of this play altogether."

"What seems to be the problem, exactly?" he asked.

"We've received reports," she said. "About strenuous dancing. And hammering at all hours of the night. The building is fragile."

"We do have dancing, and we do have sets, but they are not hurting anything." He shrugged.

She shook her head. "We're very concerned about the effects to the building. The university has given us the right to approve or deny any production, and you should have applied for permission so that we could determine the potential dangers and make an informed decision."

There was scattered applause in response.

She shook her finger at him. "Professor Lestronge, you must follow the proper channels. Our first priority is to keep our building safe."

He nodded and turned to leave, waving for me to follow.

She lifted the megaphone to her mouth and shouted, "And we must not anger our resident ghost!"

CHAPTER 2

Jean Claude and I hurried across "the green," a lovely expanse of grass around which the campus buildings circled, toward Randsworth Hall. The largest of the bunch, Randsworth presided formidably over campus as did the administrators it housed. It was surrounded by fallen orange and yellow leaves, creating a postcard-perfect autumn scene. As we approached, I pointed out my favorite gargoyles on the roof — one of the more whimsical aspects of Stonedale architecture. He said they were very nice but not in the same league as those at Notre Dame, *bien sûr.*

Fair enough.

Inside, we crossed the polished floors to the elevator that whisked us to the uppermost level. We burst into the office, hoping the chancellor's executive assistant would let us see him, though we knew it was unlikely. One does not simply pop in on the chancellor.

The woman with the steel-gray bun and tweed blazer was new — no one lasted long in that high-pressure position — and the nameplate on her tidy desk identified her as "Pearl Malden." She listened to our pleas without comment, only moving once to set her Montblanc pen carefully down on the brown leather blotter in front of her. When she opened her pinched mouth to refuse us, I placed both of my hands on her desk and looked directly through the thick lenses of her glasses.

"Pearl, could you please at least try to see if he'll speak to us?"

"He's terribly busy, as you can imagine. And it's Friday afternoon," she said primly, as if that were the most precious time of the week. She looked pointedly at her watch.

"Yes, but this is an emergency. We're scheduled to open our play in three weeks, and a crowd of people showed up today to picket us at the Opera House. Please tell him that we'll only take up a minute of his time."

"I'll make the request." Pearl pushed back her rolling chair and slipped inside the doors of the chancellor's inner sanctum.

Jean Claude and I remained where we were. He twisted the script into a roll and tapped his leg with it repeatedly. I contemplated the office, noting the sense of luxury it evoked. The carefully curated art and elegant furniture screamed money, exactly what you'd expect from the office of the most powerful person at this private university.

It wasn't exactly welcoming. Then again, neither was the chancellor.

Jean Claude could also come across as stern and impatient, and there were times that those descriptors certainly fit, but after having spent several months with him, I had seen his generous side. He went out of his way to help students struggling with lines after rehearsal. He regularly brought pastries and coffee for the company. He'd even contributed half of the money for the costumes himself, after swearing me to secrecy, when he learned that our budget was slimmer than the chance of our having a hit on our hands.

The double doors swept open simultaneously, and Chancellor Trawley Wellington strode toward us. He was about the same height as Jean Claude — both were over six feet — but that's where the similarities ended. The director was solid, scruffy, and glowering; the chancellor was trim, neat, and inscrutable.

At least until the chancellor turned toward me and assumed a look I knew well. It was the what-have-you-done-now special. He ran a hand through his silver hair and waited for me to speak.

"Hello Chancellor," I said. "Thank you very much for talking with us. We know you're extremely busy."

My proactive gratitude seemed to counter the presumed audacity of the interruption somewhat; he reduced the severity of his expression, pushed up his glasses and clasped his hands — the very picture of a patient administrator. "Hello, professors. What can I do for you?"

We filled him in on the events over at the Opera House.

"They said that even though the university owns the building, we need to check with them. That can't be right, can it?"

He smoothed his silk paisley tie as he spoke. "Ever since we were given the theater in 1991, they've been insisting that we work with them in their efforts to preserve the place. We finally established a new permissions procedure at their request a while back — it's not a legally binding arrangement, but it offered a good publicity opportunity."

He was big on good publicity, I knew from past experiences.

"We simply agreed to fill out the paper-work they've provided and" — he used air quotes — "*allow* them to give us the green light. It doesn't technically mean anything, and it's been a way to keep our association civil more than anything else. I take it Clara Worthingham was leading things?" He chuckled. "You'll find that she is quite tenacious when she sets her mind to something."

"Was the paperwork not filled out this time? Could we do it now?"

"The Theater department takes care of that in the rare instances we stage something there. We haven't had many performances at the Opera House since we have our own venue on campus. A few I could count on one hand in the past decade perhaps. We were letting the community theater rent it, but their budget dried up — a financial situation urged along, I might add, by the Wor-thinghams."

"What do you mean?" I was getting lost in the details.

"The Historical Society has always been dedicated to preserving the Opera House, but recently, they seem to have upped their game. They didn't want the community theater in the building, is the long and short of it, so they cut off their money."

I must have looked confused because the

chancellor sighed, then began to speak slowly, as if we were small children.

"Clara is distantly related to the mayor of Stonedale, and word is that the Worthinghams pressed him to" — out came the air quotes again — "*redirect,* let us say, the funding that paid for the community theater expenses, beginning with the artistic director. Therefore, in the past five years or so, there have not been any productions staged at the Opera House at all."

Jean Claude and I exchanged glances. I willed him to say something, but he remained silent.

The chancellor addressed Pearl. "Please call the Theater department chair and see what has been done with the paperwork."

As she picked up the phone, he continued. "But if Clara says it wasn't filed, then it wasn't. She has an eagle eye for the process, I can assure you."

"Would you be able to speak with her on our behalf?" I threw that one out there as a Hail Mary pass.

He looked as taken aback as I'd expected him to.

Jean Claude finally spoke up. "Chancellor, I appreciate any assistance you could provide to us. This is a very important, even significant, play —"

I thought that might be an overstatement, but I kept my opinion to myself.

"— and to cancel it at this late date would surely cause problems for many people. Especially the students."

The chancellor smiled at him. "I will take it under advisement. Let's discuss future actions tomorrow night."

Jean Claude's eyebrows shot up. "What is happening tomorrow night?"

Now the chancellor's eyebrows shot up too. In disbelief. "The reception we're hosting in *your* honor?"

Awkward.

I didn't know how Jean Claude could have forgotten. There had been email invitations streaming into Stonedale University inboxes for weeks — faculty members were all abuzz about meeting the famous director in person.

I could hear Pearl saying goodbye to someone on the phone.

We all turned to face her.

She referred to her notepad. "Clara already called him and said that since production has begun without permission, they're going to picket every single day until the play is closed for good."

The chancellor frowned. "Did he say anything else?"

Pearl paused. "Yes. He said he'd send the paperwork over to her, but he didn't know if would make a difference since Clara is," she scanned her notes and winced, "as stubborn as a dandelion in springtime."

The chancellor smoothed his tie again. "That's an accurate assessment."

"Do you think you could call her *now*?" I couldn't help asking.

"I don't think that's going to accomplish anything today." He took a step backwards to signal the end of our discussion.

I remembered Clara's parting words. "One more thing please, Chancellor. Is there anything you can tell us about a ghost at the Opera House?"

He froze, a smile playing over his lips. "Clara brought that up, did she?"

"What is she talking about?"

"It's just an old legend. Pay no mind."

Easier said than done.

As we walked away from Randsworth Hall, Jean Claude vented. First, he raged about the protestors. Then he fumed about the university (a) dropping the ball and (b) acting like their hands were tied and (c) expecting him to show up like a trained monkey and dance for the people.

I wondered where some of that bottled-up

26

fury was when we were speaking to the chancellor. It might have done some good. As a visiting professor, Jean Claude could afford to show his emotions — he was leaving at the end of the semester, after all. I, on the other hand, had a few years to go until I went up for tenure, and I couldn't risk taking on the most important person at the university.

On purpose at least.

Then again, I felt compelled to do whatever was necessary to see that *Puzzled* went forward as planned. The students had worked very hard on the production, and despite my reservations about the script, I wasn't about to let anyone deprive the cast of a chance to perform if I could help it.

Jean Claude kicked at some stray leaves. "Your chancellor means to get his money's worth from my presence."

"I hear you. The reception, at least, is intended to honor you. People are very excited to meet you."

He rolled his eyes. "More performing on demand." After a beat, he went on, somewhat subdued. "I don't mean to sound ungrateful, you understand. The work I'll be doing here will be of genuine value — it's just that although I've been to the library a few times, I haven't been able to immerse myself yet the way I need to."

It must be frustrating to come all the way to America to do specific work and be near the research files you need but unable to get to them because your schedule has been packed solid by the hosting institution. "Will you be able to focus on it after the play closes, I hope?"

"Yes," he said. "And I will simply move in to the library then. Please visit and bring wine. A lot of wine."

I laughed and said I'd do my best.

"By the way, Lila, I'm grateful for the work you've been doing. I'm promoting you to assistant director."

That took me by surprise. He wasn't one to dole out the praise.

"That's very kind of you, but —"

He raised his palm to end any debate. "I insist."

"Thank you." It certainly wouldn't hurt to add a new title to my curriculum vitae.

We passed the fountain at the center of the green, featuring a statue of the university founder Jeremiah Randsworth forever clutching a book in one hand and a rifle in the other. Jean Claude gave the statue a thorough once-over but didn't comment on it.

I touched his arm lightly. "We haven't

talked about the ghost thing yet. What do you think?"

He snorted. "I do not care if there are a hundred ghosts sharing space with us at the theater. I just don't want that Clara woman there ever again."

"Surely we can sort this out with the Historical Society."

"I intend to go forward no matter what. And as long as the ghosts don't have megaphones, they are welcome."

Chapter 3

The party was in full swing when I arrived Saturday night at The Peak House, a popular local brewery, and handed the valet my keys. The best part about driving an ancient Honda was that you didn't have to worry about the parking situation. If it happened to obtain any additional dents, so be it.

There was a sign on the glass door reading *Closed for Special Event. Please Visit Us Again.* Since the chancellor was the owner of the pub, he could do whatever he wanted. He often hosted these sorts of things at his estate, which was the kind of place featured in architectural magazines and tucked away behind high gates, but perhaps he was tired of faculty members running amok in his home. Last time we'd been there, someone had broken an expensive bust.

Not me. Thank goodness.

Inside, I found myself surrounded by people with glasses and plates in hand, chattering in small clumps around the long wooden bar to the left. The restaurant was warm and inviting, heavy on the rustic decor. I waved at Jean Claude, who was encircled by doting fans, and said hello to several colleagues, all of whom raved about the fondue and pointed me toward the source. I made my way through the enormous dining area to the party room, where a table with vats of cheese and chocolate awaited along the back wall. It had been a long day at rehearsal, and first and foremost, I needed sustenance. The variety of fruits and breads available to be dipped were almost overwhelming, in the best possible way.

As I happily picked up a plate, Chancellor Wellington entered the front door and faculty members converged immediately to fawn over him. The cluster of people grew as he crossed the room, though he eventually disentangled himself and took the last spot on an oversized leather banquette nearby. Professors continued to pay tribute, and now that he was closer, I could hear that they were also taking the opportunity to brag about their current projects. I watched from beside the fondue table, wondering if getting tenure required such nimble self-promotional gymnastics.

Finally, the last person in line stepped forward.

"Hello, Chancellor," said Tolliver, extending his hand. He was almost swallowed by the threadbare blazer that dangled helplessly and shapelessly over his extremely thin frame. His white woolen scarf, wound multiple times around his neck and draping down the front, resembled a carefully dispensed but melting stack of soft-serve vanilla. The red-framed glasses perched on his slightly pointed gray head provided the cherry on top. "Tolliver Ingersoll, as you know. Playwright." He exaggerated the last word carefully and leaned closer to the administrator. "I hope you were able to attend the final performance of *A Tale of Three Swords* last spring. It got raves."

The chancellor didn't respond.

"It was tremendous," gushed a middle-aged woman sitting next to the chancellor, who, until that moment, had been deeply engaged in her knitting project. She had long black hair with a thick stripe of white in the front, and she was beautifully dressed in layers of richly colored, delicate materials. "I absolutely adored it," she said in a loud voice to Tolliver.

"This is my lovely companion," Tolliver said proudly.

"Oh, he knows who I am."

The chancellor crossed his arms over his chest and regarded her quizzically.

"Really?" she asked, shaking her head. "You only ruined my life."

His jaw dropped open. "I — I don't —"

"Well, this is very disappointing," she said, starting to knit again. "Something so momentous to me yet so meaningless to you."

Had to admit, I was enjoying the sight of the chancellor squirming. I'd never seen him so uncomfortable before.

"Zandra Delacroix," she said, waving a needle, then pausing — with a barely audible "oops" — to unravel the mauve yarn that had become entangled with the fringe on Tolliver's scarf. "Previously of the Stonedale Theater Department."

He stared at her, his confusion palpable.

She let out an exasperated sigh and yanked the yarn back into her lap. "You didn't give me tenure."

The chancellor appeared to be at a loss for words.

She began to rewind the yarn. "Let me take this opportunity to remind you that there are real people behind those tenure dossiers. You are affecting their lives forever. Don't forget that."

He murmured something that I couldn't hear.

She bowed her head slightly in acknowledgment. "I *will* say, though, that the whole experience — although it was exceedingly painful — did allow me to focus on my gifts, which I'm now using to their fullest."

"That's good to hear —"

"I am a psychic. A medium. A ghost-talker, if you will."

The chancellor did not respond, though it was obvious that the wheels were spinning hard behind that patrician brow. He cleared his throat and returned his attention to Tolliver, trying to regain direction of the situation. "I did attend the play," he said. "It was . . ."

Tolliver leaned forward, ready to soak up additional praise.

"Interesting."

The playwright was almost able to hide his disappointment at the curt review, but not quite. He quickly plastered on a smile. "We're putting together the next one now. It's called *Puzzled: The Musical!*" His hands bracketed the play title in the air as though it were written in lights.

"So I've heard," the chancellor responded, noncommittally. "How's it going?"

Tolliver twisted both hands up in the air,

in a sort of a "ta da" motion.

The chancellor's eyebrows rose.

"It's been quite a thrill to work in the old Opera House," the playwright eventually said. "Quite the thrill indeed. Filled with such history!"

Zandra, knitting away, spoke loudly. "It's going to be a huge success."

The chancellor didn't look so sure.

"I'm not just saying that," she said, putting her knitting needles down and pointing a finger at him. "I *know* it. I can see the future."

Tolliver beamed at Zandra.

After an awkward silence, the chancellor stood up, strenuously brushing off the sleeves of his expensive suit, like he'd just emerged from a plate of crumbs. "Won't you excuse me, please?"

They nodded assent, as if it made a difference, and watched him walk away. Tolliver bent down toward Zandra and the two of them whispered energetically. She stood up and they drifted away together, through the crowd.

After a moment, I realized that the chancellor had reversed course and veered my way. Lacking an exit strategy, I stood up straighter and put down my plate.

"Dr. Maclean," he boomed. "This picketing is a nuisance. I'd like it to be over as soon as possible."

I agreed.

"So I'm counting on you to contact the Historical Society this week to straighten things out. Please take care of it promptly."

"But —"

"That would be best." He sniffed and wished me a good evening, then spun around to go wherever he was going next.

Good talk.

I was reaching for my plate when someone called my name.

"Lila! At last. I was looking all over for you." My fellow Americanist and close friend Nate Clayton appeared at my elbow. His longish brown hair with sun-bestowed highlights was smoothed back into a ponytail above the collar of his navy blazer. He looked more formal than I'd ever seen him. He tended to favor rumpled button-down shirts and khakis for teaching–and more sporty gear for his many outdoorsy pursuits.

Next to him was my petite cousin Calista James, a poet and tenured professor in our department. She wore a long sheath and jacket in a color that matched her smooth platinum blonde bob, accessorized with an intricate hammered-copper necklace and matching earrings. It was sophisticated and perfect for the event.

In contrast, I was still wearing my work clothes — there hadn't been time to stop home after rehearsal — a long black blazer over a white tee and jeans, with boots. My dark hair was gathered into a messy braid, and as I reached back to smooth it, I realized that there was a pencil sticking out. I surreptitiously removed and shoved the pencil into my pocket.

At least I'd be ready to jot something down if necessary.

"Come with us." Nate steered us to the end of the bar in the main room as I cast a longing glance at the fondue table over my shoulder. He took our drink order and transmitted it to the bartender, adding a bottle of Peak House Ale for himself. "I heard about the kerfuffle yesterday," he said, placing some bills on the bar as a tip.

"Already?"

"Faculty pipeline," he said, grinning. "But we want your perspective. Please give us every little detail."

I described the scene for them.

"Why is the play being performed at the Opera House anyway?" Calista arched a perfectly shaped eyebrow. "Don't campus productions usually take place in Brynson Theater?"

"Yes," I said. "And they just put in a high-tech sound system, so it would have been nice. But they're doing additional renovations right now."

"I heard that the remodeling there was *intentional,*" Nate said, in a low voice.

We all leaned forward to confer more quietly.

"Apparently the chancellor got ahold of the script of *Puzzled* and hated it, so he decided that it would not be performed on campus. Hence, the renovation was extended."

"That's not true, Nate," I protested. "Jean Claude said Tolliver requested that it be staged there. He likes the ambiance. The chancellor's renovations were a coincidence."

Nate shrugged. "Just repeating what I heard. And Tolliver may be trying to save face. Ask yourself why a newly renovated theater is being renovated again immediately, that's all I'm saying."

"It's that bad?" Calista asked.

"Rumor has it," he said.

"In some ways, that makes me want to see it even more," said Calista, with a laugh. "What do you think, Lil? You're in the thick of it."

I tried to put it delicately. "It's . . . like

38

nothing I've ever seen before."

The bartender plunked two sodas and a beer in front of Nate. We all took our drinks and waited until he left to continue.

Calista smiled. "I'm excited to see it. You know I love a good musical."

"I can say that there are some delightful songs."

Nate took a sip. "Tell us what you really think."

"What do you mean?" I didn't want to badmouth the show. Nor Tolliver, who, to be fair, might be a genius too advanced for us to understand for all I knew. Just because I found the play illogical didn't mean that critics wouldn't adore it. The likelihood of that was frankly slim, based on previous reviews of his plays, but still, many a literary heavyweight had trouble being celebrated in their own time period. Plus, the students were putting so much effort into it and I wanted to support them.

"You *know* what I mean." He winked and picked up a handful of pretzels from a bowl behind him.

I saw Tolliver and Zandra approaching rapidly. "You'll have to come and decide for yourselves."

"Hello, people," Tolliver said, adding a flourish with his right hand. That was

something he did, punctuate his pronounce-
ments with gestures. He had a regal wave of
greeting, a twist of both wrists to indicate
that we should know what would come
next, and a two-handed flutter above his
head that meant whatever was happening
was more than he could deal with.

We greeted them both.

Zandra stood very close to Tolliver, her
perfume cloaking us in something lush and
unidentifiable. She'd put her knitting into
an embroidered bag slung over one shoulder, but the needles poked out. One was in
danger of penetrating Tolliver's left arm. I
began to say something, but he took a step
toward us and launched into promotional
mode.

"I hope you are all saving the date for the
opening night of *Puzzled.* It's November
first."

They both nodded. Despite, or perhaps
because of, the rumors about the play's
general dreadfulness, our whole department
would likely show up to support our colleague. Tolliver had a certain charisma that
invited observation.

Some people would surely go hoping to
see him fail — *schadenfreude* and all that.
But there would be support of the arts, at
least as far as the community was con-

cerned, indicated by the attendance of the university faculty. The chancellor included. No matter what his personal feelings were about the quality of an event, he never missed a public relations opportunity.

"It is, and I say this with utmost humility, my best work yet." Tolliver bowed his head for a moment to demonstrate said humility.

"Looking forward to it," Nate said, enthusiastically.

"Me too," Calista smiled brightly at the playwright.

"I'll look forward to your detailed reviews," Tolliver said, tapping his chin thoughtfully. "Can't wait to hear what you think."

They both appeared slightly less excited at that prospect.

After the chancellor had demanded everyone's attention and thoroughly toasted Jean Claude, who appeared miserable to be in the spotlight, we felt as though we could leave. When I came through the front door toward the valet station, ticket in hand, Tolliver was already in front of his car, patting his pockets. He smiled sheepishly. "Can't find my keys. I swear the valet just handed them to me a minute ago."

"Do you need some help looking?" I

began scanning the ground around us.

Zandra swooped in, dangling some keys. "Here they are, hon. They fell into my bag." She said "my bag" as though it were the center of the universe: capital M, capital B. After she delivered the keys, she gave me a little wave, climbed into the passenger side of the car, and resumed her knitting.

"Lila, I'm so grateful for your help on *Puzzled.* We haven't had much of a chance to speak, but I wanted to let you know that your assistance is much appreciated. How do you think rehearsals are going?"

"Well," I began, stalling for time. I drew it out as far as I could, then had to commit to additional words, so I opted for something safe. "I think they're going fine."

In the light of the street lamp, I could see that he was pursing his lips. "Could you be a bit more specific?"

"The cast seems to be working hard, and the set choices are inspired." I was trying to avoid the main subject.

"But as our industrious dramaturg, do you think we are doing justice to the script?"

There it was. Honestly, I thought they'd done an incredible job making anything at all out of the script. It was almost unreadable, with stage directions that went on for pages and pages, insistently rendered in a bossy tone that made it one of the least enjoyable scripts I'd ever read. There were confusing scenes, with characters whose motivations were unclear at best and contradictory at worst, and the dialogue was incomprehensible. The best parts were the musical numbers — mostly because the songs were fun and the dancing, thanks to a talented choreographer, was wholly engaging.

"Yes," I said.

He blinked rapidly.

"I'm not sure that Jean Claude understands my vision," he said, using his scarf to clean his glasses before resettling them onto his head.

"What do you mean?"

"There are many *nuances* that he appears to be ignoring. He pays so much attention to the timing and technologies that he is simply missing the heart of the play." He paused, looking up in the air like he was accessing an invisible script. "And I can't say that I care for the way he fails to consult with me. I mean, I'm the playwright! Everything comes from my creative mind. I have much to contribute."

"I understand. Do you want me to talk to —"

"Oh no, no. Don't mention it." He put

both hands up in front of him, as if stopping traffic. "You know, I think I just needed to say it out loud."

"Say what?"

"You do know that Jean Claude has a bit of a reputation, don't you?"

"A reputation?" I repeated. "For what?"

"Oh, you don't know. Never mind then." He waved away whatever he'd been broaching.

"Is there something I should know?" His vagueness was disconcerting.

"No, but thank you for listening, Lila. You've been very helpful indeed."

I didn't know how in the world I could have been helpful in any way.

"Good night, Petal," he said over his shoulder as he walked around his car. He often called me that. I'd been wearing a silver daisy pendant the day we'd met, and it had stuck, apparently.

He tucked himself inside the driver's side and turned on the engine.

"Good night," I said, wondering what he clearly wanted to tell me but hadn't.

CHAPTER 4

Monday after office hours, I left for rehearsal. From campus, it was a short walk to the west on University Boulevard. I admired the mountains as I strolled down the busy street; on a sunny fall day like this, only the highest peaks were white, but we'd be getting the cold soon enough. Typically our first snowstorm blew in around Halloween. Until then, though, I would make the most of my favorite season. The leaves were crunching satisfactorily underfoot, and the trees along the street offered a stunning array of colors ranging from bright yellow to deepest red.

Although I was able to lose myself in the scenery, by the time I reached the Opera House, I felt a wisp of apprehension at the sight of protestors chanting and waving their signs. I skirted the circle and hurried into the lobby, only to run smack dab into the Worthinghams. Clara, in a bright lilac suit, waved her arms as if conducting an invisible orchestra. The knot of the flowered silk scarf around her neck was drifting slowly toward the back in response to her gesticulations.

Braxton was listening and nodding. "There, there, dear," he said, as I drew close. A red cashmere sweater was draped over his button-down shirt, striking a cheerful note.

"Excuse me," I said, hoping to pass them without incident.

Clara broke off her rant and whirled around. She closed her eyes for a moment, perhaps hoping that when she opened them, I'd be gone.

"Good afternoon, Mr. and Ms. Worthingham," I said.

"I prefer *Mrs.*," she sniffed. "Nothing wrong with tradition."

"Mrs. Worthingham, then. Is everything okay?"

"No," she said. "It most decidedly is not." She repositioned a white tendril into the bun at the back of her head and patted it, glaring at me all the while.

"What's happening?"

"If you must know," she looked down her nose at me, "someone broke into the Historical Society this weekend for the second

46

time this fall."

"Oh no. I'm sorry. Is everyone okay?"

Braxton, standing behind Clara, nodded reassuringly. He was rocking back and forth on his heels a little bit.

"We are physically fine," she said. "But it's extremely emotional, you know, to be violated in this way. And they have stolen very precious things."

"What did they take?"

"This time, it was my favorite pistol. It belonged to my grandmother. It's exquisite — silver with a pink pearl handle — and I am utterly heartbroken."

"I'm sorry," I repeated.

She looked down at her hands and turned the palms face up, as if she were reading a book. "The first time, which was a number of weeks ago, they took Althea's journal. You do know who Althea Gaines is, yes?"

"No, I'm sorry."

Clara's lips curled up with satisfaction at knowing something I didn't. "How about Malcolm Gaines? Do you know who he is?"

I shook my head.

"They used to *own* this theater." She waved an arm at the lobby wall covered with framed pictures and newspaper clippings. "Perhaps you should make a point of taking in your surroundings a bit more." With an air of indignation, she continued. "Suffice it to say that Althea's journal is absolutely priceless."

"Maybe someone stole it not knowing what it was?"

"That's highly unlikely, don't you think?" I persisted. "Had you photocopied it?"

"Perish the thought! We would never expose those pages to technology and risk harming them. Plus, it was intimate and detailed, not for public consumption."

"Who would have known about it?"

"Why are you so interested?" Her eyes narrowed.

"No reason. I'm just curious. But I'm very sorry that this happened. Have you called the police?"

"Of course. I'm not a child, you know." She turned sideways and gave Braxton a can-you-believe-the-nerve-of-this-one look.

Which I saw.

Which she meant me to see.

"We had to go through the same exact ri-gamarole again. The same paperwork. The same questions."

"Well, I'm sure the procedures are —"

"Oh, please. You *cannot* understand what we've been through. Plus, that horrible Professor Lestronge just kicked us out!" Her face was bright pink, and her frosted lips trembled. "Can you believe that?"

"What happened?"

"We just came here to see if he would listen to reason," she said. "But no, he wouldn't have it. He said we were encroaching —" She spun back to Braxton and repeated the word indignantly. "Encroaching!"

He patted her arm.

"On what?" I asked.

"His rehearsal time. The very thing we were trying to address." She pulled a tissue out of her handbag and dabbed her eyes, even though they weren't full of tears that I could see. "All we are trying to do is keep our Stonedale history intact. If we didn't do it, no one would."

Braxton smiled at his wife. He seemed fascinated by every word that came out of her mouth.

"Oscar Wilde tread these boards," she added indignantly. "You're an English professor, so I expect that you know who *he* is."

"Yes," I said, finally earning a point in the Do You Know Who They Are pop quiz. "How wonderful."

"It was part of his Colorado tour," she said, her voice growing stronger. She yanked her scarf back into place. "And a very famous event."

I glanced at my watch and noted that I was running late. I took a step backwards but Clara forged ahead.

"And he's not the only one. The composer John Philip Sousa was here too. You know who *he* is, I hope?"

"I do." Behind the Worthinghams, the door to the theater opened slowly. Jean Claude popped his head out, saw us, and shrank back with an expression of horror. "But I hope you'll excuse me. I need to get to rehearsal." I edged away. "Perhaps you could come back another time?"

She sniffed dramatically. Braxton automatically patted her arm again. He seemed highly capable of handling her emotional pirouettes.

I smiled at her. "The main thing is that we don't want to be at odds with you or the Historical Society in general. So if we need to have a conversation about that, let's do so sooner rather than later. Have you received the paperwork from the Theater department?"

Braxton nodded enthusiastically behind her. Clara paused and looked up at the ceiling. "Let me think," she said, apparently unwilling to confirm that we'd done what we were supposed to do. "I may have seen something. I'll have to go back and review my mail." She crinkled the tissue up and slipped it into her sleeve, just like my grandmother used to do.

"Thank you," I said. "Maybe that will give us a place to start. How about if I check in with you later?"

Braxton winked at me from behind her shoulder.

"I suppose. You probably need to be going. Don't let us stop you," she said abruptly.

I'd been dismissed.

Slipping past them and through the door, I moved down the aisle. The cast was in the middle of rehearsing "No Body Blues," which was a slow dance number, so I tried to keep it quiet.

Jean Claude was up front in our usual row. There was a table before him with a small gooseneck light angled toward his script, though he was talking on his phone instead of reading. The words were indistinguishable, but the tone was unmistakable: he was pleading with someone. I slowed down, not wanting to intrude on him, and noticed a figure in a black suit, his long arms hanging down awkwardly like Dr. Frankenstein's monster, watching the dancers intently from his position near the exit door.

After Jean Claude hung up, I moved into the row and took the seat next to him.

"Who's that guy?" I asked quietly, as I fumbled through my satchel for the script.

"What guy?" He sounded distracted.

"Over there." I snapped my head up and started to point, but the figure had vanished.

"Never mind." I returned my attention to my bag and dug around until I found a pen.

"I saw the Worthinghams outside." He scowled. "I thought I'd told them to take their — how do you say? — hats and shove them."

"They're leaving now."

"Good. I don't have time to deal with that nonsense. Let the university handle it."

"But the chancellor told me to work it out with them."

He made a sound of annoyance. "There is nothing to work out. We are here and they can't do anything about it. I told Madame she needed to accept that fact."

Oops. I'd already volunteered a conversation. "Would you mind if I tried to talk to them myself?"

His hand shot up in a swift dismissal. "Your choice, my friend. I don't want to have anything to do with those people."

Suddenly, a loud metal screech could be heard, and Jean Claude looked up. "What was that?"

A crew member ran out from the wings, skirted the dancers, and scuttled up to the director. "One of the wall brackets on the catwalk came off," he said, hastily adding a "sir," after catching sight of Jean Claude's face.

"What? Is everyone safe?"

"Yes."

"Was anyone on it?"

"No."

"How did that happen?"

"Um . . ."

"I'm not blaming you," Jean Claude said to the student, whose shoulders relaxed. "These things happen, okay? You will show me and we will fix it."

He stood up. "Take ten, actors," he yelled. "Crew, set up the party scene." To me, he said, "I may need to stay backstage to keep an eye on the catwalk if we can't repair it right away. If I'm not back in ten, please run through the party scene for me."

"Will do."

He winked at me and turned to the tech crew member. "Lead the way."

While I waited, I pulled out my phone and did an internet search for the Stonedale Historical Society. They had a website that described several locations they'd "preserved from destruction," to use their description. I clicked on the *About Us* link, which listed Clara and Braxton as president and vice president of the Historical Society. The secretary was someone named Bella Worthingham. The rest of the membership was not listed, which made it appear that the Historical Society was pretty much run by Worthinghams.

On the *Current Projects* page, there was a long, angry rant disparaging the perform-ance of *Puzzled* at the Stonedale Opera House. I skimmed it quickly. The gist was that we were going to destroy the most historical of all historical sites in Stonedale and that we must be stopped. I sighed. If the chancellor wouldn't call and the paper-work hadn't made a difference, I would have to confront Clara and Braxton Worthing-ham in their offices. I couldn't see a way around it.

After ten minutes had passed and Jean Claude hadn't returned, I called out for everyone to get in their places so we could run through the party scene. Picking up the headset, I pressed the button that connected backstage and confirmed that the crew was ready.

"Standby for party scene." Everyone positioned themselves and the stage man-

54

ager took over giving the cues. The lights came up, and the partygoers entered from both wings, talking quietly amongst themselves. After the main character, Oliver, had given his short speech about there being "a murderer among us," we hit the part of the scene that Jean Claude had been so adamant about getting right the other day. The lights went down, a shot rang out, a bright flash appeared, and there was a thud. It seemed different than last time, though I couldn't have said exactly how. Jean Claude wasn't going to like that.

Or maybe he would. You never knew with him.

When the lights came back up, Parker Lane, the student playing Oliver, took two steps upstage toward the fake fireplace where he was supposed to kick off the song, but instead he froze, pointed, and screamed.

"That's powerful acting, but — that's not in the script, is it?" I said, flipping pages in confusion.

He pointed and screamed again, then the actor playing the victim on the couch sat up, squinted into the wings, and started yelling too.

It wasn't great acting — it was genuine fear.

The whole cast was screaming as I ran up

the side steps onto the stage and into the wings, where Jean Claude lay, his eyes staring blankly at the ceiling. There was a round hole in his forehead. I yelled for someone to call 911. He didn't seem to be breathing and I couldn't find a pulse, but I administered CPR for what felt like centuries.

CHAPTER 5

Detective Lexington Archer arrived just minutes after the 911 call had been made. He'd quickly taken charge of the scene, moving the actors off the stage and into the audience seats, instructing them to stay put until the police could talk to them.

I'd begun to shake when the paramedics had taken over the CPR. Despite their efforts, it became clear that Jean Claude was gone.

The coroner arrived not long after.

Lex had brought me backstage, where I'd cried into his fleece vest for a while, then got ahold of myself. I hoped the students hadn't seen the tears, but if they had, well, it's normal to have emotions when your friend is killed.

Now Lex and I were sitting on the front of the stage, dangling our legs over the side while I drank the unpleasantly warm and overly sweet soda he'd handed me. This was a little awkward, to say the least. I hadn't seen him in over a year, and the first time we ran into each other, I shook and bawled all over him.

I snuck a long glance at the detective. Same dark hair, same muscular build, same type of dark suit. He still emanated that blend of purpose and focus that I remembered too.

He gave me an appraising look. "Feeling better?"

I turned my head and met his striking blue eyes. "A little steadier, thanks. I can't believe this is happening. How did you get here so fast?"

"I happened to be nearby."

That was lucky for us.

"So what happened?" He flipped open the black cover of his notepad. "You'll fill out an official statement later, but if you could give me a quick overview right now, something to get started, I'd really appreciate it."

"Jean Claude went backstage —" My eyes filled with tears again at the thought of him. I wiped them away and took a few deep breaths.

Lex waited patiently until I was composed. "Any particular reason he went backstage?"

"One of the tech crew came out and told him there was a problem. Something on the catwalk had broken or come loose or . . . I don't know exactly. He said he might need to remain backstage and that I should run the next scene if he wasn't back in ten. He wasn't, so I did."

Lex made notes, waving me on when I stopped talking.

"And then the scene happened. When the lights come up after the shot —"

"The shot?"

"In the show. It's a murder scene." As I heard myself say it out loud, I stopped and swallowed hard, fighting off the shakes that threatened to return.

"Take your time," Lex said, patting my arm.

After a minute, I tried again. "When the lights come up, the main character is supposed to find the victim." I paused. "The actor *playing* the victim, I mean, on the couch."

Lex nodded.

"But instead, he screamed. A real scream, not an acting scream. Then the actor on the couch screamed too. Then everyone started screaming. I ran into the wings, saw that it was Jean Claude and tried to give him CPR. Then the paramedics came."

"You didn't see him fall after the shot?"

"He was off to the side, so no. Plus, it's

pitch black. Intentionally, for dramatic effect."

"Hear anything unusual?"

"The shot sounded different. There was more of an echo or something."

He dipped his head in acknowledgment.

"And the thud sounded louder —" I froze. "That must have been his, uh, body."

The room seemed to sway a little.

He patted my arm again. "Keep drinking your soda. The sugar will help with the shock."

I took another sip of the syrupy liquid and shuddered.

"You're doing fine. One last thing: did you notice anything strange about the muzzle fire?"

"The flash? Yes. It seemed split somehow. Do you think the prop gun malfunctioned? We use a special revolver that can only fire blanks, though, so I don't know how anything could have hit Jean Claude."

Lex lifted his shoulders while jotting things down. "I can't confirm anything."

A horrible thought struck me. "Wait, you don't think the prop master —" I twisted around to see officers talking to the red-haired young man who was openly sobbing. "Sam would never hurt a soul. He's very sweet. Anyway, he was stage right, in the wings, next to the prop table." I gasped and grabbed his forearm. "There must have been someone on the opposite side *with* Jean Claude, or the actors on the stage would have been in the way. And there must have been two shots at once — from the prop gun and a real one. That's why the flash seemed split. Have you —"

"We're on top of things, Lila."

My words came out in a rush. "You should talk to the Worthinghams. Clara just told me that her pistol has been stolen. That's suspicious, don't you think? We should go see if she's still here and ask her more about that. I'll help you find her." I put my arms down to use as leverage in jumping off the stage.

He put his hand out horizontally to stop me, as if we were in a car and he was braking hard. "Please. Just stay right there. We're aware of the burglary and will perform the necessary tests to see what we're dealing with."

I stared out into the people scattered among the theater seats waiting to give their statements, wondering if the murderer was sitting there right at that very moment, trying to look innocent. The idea was nauseating.

"Anything else you can tell me? Did

anything unusual happen today?"

"What do you mean?"

"Anything out of place?"

I closed my eyes for a moment. "Oh! There was someone here during rehearsal. I didn't recognize him."

"What was he doing?"

"Just standing there. Looking at the stage. But he left minutes after I arrived."

I gave Lex the best description of the man that I could.

He slid down from the stage so that he was standing on the floor. "Thank you for talking to me, Lila. One of the other officers will take your official statement, then you'll be free to go." He closed the notebook and gave me a small smile before striding off to speak with his colleagues.

That exchange had been more formal than I would have hoped, but he was on the job, after all. I waited there until everyone had been interviewed, and the police informed us that we couldn't return to the Opera House until we were notified otherwise.

The chancellor emailed that evening. First, he acknowledged that there had been a tragedy and provided information about counseling that was available on campus. Second, he asked for our input in how to proceed. He invited all of us — students and faculty — to let him know whether we wanted to cancel the show in order to preserve a safe environment (*implied: because there is danger*) or, given the amount of time and effort we'd already put into the production, if we wanted to continue (*implied: then the danger will be on you and not on the university*).

Although I knew the chancellor was doing his job, he hadn't even mentioned Jean Claude by name. Quickly, I hit reply-all to the email, inviting everyone to gather in honor of the director on Wednesday night, specific details to follow.

I had to do *something* for our friend.

The entire company showed up at Silver's, a restaurant near campus. The lovely rock wall surrounding the patio provided a sense of privacy, but the arched windows built into the upper half created a sense of openness. Several tower heaters made for a cozy environment despite the chill in the air. The students completely filled the tables and chairs dotted around the space; they were conversing quietly.

Upon their arrival, Tolliver and Zandra came directly toward me. Both were clad completely in black, as were most of us.

"Thank you for organizing this, Petal." Tolliver took both of my hands and squeezed them gently. "You have such a kind heart."

I blushed. "Thank you for coming."

"There is one little thing I wanted to ask," Tolliver said, lowering his voice. "Have the students said anything about whether they'd like to . . . ah . . . soldier on?"

"You mean with the play? No."

"Now they *don't* want to continue?" His face fell.

Zandra put her arm around him.

"No, I mean, I haven't heard anything from them."

He lit up. "Oh, perfect. Just wanted to make sure the current was still flowing in one direction."

"We can talk about that later," Zandra murmured. "Let's go find a seat." As she pulled him away, she mouthed "Sorry" to me.

After a second, I followed them.

"What do you mean about the current, exactly?"

Tolliver and Zandra exchanged glances.

He bent his head toward me. "The student emails to the chancellor were unanimous. They want to go forward. He thinks that since it's my play, I should be the one to direct. I was supposed to send out a notification tonight — but would you mind if I made an announcement near the end?"

"That's a good idea. But let's focus on Jean Claude first?"

"Of course." He bowed his head.

I crossed the room to the rock fence and waved my hands to get the students' attention. They fell silent almost immediately.

"Thank you so much for coming. I know this has been a difficult week for everyone. Jean Claude will be very much missed. Although he was a visiting professor, he had definitely become a part of our Stonedale University family."

Their grief-stricken expressions tugged at my heart. Red-rimmed eyes met mine. We'd all been mourning, it was clear.

I pulled out a page that I'd written earlier, describing his accomplishments both personal and professional. When I was done reading, there were tears all around the room. I invited everyone to share their own stories, and for the next hour, the cast and crew related their heartfelt memories. Anecdotes tumbled out, one after the other. We laughed, we cried, and we celebrated the life of Jean Claude Lestronge.

When things began to wind down, Tolliver dabbed at his eyes with his fingertips delicately, then raised his hand. "I've spoken to the chancellor, and thanks to your support, he agrees that we should not cancel the production at this point. We're so close to opening night, and we've all put a tremendous amount of work into this. I'll be taking over the directing, and you may bring any questions to me. Rehearsals resume Friday."

The students smiled at each other.

"If Jean Claude were here, he would indeed tell us to get back to work." I pointed to the opposite wall, where servers were setting up a buffet that I'd arranged for the company. "Help yourself to some food and drink in the meantime."

Tolliver came over and beamed at me. "Very well done, Petal. And I wanted to say that I hope there are no hard feelings."

"What do you mean?"

"You're the assistant director. It would have made sense for you to take over as director after Jean Claude's . . . after."

I shook my head. "The thought never entered my mind, Tolliver. You're the right choice."

"Ah, good. Of course it would have been fabulous if the chancellor picked you." He smiled brightly, then rushed ahead. "But it's all been settled. I will lead us forward.

The show" — he performed his signature hand flourish — "must go on."

CHAPTER 6

On Friday, the students were gathered in the lobby of the Opera House. I overheard one of them sounding worried about today being Friday the thirteenth as the door swung open and the playwright swept inside, trailed by Zandra.

"Helloooooo, everyone," he said cheerily, tossing his yellow scarf over one shoulder. He walked to the box office and clapped his hands to get our attention. Then he spoke more slowly, presumably remembering the context. "I pray that the days since our last rehearsal have been gentle to you. Please remember that Jean Claude would have wanted us to go on. Let's have a moment of silence in his memory."

He looked down at the ground, and we all followed suit. I tried to be unobtrusive about wiping away the tears that welled up immediately. I heard a few sniffs from others in the group too.

After a minute, Tolliver resumed his speech. "I have been thinking long and hard about the current state of the play, and I took the liberty of making some small changes."

He nodded at Zandra, who began handing out new scripts. They'd been busy this week.

"I trust that you'll be able to process them quickly. After all, we are professionals here, are we not?"

The students looked uneasily at each other, and there were some murmurs, but no outright rebellion. Truth was, they weren't professionals yet. They were still in school. But if that's how Tolliver wanted them to see themselves, they seemed willing to rise to the occasion.

"Lila, I'll need to conference with you before we begin today. Everyone else, please take the next hour to read over the scripts, learn your new lines, and so on. Tech crew, please discuss any adjustments that will need to be made. I'll come backstage for a meeting in a bit. Is everyone clear on their assignments? Any questions?" He scanned the group. "No? Good. Then go, my ducklings. Daddy's got work to do."

People scooped up their things, took the pages from Zandra, and began to move away from the gathering.

Tolliver beckoned me over. I stepped closer as requested.

He lowered his voice. "I know that may have been a bit . . . bright in tone," he confided. "I'm devastated about Jean Claude — we all are — but the silver lining may be that we can get this production back on track to fulfilling my artistic vision. And I will lean on you as assistant director, I will. You will need to be both strong and bold." He stared into my eyes. "Are you ready?"

"Yes," I said, fighting the sense that he was about to bestow knighthood upon me.

"Very well then," he said. "My first order of business is to ensure that the cuts are reinstated. Please read through the changes carefully and I'll meet you down front in a moment."

I took the pages that Zandra was holding out and went into the theater to sit in our usual spot. Tolliver had added back in everything that Jean Claude had removed, including two musical numbers and a very long stream-of-consciousness monologue where the main character covers the entire history of the mystery genre for the audience.

As Tolliver careened down the aisle, I

called him over. "May I ask you a quick question?"

"Of course. Proceed."

"Are you sure about the monologue? It seems a little . . ."

He waited, practically twitching. "A little what?"

"It slows the action down quite a bit."

His eyebrows drew together, but he didn't say anything.

"I mean, the pacing is superb everywhere else," I mentally crossed my fingers behind my back as I stretched the truth a tad. "And this brings things to a standstill."

"That's precisely the point, dear. It's intended to contrast the enthusiastic tension that characterizes the rest of the play. Give the audience some time to reflect."

I wasn't so sure audiences *wanted* time to reflect built into their play-watching experience for them.

Tolliver launched forward. "You're a literature person and not a drama person, Lila, but there's something that has to be sensed about the three-dimensional experience that only comes with years of training, as I have."

I counted to ten. Well, five.

"Let's come back to this after the rehearsal, Tolliver? Once we have a chance to see it in action."

He seemed satisfied, if still slightly annoyed that I'd dared to ask in the first place, and he went off to talk to the tech crew.

It was true that I didn't have years of training in theater. But I'd taught many plays and I had been to many plays, and I had never encountered anything as dreadful as that monologue. It wasn't even on the amusing side of ridiculous, like the rest of *Puzzled* had potential to be. It was straight up deadly boring and went on forever.

I had to say something. They'd hired me to consult, after all; certainly offering an occasional strong opinion was warranted, right?

I straightened my shoulders with new resolution and returned to the script, recognizing a twinge of empathy for the students, who not only had to deal with their feelings about having seen the tragic death of their director but also had to reinstate lines they'd long abandoned. We'd been off book for weeks. It was a tall order.

The empty seat next to me triggered a fresh wave of sadness about Jean Claude. It was as though he'd simply disappeared. Someone with that much passion for life. Here one day, gone the next.

And none of us knew who had shot him.

Which reminded me: here we were, back again in the same place, with the same people. One of whom might be responsible for murdering him.

Who could have done it? I studied the faces of the cast members, seeking an outward sign, but no one looked overtly guilty.

The base of my spine tingled. In college, a psychic my friends and I once visited on a lark had claimed that the sensation was the spirits' way of telling me to pay attention. I'd laughed about it back then, but ever since, I had indeed paid a little more attention when it happened.

I took another look around. Everyone was acting like they usually did, if a bit subdued.

It was unnerving to be here, but I wasn't sure what the alternative was, if anything. We either had to stop the production altogether — and deprive the students of performing — or go forward warily.

The good news was that we had two police officers joining us for a week, at the chancellor's request. I appreciated that the chancellor wanted to make the students feel safer as we eased back into the production.

Or maybe it was an insurance thing.

The sooner we got through this mess, the better.

A thought struck me, and I made my way up the stairs, stage left, to the spot where Jean Claude had lain. There was no discoloration on the floor to mark it, but he'd been behind the second leg, the vertical black curtain intended to obscure any view of the wings from the audience.

I glanced around uneasily, realizing that it might look strange for me to be standing there. But the actors were running lines or chatting with one another, and no one paid any attention.

After walking in a semi-circle around the spot, I closed my eyes to summon up the memory of the last time I'd seen him here. I braced myself for the inevitable wave of grief, then concentrated hard on the image. He'd fallen with his head toward the stage, which suggested that the shot had come from deep in the wings.

I moved quickly to the wall and turned around, studying the stage. If someone had shot him from here, the only possible exits were down the steps into the house seats or through the backstage area. In either case, during rehearsal, there were actors and tech crew members in both places.

How had someone walked right through the middle of everything — with a gun, no less — without anyone seeing them?

Parker stood center stage, deep in his performance as Oliver. A short and somewhat pale young man, he had a long face and high eyebrows that granted him an air of perpetual surprise. He wore a trench coat and Sherlock Holmes-style cap; in his hand was an unlit pipe, which he waved around for emphasis at certain points. He had made it through half of the monologue and was easing into celebration of the Golden Age. The rest of the company had found seats and most of them were staring at their cell phones.

I didn't blame them. I was squirming in my seat myself. The monologue was just too long.

Tolliver, however, stood watching in delight, mouthing the words along with Oliver. His hands were clasped in front of him.

I stared at the actor, trying to absorb the words, but my mind kept wandering to the grading I had waiting for me after this. I was teaching Mystery this term, along with an American Literature survey, and I was thrilled that the course was being offered concurrently. A number of my mystery students had volunteered to help out with the play, and Tolliver had put them onto the publicity team. They'd been very inventive about blasting updates and memes via social media and were generating a helpful buzz about the play on campus.

I turned on my phone, angling the screen away from Tolliver so it wouldn't bother him. Glancing over, I confirmed that he was still transfixed by the endless recitation and not even aware of what I was doing.

The Instagram account had action shots of various musical numbers and seemed to be garnering a steady stream of likes. I opened Twitter next and saw that there was a respectful acknowledgment and expression of sadness about Jean Claude's passing. Someone had retweeted it, and I clicked to see, more out of a desire for something to do until the monologue ended than anything else. It went to the Stonedale Historical Society account, with the words "One obstacle down."

Oh no. My throat clenched.

That was beyond unacceptable. Now I was definitely going to pay them a visit. I pulled up their website to find their office hours and saw a new post on their blog.

"Protest Successful!" was the headline. Below, it detailed how they'd arrived "en masse" at the Opera House and "made our case in no uncertain terms." There were descriptions of the various contributions of Clara, Braxton, and the "committed and single-minded" crowd members, along with claims about how they were making it difficult for us to "continue the destruction of our beloved building." Basically, they wrote a battle story, and we were positioned as the bad guys.

My face heated up. I was more than a little bothered by the tone of the piece, which sounded like Clara all the way. They made it seem as though we were doing something harmful to the Opera House, when in fact we were honoring its original purpose: to provide entertainment.

Suddenly, the members of the company gasped all around me, almost as one. I looked up to see Parker in a heap on the floor of the stage.

CHAPTER 7

Turned out that the wool trench coat and cap, combined with the heat of the spotlight and the length of the speech, overheated our leading man. After a brief rest, some cold water, and vigorous fanning by friends holding scripts, Parker was back to himself again.

It was the end of rehearsal, though, and Tolliver called it a day. The students began to leave.

"Wow," I said to Tolliver as I packed my satchel. "That was something. What should we do? Change the costume? Alter the lights? Streamline the —"

He frowned. "I suppose you'd like to shorten the scene."

"That would be better for Parker, probably," I agreed.

"But," he said, shoving the script into his bag, "the whole point is to focus the audience's attention on the magnificent traditions of the genre. I'm not sure that scrapping it is the answer."

"I wonder," I said gently, "if we might include the monologue in the program instead of in the play?"

He pursed his lips. "Continue," he said, circling his hand gracefully.

"It might serve as a helpful guide to audience members, especially those who are not as familiar with the history of the mystery as you are?"

He straightened his shoulders and sniffed. "Yes, I suppose that would be useful. It would be a shame to lose such a masterful speech completely."

I held my breath. The play was a thousand times better without it.

"And this way they could carefully read it." He pushed his glasses further up on his nose.

"And re-read it."

"They could savor every word, you mean?" He tapped his chin and looked up at the ceiling, presumably imagining all of the savoring.

"As much as they wanted to, yes."

Finally, he clapped his hands and rubbed them together briskly. "Let's do that." He started to walk away, then turned back to face me. "You know, Lila, I wasn't sure about having a consultant around. Especially one more entrenched in the written word than in the stage world —"

I managed not to take offense to that. Again.

"— but now I'm starting to think that you're earning your keep."

"Thank you." Then it occurred to me: Jean Claude had been the one who hired me. It wasn't much of a stipend to begin with, but in any case, he wouldn't be paying me anymore.

Tolliver must have realized the same thing. "Was Jean Claude footing the bill for your assistance?"

"Yes. So if you don't want me to continue, I'll understand." For a split second, the promise of time gained danced before my eyes. But then I remembered the students and felt guilty for even thinking of walking away.

"No, no. We need you. It's only another two weeks. Do you think you could manage it pro bono?"

"Absolutely."

He beamed at me. "I knew you wouldn't want to miss out on being a part of my masterpiece."

Sure. That's what I meant.

■ ■ ■ ■

The Stonedale Historical Society was located a few blocks away. After elbowing through the protestors who had showed up while we were rehearsing — a much smaller group today, perhaps in deference to Jean Claude — I strolled along the sidewalk of University Boulevard, past the little shops mixed in among the restaurants and bars. Students had access to pretty much everything within walking distance, from vintage clothes and used books to computer services and cell phones. Stonedale was fond of its small-town ambiance and had worked hard to cultivate its appeal by adding streetlamps, statues, and fountains everywhere you looked. The citizens made sure the big box stores were relegated to the outer edges of town. No doubt led by vocal opponents such as the Historical Society members.

On the way, the cool breeze whipped my hair around. I made a valiant attempt to braid it as I walked, musing over what I already knew about the society. One, they liked to be in control. Two, they seemed to be presided over by Clara and Braxton. Three, they knew how to organize and even if it was just a small crowd, it could still make a fuss.

Clara seemed like the kind of woman who longed to be recognized as alpha and didn't let anyone else's opinion make a dent in her plans. It was pointless to argue with those kind of folks — they were so convinced of their own rightness that all it did was make you crazy.

The Historical Society was a brick cottage surrounded by a white picket fence. A garden took up the space between the road and the house, with neatly trimmed bushes and small trees. It was probably a riot of color in the spring and summer, but this late in the fall, only one red plant still had blossoms. The whole thing had an air of welcome, though I didn't anticipate feeling welcomed inside.

I went through the gate and up the steps, then rang the doorbell located to the left of the arched wooden door, next to a sign that said *Please Let Us Know You're Here.* It played a few melodious trills, and the door was answered by a slender young woman with large brown eyes and long, caramel-colored hair. She opened the door slightly, so that I was theoretically invited in but couldn't squeeze through unless I pushed her out of the way.

I didn't, of course.

"I'm Lila Maclean from Stonedale University," I said. "English professor."

"Bella Worthingham," she said quietly, with a slight dip of her head. "Historical Society Secretary."

"Nice to meet you."

"Likewise."

"Is your mother here, by any chance?"

She stared at me.

"I'm looking for Ms. Worthingham," I repeated.

Something moved in her eyes and she stepped back, pulling the door fully open this time.

"Please follow me," she said, moving down the short hallway. The walls were completely covered with landscapes in ornate frames. "Wait here," she said, pausing just before a set of double doors. She slipped through and closed them behind her.

The paintings on the walls were all tranquil scenes — the artist had an eye for detail despite the overenthusiastic use of pastel shades. Standing in the colorful hallway was like being smothered by Easter eggs. I moved to read the signature on the closest painting and could just barely make out the letters "CW."

"Dr. Maclean?" Clara stood in the doorway, looking down her nose at me. All she had said was my name, but the tone was so disapproving that I almost couldn't bring myself to respond.

"Hello, Ms. Worthingham. Could we please talk for a moment?"

She made a *tsk* of displeasure. "Again, I prefer *Mrs.*"

"I'm sorry. I won't forget again." I would try not to, anyway.

She gave me the once-over and gestured me in. "I am *very* busy today, though," she said over her shoulder. "I only have a few minutes."

I followed her in and settled on the wingback chair in front of her desk when she patted the air to indicate that I should sit down.

"Your paintings are —" I began.

She cut me off. "As one of the sole remaining etiquette teachers in Stonedale, I feel I should advise you that it's not polite to drop in on someone unannounced. It's not ladylike."

"Sorry about that," I said, though being ladylike would never make my list of concerns in this lifetime. "Thanks for seeing me. I had a little window of time and took a chance. I wanted to make sure you'd received the paperwork and ask if there was anything I could do to help sort things out."

Her thin white eyebrows rose. "Sort things out?"

"Yes," I said. "Make sure that we can proceed with your blessing."

A very unladylike snort followed that. "You'll never have our blessing. But permission is quite another thing."

I smiled at her.

"Let me see," she said, sorting through the neat stacks on her desk. I could tell she knew where every single item was located, but she made a show of having to check each pile until she reached the last one. "Ah, here it is."

Clara grabbed the reading glasses attached to a long gold chain around her neck and applied them to her nose, then turned her attention to the page in her hand. She used a finger to tap paragraphs as she skimmed the words.

"Everything is in order," she pronounced. "So the final approval depends upon our inspection."

"Inspection? What does that entail?" Seriously? Was she just making it up as she went along? No one had mentioned an inspection before.

"We need to attend a rehearsal, view the scenery, observe the company in action, that sort of thing. To make sure that no damage is being done to the theater."

"I can assure you, Mrs. Worthingham, no damage is being done."

She tittered. "Fine, but we need to see that for ourselves, Dr. Maclean."

I imagined what Tolliver's face might look like when he heard the news. I'd have to deal with that later.

"How about next Friday?" I asked. That would give us a week to prepare. "And could the protests at least be suspended in the meantime?"

She pulled her desk calendar over and perused every hour of the day, again sliding her finger down the list, before agreeing to the appointment — but not the suspension.

"Well, it's your right to protest, but honestly, we don't need to be at odds."

She visibly recoiled. "We most certainly do."

"In light of recent events —"

She affected a puzzled expression. "To what are you referring?"

She would have known if she'd let me finish my sentence. But pointing that out wouldn't help the cause. "Jean Claude."

She nodded, slightly.

"Well, the students — all of us, really — are grieving. The tweet about Jean Claude and tone on your blog, when you write about the Opera House, is . . ." I put it as delicately as I could, "very upsetting."

Clara pursed her lips. "Well, the whole situation is very upsetting to us too."

"I understand that you have a goal. But a life has been lost. The life of someone we cared for. Do you think it would be possible to please soften the tone?"

She blinked rapidly.

"Even temporarily?"

"I'll speak to our team." Unsurprisingly, she made it sound as if she wasn't the one responsible, even though I'd seen her out there waving the megaphone and leading the charge.

"Thank you. By the way, did you talk to Jean Claude again after the rehearsal?"

She bristled. "I should think not. Why?"

"Just curious."

"What would we have to talk about?"

"Well, you did seem angry. And your social media posts suggested —"

Her eyes widened. "You don't think I had anything to do with . . . no. How preposterous! I am not a *murderer*."

"I didn't say you were," I said calmly. "I was just wondering how often you'd spoken."

"Are we done? I do need to return to my

work." She stood and before I knew what was happening, she had shepherded me out of the office and halfway down the hallway. She paused in front of a closed door and knocked. "Brax? It's almost time for our meeting with the mayor."

"Hi, Mr. Worthingham," I heard myself say to the door. I don't know why.

Clara shushed me. "Don't disturb him. He's an absolute beast when he gets angry."

Remembering his general demeanor in the lobby, I doubted that very much.

"One more thing," I said. "Circling back to the protestors, will you be calling them off now that we're following procedure?"

She frowned.

"Please think of the students." I smiled at her.

"I *am* thinking of the students," she snapped. "They're the ones doing all the damage to our cherished Opera House right now. Even P.T. Barnum's circus did less harm!"

I ignored the dig. "I hope you'll see during the inspection that everything is as it should be. We're being careful, I assure you."

She rolled her eyes.

It took all of my willpower not to do the same.

"Good afternoon, then," she said, as she practically pushed me out the front door and slammed it behind me.

I'm no etiquette expert, but I'm fairly sure that's not how one says goodbye properly.

CHAPTER 8

"Come in at once! We're having drinks." Francisco de Francisco, a tall African-American man with short dreadlocks, waved from the front door of Calista's bungalow, a cocktail in hand. My cousin had texted an invitation as I'd been walking home — just the antidote I needed after the frustrating conversation with Clara.

Calista, Francisco, Nate, and I, along with my next-door neighbor Tad Ruthersford — who was currently out of town visiting his boyfriend — were all thirty-something professors of English who had become great friends.

"I'm getting an earful about your play from Nate and Cal," Francisco said. "Need you to fill in the blanks."

As tired as I was, his good spirits were infectious, and I waded quickly through the crackling leaves toward him. The smell of cinnamon greeted me as I walked into her lovely house — decorated with numerous art prints and brightly colorful furniture.

Francisco gave me a hug and studied me with his kind blue eyes. "You doing okay?" he murmured. "Hear you've got a lot on your plate."

I nodded, grateful for the check-in, and asked about his trip. He'd been on quite a roller coaster during the past few years. He was finishing up a long and complex scholarly study when a scandal involving the author broke out, which he'd worried would render all of his work useless. On the contrary, though — it went mainstream, became a bestseller, and Ivy League schools had come courting. So far, he'd decided to stay at Stonedale, but he was in demand as a speaker and traveled often. Also, since the administration knew he was being wooed, they had given him a raise as incentive to stay. It was like an academic fairy tale happy ending.

After he'd covered the highlights of his most recent presentation, he led me to the front room where Calista and Nate were waiting.

"Cheers!" said Nate, lifting a bottle of Peak House Ale.

"Nice to see you're supporting the chancellor's brand."

Nate winked and waved me over, moving sideways on the purple sofa. I plunked down, glad to let my heavy satchel rest on the floor instead of my shoulder.

Without a word, Calista picked up a glass from the lacquered tray next to the sofa and handed it to me: she'd made me a cabernet with ice. I leaned back against the soft cushion, spinning the glass slightly to get my wine slushie down to the arctic temperature I preferred.

I never claimed to be fancy.

After thanking her, I took a sip, savoring the blackberry and vanilla tones. Heavenly.

Francisco sat down next to Calista on the loveseat. "So Nate was just recounting some tale about a play that you're involved with, Lila. Written by Tolliver?"

I glanced at Nate, who did his best to keep a straight face. "And what has Nate been telling you?"

"That it's the worst play ever written and that you're a consultant on it."

I elbowed Nate. "Seriously? That's how you described it?"

He laughed. "I may have said something to that effect."

"It might end up being entertaining, when everything's said and done." I sighed. "Or it could be terrible."

There was a long silence.

"Why are you consulting on it?" Francisco asked.

"Jean Claude —" A sudden lump in my throat cut off the rest of my words.

Calista came over and gave me a hug, during which I tried valiantly to keep the wine glass in my hand from tipping. "We're all so sorry, Lila. We were talking about it before you got here. I know you cared about him. Are you okay?"

"Not really."

She regarded me for a long moment, then hugged me again. "Anything you need, you just ask."

Nate and Francisco nodded.

I blinked back tears and swallowed hard. "Thank you. Anyway, Jean Claude heard that I taught the mystery class — *Puzzled* is a postmodern murder mystery — and hired me. He also promoted me to assistant director."

Calista moved back to her seat. "You didn't tell me that. Congratulations!"

"Thanks, and I'm sorry. I know I haven't been in touch very much. I miss you all. The rehearsals are keeping me so busy —"

"No worries, Lil. You mentioned that you were feeling overwhelmed by the play. And now there's the rest of it too." She bit her lip, and her expression softened. "But soon, when the play is done, you can get back to being overwhelmed by the usual things. With us, where you belong."

"Looking forward to that." I smiled at her.

Francisco set down his glass. "How did Jean Claude become involved with the university's production?"

"I know this one," Nate jumped in. "He's on sabbatical, doing some research in our library collection." Pennington Library had a vast collection of materials related to American theater productions. "His primary focus is on Damon Runyon."

"The one whose stories were the basis for *Guys and Dolls*?" Calista asked.

"Among other things."

"But," I thought back to the reading I'd done in preparation for teaching Runyon's true-crime piece "The Eternal Blonde" in my mystery class. "His papers are collected elsewhere . . . one of the Ivy League schools, I think."

"Well, there's *something* here from when Runyon lived in Colorado. Jean Claude gave a terrific lecture when he first arrived, explaining what he hoped to accomplish." Nate took a swig of his beer and set it down on a coaster. "But I wouldn't do it justice if I tried to paraphrase."

"That was before he asked me to work on the play, so I missed the lecture, and I'm sorry now. I bet it was fascinating." Another wave of grief ran through me, and I tightened my grip on the wine glass.

"He also had quite a reputation," said Francisco. "I always wondered about that."

"Tolliver said so too," I confirmed. "But he didn't elaborate. What kind of reputation?"

"For being controlling," added Nate.

"Rather an understatement," said Francisco.

"Okay, for being a monster control freak." Nate turned to me. "Google him, Lila. There are all kinds of stories about how he lost his temper and threw furniture around the stage, or shredded peoples' scripts, fired the whole cast. Stuff like that."

Wow. I did not recognize the Jean Claude I knew at all.

"How did he and Tolliver get along?" asked Calista.

I hesitated. But just for a second. This was my third year at Stonedale, and my friends had proven themselves to be trustworthy.

"Just between us . . ." They all nodded eagerly. "I think Tolliver wasn't exactly thrilled about the direction Jean Claude was going in."

"Why?" asked Calista, her gray eyes alight with curiosity.

"He just mentioned in passing that he didn't think the production was fulfilling his vision."

I took another sip of wine.

They seemed vaguely disappointed. Then Nate raised one finger. "At least you've got the Opera House ghost thing to keep you entertained."

"What?" I stared at him.

His eyes grew rounder. "You don't know the legend?"

"I'd forgotten about the ghost. I only heard it mentioned by Clara the day they started protesting."

He pointed at Francisco. "You tell it. You're the one who told me."

A slow smile blossomed on Francisco's handsome face. He settled back in the chair and took a long sip from his glass, gearing up to tell the story.

"Back in the early 1990s, there was a Theater professor at Stonedale University named Camden Drake. He was a playwright as well as a composer, both attractive and brilliant. Students adored him. His classes were so popular that they were moved from the classroom to the lecture hall. His office hours overflowed with students lined up, eager to be able to say they'd had a conversation with him. He —"

"You're making him sound like a magical unicorn," Nate laughed.

"Are you done?" Francisco asked Nate, who grinned at him. "I'm just telling the story how I heard it. He was a remarkably popular professor, okay?"

"I'm sorry." Nate put his hands up in acquiescence. "Go on, Professor."

"Camden was one of those people who oozed charisma. One of his musicals was staged at the Opera House, and Althea Gaines was cast as the star. On opening night, the audience was too large to fit inside the building. People flooded the streets, hoping to hear the new melodies from outside. It swelled into such a large crowd that eventually some windows were broken. At this point, the owner of the theater, Malcolm Gaines, who was also Althea's husband, became enraged. He came out to address the audience and cancelled the performance altogether. They complained, but he had his ushers move the crowd."

"But it gets better," interjected Nate enthusiastically.

"Yes, it does," Francisco agreed. "When Camden stormed offstage, Althea left with him. They walked down the street followed by the townspeople, went into Brynson Hall, and held an impromptu concert. Camden played the songs from his play, Althea sang, and it was, by all accounts, an unforgettable evening."

"Wow," I said.

"Malcolm heard about how glorious that was for weeks afterwards. He was the Theater department chair at Stonedale, and you know how campus gossip works." Nate looked thoughtful. "That must have stung."

Francisco nodded in agreement. "Especially since Camden was one of his colleagues. Malcolm had pushed everyone to hire him, in fact. Afterwards, Camden offered to pay for the broken windows, but Malcolm wasn't having any of it. He banned Camden from ever setting foot in the Opera House again, and he took to wearing a gun as a warning."

"A gun?" I shook my head.

"What was the point of that?" Calista asked. "Seems kind of extreme."

"Probably just pride," said Francisco. "He'd lost face with the entire community, and his wife had contributed. He didn't want Althea and Camden to work together again, and her work was in the Opera House."

"But there's more!" Nate said, patting the arm of the sofa rapidly in anticipation.

Francisco resumed the story. "Weeks went by without further incident. But, one day, Malcolm found Althea and Camden in a compromising position. The most compromising position, in fact. In the Opera House, no less, where Camden had been banned. It pushed Malcolm over the edge. He struck Camden, which turned into a brawl and Camden left town, never stepping foot in Stonedale again. Much to the disappointment of both students and townspeople."

"He just left Althea behind?" I couldn't believe it.

"And she had a baby."

I found myself leaning toward Francisco.

"But then Althea disappeared too."

My mouth fell open. "What do you mean 'disappeared?'"

"She left to be with Camden," he said, matter-of-factly. "But she didn't announce it to anyone, so the town thought for awhile that she went missing."

"They were in love," Calista added, dreamily.

"What about the baby though?" I asked.

"Okay, well, this part riles me up." My cousin shook her head.

"Well, that's another sad turn. Malcolm dropped off the baby at the neighbors —"

"Literally in a basket," Calista interjected. "Like in the movies."

"— then hung himself in the Opera House."

"Right on the stage," she said, then stopped when she caught sight of Francisco's expression. "I want to make sure she has all the details. Sorry I interrupted, babe."

He acknowledged her apology and took a long drink.

"Oh, how tragic," I said.

"And now . . ." Nate said, waving his hand in the air to urge Francisco to continue.

"There's more? I don't think I can take it," I murmured.

"Yes." Francisco set his glass down carefully on the coffee table. "There's more. Now, Malcolm's ghost is said to haunt the Opera House."

"Wait, what? For real?" I took a sip of wine for fortitude.

"Ever since that day, people in the Opera House have reported all sorts of events —" Nate said.

"Supernatural events," clarified Francisco.

Nate picked up the thread, affecting a deep voice and wiggling his fingers. "Lights

100

flickering, doors opening and closing by themselves, inexplicable sounds."

"Well, couldn't those be explained by —" I began.

"Also, objects moved from room to room overnight, air so cold that no one can stand in that spot, and a piano that plays music even when no one is in the room," Nate finished gleefully.

"Yeah, that's a little harder to explain," I admitted.

"Plus, there have been sightings," he added, just as I took another sip.

I choked. "Sightings? As in full-body-manifestation kind of thing?"

"Yes," he said, nodding vigorously. "I can't remember where I saw this, but there were even some photos that claimed to have captured him on film."

I sat back, stunned. "Why is no one talking about this? Not a single person involved with the play has mentioned anything."

"Probably because it happened such a long time ago," Francisco said. "It's very old news."

"It's new to me," I said. "You'd think there would be at least a mention of it somewhere in the theater proper. A framed newspaper article or something next to all of those pictures of performers in the lobby —"

"Those photos were already on the wall. The theater itself is exactly as it was when Malcolm left it to the university," Nate said. "The school hasn't done anything to it. It was viewed by the board of trustees as an annoyance." At my confused expression, he continued. "You know, like when someone gives you a gift that's quite valuable but is not anything you ever wanted? You would feel guilty giving it away, so it just sits there and collects dust."

"It's not been loved the way it deserves." Calista sighed.

"That's exactly what the Historical Society would argue. Why didn't the school just give it to them?" I looked around the group.

Francisco smiled at me. "Because it *is* actually worth something. The university hasn't figured out how to benefit from the theater yet."

I set my wine down on the table. "This is a lot to take in."

Calista leaned forward. "Keep me posted, please. I'm dying to hear about anything strange you experience there. Anything at all. Human or . . . otherwise."

CHAPTER 9

On the morning of the Historical Society's scheduled visit, I awoke after a troubled sleep. Bits of my dreams came back to me as I walked to campus for a department meeting: a piano playing off-key slowly, sadly; the sound of footsteps running across the floor above; my breath a visible cloud in a room so cold I could see ice forming on my skin. My brain was clearly processing the story my friends had told me, but knowing that didn't make it any less unsettling.

Some unexplained things *had* happened during rehearsals, now that I thought about it: plenty of props had gone missing, lights flickered unpredictably, and it did sometimes feel as though you were being watched. Once, I'd been working late, alone, and looked up from my script to see a human-sized shadow moving steadily across the stage behind a scrim. I'd run up to look, but no one was there. That night, I figured I was just overly tired. And I'd never thought of any of them as particularly odd, but now that I had some context, it was somewhat disconcerting.

By the time I passed the gryphons positioned on either side of the wrought-iron-gated campus entrance, I'd decided to talk to Tolliver and Zandra about the specific details of the ghost story. I wasn't sure why I felt it was important for them to know what my friends had said . . . it wasn't like I was expecting a specter to come flying out of the wall during a performance or anything. But, forewarned is forearmed, as they say.

That afternoon, I zoomed past the protestors as if they weren't there at all, pulled Tolliver and Zandra out into the lobby, and told them what I'd heard.

When I'd finished, they stared at me for a moment.

"Of *course* we know," Zandra said. "Malcolm has been very active the whole time. I just haven't mentioned it."

Now I stared at her.

"Psychic," she said, pointing at herself. "Remember?"

My cousin had said that to me once. Great, now I had *déjà vu* on top of everything else.

"But now that I know you're interested, I'll be more open —"

The sound of the glass door slamming interrupted our conversation.

Clara Worthingham walked vigorously toward us. Braxton trailed a few feet behind her, his crisp white shirt and black trousers with nary a wrinkle. Her royal-blue suit was immaculate as well. But her matching pillbox hat was slightly askew, and she huffed at the small veil floating above her forehead as she entered the lobby.

"Lila, I need to speak to you. Don't move a muscle." Tolliver and Zandra made a hasty exit. Couldn't say I blamed them. Her outrage was palpable.

I wondered what transgression had been added to her list of complaints this time.

"Hi Clara. Hi Braxton," I said. If she was going to leap willy-nilly into first-name status, I was too.

He smiled at me.

"Have you heard the ghastly news?" She clasped her hands in front of her as if at a recitation. "A developer is *this close* to buying the Opera House! He's been trying for almost a year, but it has never seemed possible until now. Your chancellor has been refusing the offer — for which we were extremely grateful — but he has changed his mind."

"What? No, I don't know about that. Who is it?"

Her expression sported an odd combination of anger about the gossip and visible delight at being able to spread it. "He lives in New York City —"

She turned to Braxton and repeated, "New York *City*!"

Now was not the time to tell her that I hailed from there as well.

He patted her arm gently before she spun back around. She moved so close that her violet scent wafted onto me and I could see a spot of frosted pink lipstick on her front tooth.

"He wants to tear the Opera House down and build a new theater instead."

"A new theater?"

"Yes. State of the art, he says. With automatic everything. Soulless. Doesn't it sound awful?"

I definitely didn't want to get into a debate about the merits of new versus old with her, so I moved on to the more pressing point. "This is really happening?"

Braxton, behind her back, nodded vigorously.

Clara clutched her head. "I can't possibly

imagine why he needs to destroy our theater. It's historic! And we need to put a stop to it immediately."

"Let's see if we can find out more information," I said. Suddenly I realized that we had become aligned against the third party, united rather than opposed. The thought heartened me. Perhaps they'd let the whole protest issue slide if the alternative was complete destruction.

"We must! We simply must. Or . . ." she tilted her head as she processed a thought. She turned to face Braxton again. "Dear, maybe we should buy it! If it's up for sale? Oh, wouldn't that be the answer to our prayers? Then we could prevent anyone from ever stepping foot in here ever again!"

Opposition back on.

I sighed.

Clara was spinning a plan with her husband who stood smiling patiently in the face of her storm of words.

After a minute, I raised my hand. "Did you still want to see the rehearsal?"

"Wouldn't miss it," Clara said.

"How long would you like to watch?"

"An hour," she said. "Then we need to tour downstairs." She opened her purse and removed a notepad and pen. "Proceed."

I led them halfway down the aisle and

gestured to some seats on the left. Clara began writing as soon as she sat down.

The cast was working on a scene where Sherlock Holmes, Miss Marple, and Oliver were arguing over whose interpretation of events was correct. It was particularly tricky because it called for the ghost of Edgar Allan Poe to descend from the ceiling and referee at exactly the right moment.

Yes, like Batman. No one really understood why, but it was part of Tolliver's vision.

The actors on stage were frozen in position, waiting. There was a clank, then a banging noise from above. The catwalk had been repaired and triple checked for safety, but I'd wager the sounds were coming from the old pulley system. The three sleuths did not break position, but glanced at each other as if silently trying to reach agreement about what to do next.

Finally, Tolliver called for them to stop. I hurried down to where he was standing, shoulders slumped.

"I cannot work in these conditions!" He threw his hands up into the air and his volume escalated. "This theater is a bag of bones. We need to get someone from the engineering department in here to rip out the rubbish and revamp the entire thing."

I tried to get him to lower his voice. Those were exactly the kinds of changes that the Historical Society was anxious about.

"Tolliver, the Worthinghams are here," I whispered into his ear. "Right behind us."

"I do not care." He began to pace back and forth, waving his arms. "We have a crisis, Lila. I *must* have creative control. I am an *artist*! And if we cannot bring my idea to life, then I quit!" With that, he stormed up the stairs on the side of the stage and out of view.

The students remained on the stage, looking around uncertainly.

"Break for lunch, everyone," I yelled. "Come back in an hour." I repeated it into the headset Tolliver had left lying on the table. It was early for lunch but I had to buy time in order to see if I could get Tolliver back and shoo the Worthinghams away.

My cell phone buzzed. It was a text from Tolliver. *I'm not quitting. But get those people out of here. Zandra and I are in the front office, and I don't want to speak to them again.*

I felt a tap on my shoulder.

After Tolliver's outburst, there was nothing I wanted to do less than turn around to face the Worthinghams. But I did.

Happily, it was Bella. "Clara is wondering if she could go downstairs now." She smiled tentatively.

I wondered why she referred to her mother by her first name. Probably another one of Clara's preferences. She sure had a lot of them.

"Now would be fine," I said, smiling at her. Might as well get it over with.

Bella scurried up to retrieve Clara, who marched down the aisle, complaining loudly. "Now I'm even more anxious to see the damage you've done. Did you *hear* what that director said? I have half a mind to shut things down right this instant."

"He didn't really mean it, Clara. He was just frustrated." My explanation only seemed to irk her more.

"No, Lila." She reached back to clutch Braxton's forearm for strength. "That man announced that he plans to — and I quote — 'rip and revamp'!"

Braxton nodded to corroborate her claims, his eyes wide.

I smiled at them reassuringly. "Don't worry, Clara. He doesn't have the power to rip or revamp anything. He won't do that, I promise."

She turned around to Braxton and muttered a few more things I couldn't quite hear. She added another item to her notepad and showed him. They conferred further.

I waited, suppressing the urge to tap my foot. After her indignation had sufficiently subsided, she allowed me to lead the way downstairs, where the storage and dressing rooms, along with a combination workshop/prop room were located. We called it "below stage" in contrast to backstage, which was used primarily to store scenery and to act as a crossover area during performances.

At the top of the steep cement stairs, I asked them to please use the metal handrail.

"Look at all the crumbling!" Clara exclaimed. "No doubt from all the cast and crew parading up and down."

I kept walking, pretending I didn't hear her.

She raised her voice. "Lila, the steps are wearing away to nothing! That's exactly what we are worried about."

I made a noncommittal sound.

At the bottom step, the temperature dropped sharply, as it always did. The lower level gave me the creeps: it was narrow, damp, dark, and very cold. There was something else too, a sort of disquieting energy that emanated from the walls.

I shivered and led them to the nearest room, which was used for storage.

"Do you want to go inside?" I spoke to Clara, as she seemed to be in charge of the inspection. Tour. Whatever it was.

She poked her head inside. "This is dreadful. It needs a thorough cleaning." After giving me a pointed look, she wrote furiously in her notepad of grievances.

When she was done making her notes, we continued down the hallway toward the dressing rooms. As we reached the section with brighter wall sconces, I silently counted to three, knowing Clara was going to resume her litany of complaints now that she could see more clearly.

She gasped. "The paint is positively falling off the walls! Braxton, look!"

It was true — there were chips and scrapes all the way down the hallway. The point I was passing even seemed to have claw marks. How bizarre.

"The paint was like that when we got here," I reminded her. "Haven't you ever noticed it before?"

She harrumphed and scribbled.

We continued down the hall past a variety of small dressing rooms. The doors were open and the lights were off. I explained that they were being used for members of the cast. She peered in, then made a sound of disapproval and another note.

112

Finally, we reached the corner, where the largest dressing room was located. The heavy wooden door was closed.

"This has traditionally been given to the star of the show," Clara informed me, even though I already knew that and she knew I knew that. She asked if we could go inside. I knocked, and there was no answer, so I turned the old metal knob and pushed open the door.

I felt along the wall for the switch. The instant the light came on, she charged in. I remained by the door as Clara stared intently at the rose-papered wall along the right side, which had a large diagonal crack. Her expression reminded me of Cady, my cousin's cat, when she was hunting something — completely focused and poised to spring.

"That crack was already there too," I said firmly.

She didn't reply but continued inspecting the wall carefully, as Braxton sidled up to her.

Bella stayed in the hallway, shifting her weight from side to side.

"Would you like to come in and join us?" I invited her.

She edged into the doorway and swept her gaze across the room. "It's beautiful," she breathed.

I wouldn't have thought to call the old blotchy mirror or wobbly vintage table beautiful — both had multiple cracks and chips, like the walls — but they were pleasant to look at nonetheless, and the velvet chair before them was an appealing deep wine color. A floor lamp in a baroque chandelier style with black crystal drops graced the corner. The room must have felt quite luxurious once.

"Have you been down here before?" I asked.

She tilted her head. "When I was very young, I think. But these days, only Clara and Braxton come down here when there's not a production. They prefer that the rest of us stay upstairs so as not to damage anything. It's all so fragile, you know."

What a weird society. Two people seemed to have all the power and everyone else just followed their random rules.

When Clara was done scrutinizing the room, we headed around to the large area beneath the stage, which housed a workshop with tools hung neatly on pegboard, shelves for storing props, and assorted building materials.

"There are supposed to be mattresses

there," Clara pointed to the middle of the floor.

"Not for sleeping, surely." Bella looked slightly aghast at the thought. Couldn't blame her.

"Of course not. How silly." Clara's pointer finger rose toward the ceiling, her large diamond catching the light and flashing. "That's the trap door. Harry Houdini himself used it, you know."

"How remarkable," I murmured.

"Yes. It is. A triumph for Stonedale, as his performance was covered nationwide." She cut her eyes to me. "Is the trap door involved in this particular play? It's very dangerous, you know."

"Yes," I admitted.

Clara had just opened her mouth to say more when the lights went out.

CHAPTER 10

We were plunged into complete darkness. I don't know why the go-to response is sheer panic, but it was coming on hard.

I tried to swipe my cell phone screen with just the right amount of pressure to turn on the flashlight app but couldn't get it open.

"Don't move, anyone," I called out. "There are a lot of things lying around, and I don't want you to hurt yourself." I sounded much calmer and in control than I felt.

After several more attempts, the tiny beam kicked on, and I swung my phone around in an arc. Bella was right next to me, her arms wrapped around herself, standing complete still.

"Is everyone okay? Would you mind turning on your phone flashlights too, if you have them, please?"

One by one, their beams joined mine. I instructed them to aim their lights ahead of us so that we could move as a unit through the dark. We took it very slowly and had almost made it to the corner when there was a loud bang.

"What was that?" Clara screeched.

"Swing your flashlights over to the right," I directed.

There was nothing in the hallway.

"Why is the dressing room door closed?" Bella asked. "Didn't we leave it open?"

I stared at the door. "Let's go inside."

"No!" exclaimed Clara. "Are you crazy, child?"

"There was nothing in there before," I said. "And the doors do close by themselves sometimes here. It's an old building —"

"You don't have to tell *me*. I've been looking out for this building long before all of you folks arrived." Clara's flashlight circled in concert with her angry gesticulations. "And don't be stupid. The door was open. Now it's closed, that means someone else must have been down here with us."

"It may have been an actor," I said, gritting my teeth.

Suddenly, lights flooded us. Power had been restored.

I pushed on the dressing room door. The room was empty. "All clear, everyone."

As soon as the words were out of my

mouth, I saw that part of the wall seemed to be missing. Then I realized that a door in the wall had swung outward, revealing a perfectly rectangular shape.

They filed in behind me.

"A secret passageway — how magical!" exclaimed Bella, clasping her hands in front of her. "Have any of you seen this before?"

"No," Clara said, frowning. It must have pained her to admit that she didn't know everything about the Opera House.

Braxton shook his head as well.

"New to me. Should we see where it leads?" I asked.

"What's wrong with you, Lila?" Clara yelped. "Don't stand around here all day quizzing us. Go on." She made a shooing motion with her hands.

"Follow me." I crossed the room and peered inside the opening.

"You should be first, in case it's not safe," Clara added.

Gee, thanks.

I aimed my flashlight beam around the recessed area. The floor was noticeably raised compared to where we stood, and I warned the others to watch their steps as I climbed up. On the far side, cement blocks formed a spiral staircase. Not even the thought of potential danger could have stopped me from seeing where that went.

The stairs were remarkably sturdy. In fact, they were probably the sturdiest in the Opera House. Maybe the staircase had been added later. I said as much to my companions behind me.

As we ascended, I tripped on something. My flashlight revealed a small black shape about the size of a bread box. I picked it up and brought it with me so that no one else would fall.

Within seconds, I reached the top and pushed gently on the wall. A door swung open, outward, and after going through the opening, I came out in the wings, stage left.

So *this* must have been how the person who shot Jean Claude got away. I had to tell Lex as soon as possible.

The others soon emerged blinking in surprise.

I looked down at the battered black case in my hands and set it in the center of the stage.

We formed a semi-circle, staring down at it.

The dark leather on the rectangular case was pocked with scars, the handle on top was worn, and the silver latch on the front was tarnished.

"Should we open it?" Bella ventured,

earning a glare from Clara, who probably had wanted to be the one to say that.

"What if it's an explosive?" Clara countered, switching positions just as a power play. We all thought about that for a moment.

Braxton joined us on the stage, leaned down, and listened. "No ticking," he pronounced.

"Open it." Clara smirked, happy to be the one to say it this time.

No one moved.

"I meant Lila," she said. If someone was going to blow up, she wanted it to be me.

The latch opened easily. Placing one hand on either side of the lid, I gently pushed it up. Aside from making a creaking sound, the case was inactive.

Thankfully.

On the top was a pool of fabric. I pulled it out and shook it. A beaded black negligee formed itself into proper shape.

Braxton cleared his throat self-consciously.

I set it carefully on the stage.

A roll of velvet was the next item. I put it down on the floor and unfurled it slowly. A silver letter opener glinted in the bright lights. It was tarnished as well but still reflected. The letters "AG" were engraved on the handle.

120

I went back into the case to retrieve the last item: a bundle of envelopes with neat cursive handwriting tied with a ribbon.

Clara's eyes were gleaming oddly.

"What are they?" Bella asked, her voice catching in her throat.

"Letters of some sort," I said, untying the red ribbon.

Clara made a snatch for them, but I was too fast for her. I pressed them to my chest and faced her. "What are you doing?"

"They belong to the Historical Society," she said. "All of this does."

"No they don't," a voice boomed. "They belong to me."

A tall man strolled onstage; his face was tanned below heavily gelled and rakishly angled black hair. He wore a charcoal suit and shiny black leather shoes. When he reached us, he smiled widely, his teeth unnaturally white, and handed a business card to each person. Then he held out his hand to shake ours, one by one. It was a whole production.

"Chip Turner," he said. "Nice to meet you."

Clara pulled herself up and shot him a withering look. "You're the Mr. Turner who is attempting to destroy our Opera House!"

He made a little frown, pretending she

had hurt his feelings. "I wouldn't say destroy. I'd say improve. And, I'm sorry, I didn't catch your name."

That ruffled her feathers, I could tell. She was used to people knowing who she was. In a small town like Stonedale, everyone knew their places in the food chain, and Clara saw herself at the top.

"I am Mrs. Clara Worthingham and this is my husband, Braxton. We are with the Stonedale Historical Society. You have been pestering us by email for the better part of the past year." The feather on her hat bobbed with every syllable as she over-enunciated. She reached up to straighten it and wavered a little.

Bella stepped closer and steadied Clara, who pointed at her in return. "You've been pestering Bella too. And I —"

"Hello, Worthinghams." Chip turned to Bella, which further irked Clara, as she had something else to say. "Hello, Bella." She murmured a greeting. He regarded her for a long while before moving his dark blue eyes to me.

"Lila Maclean. I teach at the university."

"Oh, a professor. I was not much of a student myself, I confess. Far too distracted by all the social opportunities. Barely graduated."

I wasn't sure what to say to that. Out of the corner of my eye, I could see students filing into the auditorium. It was time for rehearsal to begin. I jerked my head toward the lobby, hoping everyone would take the hint and move off stage with me, but nobody budged.

"What did you mean about these belonging to you?" Clara addressed Chip, pointing to the letters I was still pressing to my chest protectively.

"Right. I'm in negotiations to purchase this fine property. Just taking another look-see today, making sure everything is in order."

"It's not a property, it's a historical *treasure,*" Clara hissed at him. "And we're doing everything in our power to preserve it."

He bobbed his head to the side, acknowledging her words. "Well, it won't need too much preservation given that I plan to knock it down and build a world-class entertainment complex here."

"A complex?" Her hand flew up to her heart. "But Mr. Turner, that would be a tragedy. Even worse than a new theater."

"I understand that you're attached to it. But this will bring jobs and visitors to Stonedale. It will be great for the town."

Clara gasped. "But we don't *want* more

123

jobs and visitors here. Stonedale is perfect the way it is."

Braxton and Bella exchanged a glance. They'd surely heard Clara's views on Why We Need To Keep Stonedale The Same for years.

"Well, we're going to have to agree to disagree on that one," Chip said. "There will be a big improvement, I promise you."

"Why is that?" Clara's laser-hot glare could have burned a hole through wood.

"There is so much potential here. Look, I love theater. Once upon a time, I even tried to be a director, but I couldn't make a living at it. So now I'm a developer." His eyes lit up. "And I'm in a position to bring culture to small towns all over America."

"Are you saying we don't have culture —" Clara clutched her pearls.

"Not like in New York," he said. "And I've been thinking to myself: why not share it with the world?"

"I can't stand here and listen to this for one more minute." Clara went pale and swayed slightly, then stomped away, towing Braxton behind her. At the edge of the stage, she rallied with a parting shot. "Your plan is a travesty, Mr. Turner. I . . . I curse you and your project! And I curse Tolliver Ingersoll and everyone who wants to dam-

124

age our beautiful Opera House too!"

Everyone froze under the weight of her unexpected venom.

Even Clara looked surprised after her outburst, and she sagged against Braxton, clutching her hat as if someone might snatch it from her. He bustled her firmly down the steps.

"Sorry," Bella whispered to the developer after Clara had passed him. "She just loves this building."

"Got it." He didn't seem to be bothered by the tirade.

As they walked up the aisle, I could hear Clara angrily continuing to voice her displeasure. Bella looked back once over her shoulder.

Once the trio had departed, I smiled at Chip. "Well, I guess that's that. Is there something I can help you with? We've got a rehearsal to finish. We're putting on a production of a new play and we don't have much time before opening night."

"Understood. I'll be going then." He held out his hand. "The letters, please?"

I stared at him.

"They're part of the theater, no? Everything in here is included in the sale."

"Right now the school owns everything. And I'm working here as a university representative, so I have the authority to hold onto them." I had no idea if that was true or not, but I said it firmly.

He considered this, then shrugged.

"See you next time, Lila."

I watched him leave.

New York did have incredible culture, no doubt about that. I'd lived there for years with my mom and Calista, who came to live with us after her parents were in a fatal car accident. No matter how often we traveled around the country due to my mother's various art engagements, New York was home. Yet even I felt that Chip's attitude was a wee bit insensitive.

The thought shook me a little. Was Stonedale rubbing off on me? If so, I didn't know how I felt about that.

The crew rolled out the backdrop for the first scene. Actors lined up in the wings. It was time to get back to business.

"Dr. M?" One of the students came over with a script in hand and an inquiring expression. We went over one of the lines together and sorted out his motivation for it, then I went back down to the front row and began preparing for the rest of rehearsal.

A few minutes later, Tolliver and Zandra joined me. We were settling in for the next scene when Zandra gasped.

"The ghost is here." She pointed at the stage. "And he's not happy." She closed her eyes and pressed on her forehead with two fingers. "Yes, I hear you, Malcolm." After a moment, she looked up. "Who has been rummaging through things that don't belong to them?"

That would be me. I glanced down guiltily at the packet of letters in my bag.

"We found a trunk in the secret stairwell —" I began.

"The what?" Tolliver turned to me, his eyebrows nearly summiting his head.

"The stairwell that leads from the corner dressing room to the stage."

He shook his head blankly.

"The door is almost invisible, it's blended in so well with the wallpaper, but there's a spiral staircase behind it. And we found a trunk inside. It's over there." I pointed to the items still sitting on the stage.

"Who's we?"

"I was giving the Worthinghams a tour and Clara —"

He cut me off again. "You gave that woman a tour? What were you thinking?"

"Remember I told you we had to do that? It's part of the final approval process for the permission form."

He tore his glasses off and flung them onto the table.

Zandra shrank back into her seat and reached for her knitting.

"Yes. I'd forgotten. Well, now it has been done and I cannot take one more second of their harassment. You will not aid and abet those . . . those . . ." he scowled, "thieves of art! What self-respecting society dedicated to preservation would obstruct an active work of genius?"

My face warmed as I became aware of the cast onstage watching his blow-up.

"I hear you," I said quietly. "But you're going to have to face facts, Tolliver. They have managed to take control of whether or not we can continue with this production, and someone has to deal with them. If you will not, then it must be me."

His face grew redder. "I am the director," he spit at me.

"Of course you are. I am here to help you. But we need to handle this. And we're very close to being shut down."

"Can they even do that?" He made angry jazz hands. Which, until that moment, I wouldn't have imagined could be a thing.

"I don't know," I admitted. "But the chancellor said the Worthinghams were able to make the funding disappear for the community theater, so they do have power."

"She's very influential in this town," Zandra agreed. "People listen to her and she could demolish our ticket sales."

Tolliver groaned.

"Let Lila handle it," Zandra said calmly.

He simmered, visibly, then his shoulders relaxed and he rubbed his hands together. "I'm done with this, okay? I don't want to hear about those people ever again."

He looked over at the items from the case. "And will you please move those things so no one trips over them?"

A bunch of beeps went off from cast members' phones. The students began conferring with one another and pointing to their screens.

"What's happening?" I called out to them.

Rachel Hernandez, our Miss Marple, jumped down from the stage, landing on her sneakers with a thump. Her brown eyes were sparkling with delight. She flipped her long hair over her shoulder and showed me her phone screen. "We all have alerts set up for anything about the play. The *Stonedale Scout* just published a story about us on their website! They said we're haunted and —"

I squinted at the screen but couldn't see anything from my angle. "Do you mind if I look for a sec?"

She smiled and handed it over.

The headline read "STONEDALE THE-
ATER PRODUCTION CURSED!"

CHAPTER 11

News travels fast, they say, and in this case it turned out to be practically instantaneous. I don't know who texted the scoop to the paper seconds after it happened, but when the story ran, everything changed.

On Saturday morning, we had a new crowd at rehearsal. Surprised to see them when I walked in, I asked around and quickly discovered that the friends of cast members had been so interested in experiencing the "hauntings" for themselves that they'd simply accompanied whomever they knew into the theater. They didn't seemed fazed at all about crossing the picket line out front.

Tolliver was practically hopping across the stage. He swept his arm out, gesturing toward the gathered students.

"Lila, look! The play is garnering so much attention that we've already gotten groupies."

I walked up the steps. "Tolliver, they're here for the curse. Or the ghost. Or both."

"Oh." The crestfallen look made me want to comfort him, even though I was a little wary from yesterday's explosion.

"Maybe the ghost story will sell tickets," I said. "While it's an old legend, it appears to have been revitalized by the newspaper."

"Do you think so? Oh — wait! I have a magnificent idea: what if we added some ghosts to the play? Oooh, and maybe some werewolves." He peered off into the distance and muttered something about vampires.

Oh no.

"That seems like we'd be moving into a completely different genre, Tolliver. You've already got a lot going on."

He grinned. "But I'm known for breaking the rules, Lila. You know that."

"True, but in this case, we're so close to dress rehearsal that maybe we could just go with what we've been practicing all these weeks. Think of the students."

"The actors come second to the art, darling. But I hear what you're saying." He lowered his voice and whispered into my ear. "And can you please get rid of the groupies now so we can begin?"

Sigh. I turned to the students and said hello. They quieted down and looked up at

132

me expectantly.

"May I have everyone in the company come up on stage? Please take a seat in a circle." Individuals made their way up the steps on either side, then followed my directions.

I addressed the remaining people. "Thank you all for your interest. We have a lot of work to do, so I have to ask you to leave. But we open November first, and we'd love to see you back here then."

No one moved.

"In other words, this is a closed rehearsal. If you're not in the play, I'm sorry, but you won't be able to stay."

After a few groans and sounds of disapproval, they began to shuffle up the aisle, thank goodness. Many of them were snapping photos on their way out. I wasn't sure what I would have done if they ignored me.

I turned back to the cast. "Hi, everyone. We need to talk."

A circle of bright eyes met mine.

"The story that came out yesterday is likely to draw a lot of attention to the play."

Tolliver squiggled a little bit. That part made him happy.

"Did anyone here talk to any reporters?"

I didn't expect them to volunteer that information, but I thought maybe I'd be able to tell from body language.

"You're not in trouble," I added. "It would just be helpful to know what the source was for his descriptions."

The students looked around the circle at one another, uneasily.

After it became clear that no one was going to say anything, I moved on.

"Well, has anyone experienced anything . . . unusual?"

The students twisted their necks expectantly.

Parker finally blurted out, "It feels like someone's watching me all the time."

There were numerous sounds of agreement.

Several students mentioned hearing loud bumps with no logical explanation.

Others mentioned the lights flickering or going out.

"And . . ." Parker raised his hand.

"You can just talk," I assured him.

"I came in early last week to work on lines in the dressing room. I kept hearing skittering sounds up and down the walls." He shivered.

Rachel nodded enthusiastically. "I've heard that too, in the prop room."

Another student described hearing someone singing, but when she looked into the other rooms, no one was there. Several cast members concurred. A discussion followed, which ended with agreement that they couldn't make out the lyrics of the melancholy song.

"Oh! And one time," Parker said, "I thought I saw a . . . um . . . ghost go into our dressing room."

Rachel grabbed his hand. "Was it a man in a black overcoat?"

His mouth fell open. "Yes."

"I saw him too." They high-fived.

"Are you sure it wasn't an actual man?" I pressed a little. "Can you describe him?"

Parker shook his head. "No. I only saw him for a second from the end of the hallway. Then when I got to the room, he was gone."

Rachel nodded again. "I'm so relieved. Thought I was going crazy."

"Of course you saw him." Zandra walked out onto the stage. "It's Malcolm Gaines, the previous owner of the Opera House. He's been talking to me."

Here we go again.

"I didn't want to scare anyone," Zandra continued. "I have to be careful with my gift." She bowed her head for a moment, then addressed the group. "You read about his demise in the paper, right?" The students

135

indicated that they had. "Well, Malcolm has feelings about us being here."

"What kind of feelings?" I didn't know if I wanted to hear the answer.

Zandra glanced up at the ceiling, either thinking or conferring with Malcolm. "It's complicated," she said finally. "Hard to put into words."

"Are they positive feelings or negative feelings?" Parker was the one who pressed her, but we all wanted to hear the answer.

Her smile was enigmatic. "Both."

I was just about to leave when Bella walked down the auditorium aisle. She tucked a lock of hair behind her ear and asked if Clara had left her bag anywhere. Apparently, her dramatic exit hadn't involved picking up her things.

"I haven't seen it," I said. "Do you want to do a quick scan in the wings?"

"Or maybe downstairs? She thinks she left it in the room where the lights went out."

I nodded and went through the door on the side that led more directly to the lower level. The Opera House had a kooky layout and it was not particularly helpful to have to go up and down stairs all day long, but at least we got a workout.

When we reached the prop room, she

poked around for a few minutes until finally locating what she was looking for. Straightening up, she popped the short handle of the small purse over her arm and patted it. "Thank you so much. I was afraid to go back to the office without it. She's already so upset."

"How's she doing?"

"Better, now that she's had some tea and time to rest." She cocked her head and smiled. "I know she seems . . ."

"Committed?"

Bella laughed, her white teeth flashing and her nose wrinkling up in a charming way. "That was very diplomatic of you. Yes. She just really loves this place."

As we moved down the corridor, she stopped by the large corner room and peered inside.

"Do you want to go in?" I remembered her wistful look from earlier.

Her brown eyes widened and she clasped her hands together. "May I?"

"Absolutely." I switched the light on and gestured for her to go first. As she walked inside, I glanced at the secret staircase. The closed door blended seamlessly into the wallpaper. I wondered how many people knew about it.

She walked around the room slowly, taking everything in. As she passed the dressing table with the mirror, she trailed her fingertips along the top slowly. Something emanated from her — a sadness, perhaps. Or a longing for something. I didn't know what.

"Why don't you sit down at the table?" I invited her.

She froze, her back to me, then twisted around so that she could lower herself into the velvet chair facing the mirror. Staring at herself in the glass, she burst into tears.

"Bella, what's wrong?"

She put her hands over her face and sobbed. I patted her on the back, unsure what else to do. Finally, when the storm had passed, she looked up and delicately wiped her face. "I'm so sorry, Lila. It's just —" She paused and sniffed and took a deep breath before continuing. "This was my mother's dressing room."

Our eyes met in the mirror as she spoke.

"Althea Gaines is your mother?"

"Yes." Her shoulders sagged. "I never met her. She left right after I was born, to be with the man everyone believes is my father."

"Camden Drake."

"Yes." Another tear ran down her cheek.

I knelt and put my arm around her shoulders. "I'm so very sorry."

"I just wish I had known them. And I wish I knew why they left me behind. They've never even tried to reach out to me. I can't find them online, either. Clara said they probably changed their names to avoid being connected to the scandal. She also believes that all they care about is themselves. And she knew them, so she may have some genuine insight about it all, but still . . . it hurts."

She cried a little more, then eventually calmed down. I pulled a tissue from a box on the table and offered it to her.

Bella dabbed at her face. "Maybe we could go back upstairs."

"Of course."

I followed her out of the room and turned the light off.

"To be around the places where my parents were makes me feel closer to them," she said as we walked.

It occurred to me that Malcolm Gaines, the man married to her mother who could also be her father, had died here by his own hand. I wasn't going to bring it up right now, though. "How long have you been connected to the Opera House?"

"Since as far back as I can remember. The Worthinghams have been involved with it since Malcolm Gaines gave it to the university. And they raised me."

"Oh, I didn't realize that. I wondered why you called Clara by her first name if she was your mother."

"Yes, that throws people sometimes. They adopted me, and I took their last name, but her preference was that I call her Mrs. Worthingham when I was growing up. She may have wanted to distance herself from the scandal or something. I don't know. I can't complain. She's a complicated person —"

That's putting it nicely.

"— and it was incredibly kind of them to take me in after finding me on their doorstep. They lived next door to my father, you know. Or perhaps I should say next door to my mother's husband." She paused on the top step and turned around, looking into my eyes. "It's very difficult to tell a story when you don't know if your father is one man or the other. Though I think of them both as my father in some ways. That probably doesn't make sense."

The lights flickered briefly.

"I don't know who my father is either," I admitted.

"Really?"

I nodded. "My mother never told me."

"I'm sorry, Lila." She put her arm around

my shoulders and pulled me in for a side squeeze.

The simplicity of her statement could only have come from someone who understood how complicated it was not to have an answer for something so many took for granted. Most people peppered me with questions, and I had no answers for them. No, I didn't know why my mother wouldn't tell me his name. No, I didn't know who he was. No, I hadn't tried to find him. No, I didn't want to explain why. And so on.

"We're more alike than I thought," she said, regarding me thoughtfully. "If you ever want to talk, I'm here. Not to be pushy. Just an invitation. I have certainly had my share of emotional turmoil related to daddy drama."

The lights flickered again. I didn't want another blackout experience, especially when we were the only two people in the whole place. I hurried us both up the aisle and into the lobby.

She stopped at the wall across from the box office, which had a number of framed pictures of actors and guests of the Opera House, and pointed to one right in the middle.

"There are lots of pictures of her on this wall, but this one is my favorite. The costumes are gorgeous, and they both look so happy."

I stepped closer to take in the color photo of a woman in a dark red gown with a fitted bodice and full skirt. Her hair, pinned up in an intricate manner, was a caramel shade identical to Bella's, and her generous mouth was stretched into a radiant smile. Her left hand rested on the shoulder of a man with black hair who was seated at the piano.

"Isn't she beautiful?" Bella's face was aglow.

"She's lovely," I agreed.

"That's Camden," she said, pointing to the piano player in a dark suit. His back was perfectly straight, and his hands were poised gracefully over the keys. He was only visible in profile, but they made an attractive couple nonetheless.

"He looks very elegant."

She gazed at the image for a long moment, smiling, before pointing at another picture below. "And that's Malcolm."

The blond man in the photo leaned against the box office door, arms crossed over his chest. His sleeves were rolled up, revealing strong, muscular arms, and he was laughing. He wasn't at all what I'd been imagining. Probably because I knew the end of the story.

"He looks like he has the kind of personality that would fill up a room."

"Clara and Braxton said he loved to laugh. At least until my mother left." Bella took a step closer and peered at it. "I don't know why he had to leave me too, though. I would have laughed with him."

Words failed me in that moment. What does someone say to that?

She turned to me and said, "Let's get out of here."

Best idea I'd heard all day.

CHAPTER 12

We were hard at work the next day on the penultimate number, "Curtains for the Culprits," where Oliver gathered all of the suspects into the drawing room of the country manor house for the big reveal. The script called for Oliver to have a spirited debate with the various sleuths over the identification of the murderer and then to prove them wrong using information he'd collected through an instance of time travel. To cement his case, he introduced an alien, a self-proclaimed "interstellar sleuth," to bear witness.

It was hilarious, though I didn't know if that was intentional.

Tolliver was giving adjustment notes to the lighting crew, and I was chatting with Luciana Trevalti, the costume designer, about how to correct an issue with Sherlock's hat. She had just come up with the solution when I noticed the actors on stage staring at something behind me.

Spinning around, I saw six men walking down the aisle with all manner of gadgetry and cameras. I excused myself from the conversation and headed their way.

The man leading them had a surfer vibe — a shock of blond hair falling over his temple, a dazzling smile, and a deep tan. When he reached us, he extended a hand. "Are you Tolliver Ingersoll?"

I shook his hand and pointed to the director. "That's Tolliver. I'm Lila Maclean, the assistant director. May I help you?"

"I'm Vance Myers, and this is my crew. We're from *Spirit Wranglers,* and we're here to do some filming."

Spirit Wranglers was one of the more famous paranormal reality shows. It typically featured an intrepid group of people who went into locations that were said to be haunted. They used different kinds of equipment to prove, or more often to disprove, the legends.

Tolliver bounded down the stage steps, waving his hands wildly. "Who gave you permission to film? It's absolutely unthinkable. We're in the middle of rehearsal here." He came to stand next to me, radiating fury.

Vance smiled widely at him. "Mr. Ingersoll, I'm so thrilled to meet you. *A Tale of*

Three Swords is one of my favorite plays. When I was out here visiting family, we went to see it four times."

The fury dissipated instantly. Tolliver clapped him on the back. "Four times? How splendid."

"Yes. I thought it was brilliant. Perhaps one of the best plays in the current century."

"How kind." He bowed slightly. "Though why limit it to the current century?"

Vance released a surprisingly loud bray of a laugh.

"I'm joking, of course," Tolliver said, reaching for modest but failing.

"No need. I revise my assessment, sir. One of the best plays of *all* the centuries."

There was another round of back clapping, this time by both men.

I looked rapidly back and forth between them, engaged by the confluence of fawning and narcissism.

"It's an honor to meet you, Tolliver. Listen, we've been given permission by Dr. Frinkle in the parapsychology department at Stonedale. We ran into him while we finished up some reshoots in Estes Park, and he sent us here."

"Were you at the Stanley Hotel?" I took a guess. It was famous for being the inspiration for the Overlook in Stephen King's *The*

Shining. The hotel offered ghost tours and so forth.

Vance nodded gleefully. "We got some great stuff on tape."

"And now you're going to film here? I don't know how that will work since we're using this theater." I turned to see what Tolliver's reaction was.

"We won't interfere with your rehearsals," Vance said quickly. "We shoot mostly at night after you've gone home. And we only have a few days to do this, so we will be in and out before you know it. We were hoping to get set up now, though, if you don't mind."

"Well, as long as you won't be in our way," Tolliver said. "Carry on."

An hour later, it was clear that they would very much be in our way. There were cables here and cords there and cameras everywhere. Although they weren't technically shooting while we were rehearsing, they were definitely *here*.

Tolliver, despite having given permission, was regretting it. Clara was going to pitch a fit if she found out, which I prayed she didn't.

At least not before she signed off on the paperwork.

The students, however, were extremely excited. When they weren't onstage, they hovered on the edge of the *Spirit Wranglers'* central location, set up in the back of the theater, where three guys were fidgeting with video equipment and other devices.

"Do you need anyone to be in your show, like for interviews?" I heard Parker asking Vance.

"We might. Go talk to Joe — he's the one who coordinates talent." He pointed to a man with curly brown hair speaking into a headset.

Parker, followed by every single actor within hearing distance, zoomed over.

Tolliver called for a dinner break and faced me. "I know I told him to carry on, but you have to find a way to shut this down. It's intolerable."

"I understand, Tolliver. It's frustrating. But if the university already gave permission, we need to make our peace with it. They're only going to shoot at night."

"You might be right," Tolliver said begrudgingly.

"Maybe you could even participate. Be on television."

He perked up at that thought.

Zandra joined us. She flung an arm over the director's shoulder. "Tolly, I have a message. Our ghost wants *Spirit Wranglers* to be here. He has much to tell us."

"Is that so, Z?" Tolliver looked fondly at her.

Zandra curved her lips into a mysterious smile. "It is so."

I began to ask for more details but broke off at the sounds of shouts and thumps.

Students surrounded Chip Turner and Vance Myers, who were crouched and circling each other onstage as if they were at an impromptu wrestling match.

"What in the world are you doing?" Tolliver bellowed at them.

"The ghost chasers need to leave!" Chip said angrily, jabbing his fist forward, though Vance was safely out of reach. "This is my private property."

"It's not your private property yet," I reminded him.

"We have written permission from the college to be here," Vance retorted, angrily swiping at his hair, which kept falling into his eyes. "It doesn't matter if it's private or not. And who are you to come in here and start insulting our show, man?"

"I was just joking around," Chip muttered.

"It wasn't funny." Vance lurched at him, but Chip skittered out of the way.

I marched into the space between them and put my hands out on either side. "Guys, you have to stop."

Tolliver joined me. "Yes. This ends now. Mr. Turner, please leave."

Chip's head snapped back in surprise. "Me? I have to leave? But I'm not doing anything wrong."

"You are, actually. Please leave," Tolliver repeated.

I wondered why Chip kept showing up here. It was true that the theater wasn't locked during rehearsals, but doesn't a potential buyer need to be accompanied by a realtor? What made him so entitled?

Come to think of it, maybe the fact that anyone could stroll right in was a problem. The police were no longer stationed anywhere at the theater, having ended their promised week of coverage.

Chip finally straightened up, jumped off the edge of the stage, and left the theater.

Vance flashed a wide smile at the students. "How'd you like that?"

They laughed and applauded.

He flexed his muscles and made a playful roaring sound.

"You didn't win anything, you know," Tolliver said.

150

"Feels like it." Vance winked and sauntered away, whistling.

We were almost done with the second act when Tolliver leaned over to me. "Where are the ghost busters?"

"They're below stage."

"Will you go check on them?" he asked. I slipped out of the row while he grumbled and Zandra listened sympathetically. Now that the delight at Vance's flattery had worn off, the presence of the spirit wranglers was aggravating him.

I made my way down to the lower level and through the cold spot. It was always just as abrupt and startling as it had been the very first time. As I entered the prop room, I bumped into Vance.

"Sorry," I said. "Didn't see you there."

"It's all right, Lila. I'm looking at shot angles. What can I do for you?"

Another crew member came up to him with a confused look and pointed to the digital screen on a small box. Vance moved a switch and regular numbers appeared.

"Okay, we are go for tape, everyone," said Vance. "You can watch if you want, Lila. We're going to shoot the first segment." The crew members took their positions behind the cameras. Vance moved to the center of the room, beneath the trap door. They'd moved the mattresses to the outer perimeter. Tolliver wasn't going to like that.

"Sorry to interrupt, Vance, but could you guys please put everything back the way you found it afterwards?" I tried to say it gently.

"No prob." He grinned at me, then looked around at the crew. One of them counted down and the camera light went on.

"Hi, all you ghost hunters! I'm Vance Myers of *Spirit Wranglers.*" He smiled brightly. "Today we are in Colorado, at the Stonedale Opera House, said to be the site of a terrifying haunting."

I wouldn't say terrifying, exactly. More like annoying.

"Legend has it that the spirit of a professor — the owner of the Opera House — is trapped here. His wife was said to have had an affair with another professor from nearby Stonedale University. And after he discovered it, he hanged himself onstage."

After an appropriately grave pause, Vance perked up. "There have been numerous hauntings — including multiple full-body sightings — reported in the years since. Using our state-of-the-art equipment, we're going to get to the bottom of this tragic tale and see what the spirit himself has to tell us. Stay tuned."

He held his bright smile until the camera light went out. Vance came over to me, holding a microphone. "Hey, would you let us interview you, Lila? It would be cool to have another Stonedale professor, aside from Dr. Frinkle."

The last thing I wanted to do was go on camera and talk about ghosts. I was pretty sure that wouldn't help my tenure bid down the road — in fact, it might even hurt it. "Oh, I don't really have anything to say. You know as much as I do, basically."

"Could I just ask you some questions, then?"

I looked pointedly at the microphone in his hand. "Is that thing on?"

"Nah," he said. "It's just you and me talking. So. You've been here for a few months. Ever see anything strange?"

I craned my neck toward the camera man to make sure he wasn't surreptitiously filming. No lens was pointed in my direction as far as I could tell.

"Anything at all unusual?" Vance persisted.

"No."

"Maybe I should ask if you have ever *experienced* anything? It doesn't just have to be something you saw. Sounds, sensations, stuff like that."

"Well, the temperature down here always

surprises me. It's cold all the time. It could just be because it's below ground, though, right?"

He tilted his head. "Maybe, but it could also be a sign of paranormal activity. Good. What else?"

I hesitated.

He took a step closer and lowered his voice. His aftershave was spicy and not unappealing. "You can tell me, Lila. I won't think you're losing it. You'd be surprised how many people talk themselves out of believing something they definitely experienced just because it sounds crazy."

"Well, I have heard knocking or scratching in the walls, though that could be squirrels."

"Or not." He gave me a you-never-know shrug.

"And the lights often go out, though that could be just be the old electrical system. The main breaker literally sparks when the lever is moved."

"Or not. Though they should get someone to fix that," Vance said. "I mean, ghost hunting aside, it's a fire hazard. I'm surprised the university hasn't taken care of it."

"The school doesn't usually stage productions here. The chancellor and Tolliver came to an agreement about that. Tolliver said he likes the ambiance. Plus, we just found out that they're probably selling the building, so perhaps they aren't too concerned about updating everything."

He nodded thoughtfully. "Thanks for the information. It jives with what the students are saying too. Though a few of them reported having seen a full-body manifestation as well . . . a man walking down the hallway. Have you ever seen that?"

"No," I said. Thank goodness.

"Let me just run down a few other things if you have a minute. Any orbs or unexplained light phenomena?"

"No. Aside from the lights going on and off."

"Well, I'd say that counts."

"It's an old building," I insisted.

"Any doors, windows, or cabinets opening or closing by themselves?"

"Doors have been known to slam. But that could be because the building foundation has shifted. It happens a lot in Colorado, I've heard, because of the soil."

He ignored that explanation. "Any screams or groans or other sounds?"

"No. Oh, wait. Several students have heard singing. But I don't think —"

"Good. Okay, how about any floating or falling objects? Or items moving locations without explanation?"

"I did find a small trunk sitting in a stairwell once. But it could have been left there by anyone. I don't know if it moved —"

"How about unusual marks on any objects?"

"No. Oh. Well, there are the claw-like marks along there." I pointed to the wall near the dressing rooms.

"Saw those." His eyes lit up. "You do realize that you've said yes to almost everything I've raised, in one way or another, don't you? I think we may have an actual presence here. Maybe even poltergeist. This could be very exciting."

"For you, maybe. Not so much for us."

He laughed. "Lila, part of what our show does is help people come to terms with what's already happening. You'll feel better afterwards, once you know what you're dealing with, I promise."

I wasn't so sure.

CHAPTER 13

Later that night, I lay awake, staring up at the ceiling while I ran through my to-do lists. Cady, a lovely brown cat, was curled up next to me — Calista had asked me to cat-sit while she attended a conference — and her warmth was comforting, but I couldn't fall asleep. The rehearsals were getting longer and more exhausting, and it was all I could do to keep up with my normal class load. I was afraid my classes were getting the short shrift, but no matter how late I stayed up, I couldn't accomplish more than the bare minimum.

I also needed to call Clara to ask for the signed paperwork, just so we had it. She'd completed the tour, which was the final step, but we had never received anything official. Although the chancellor had said the paperwork was merely a formality, it was clear that Clara didn't view it quite the same way. It was also clear that she would take oppositional action — discourage people from attending at the very least — if she wasn't happy.

Maybe I shouldn't talk to her about it. What if she said no? What would we do then? What would *she* do then?

Turning onto my side, I tucked my arm under the pillow. Cady shifted slightly and blinked her yellow eyes at me but didn't meow any complaint.

I ran through the conversation with Vance again. The comment he made was bothering me — that I'd checked off almost all of the boxes on his paranormal activity list. How could there have been so many signs, and why weren't they on my radar sooner? I mean, I wasn't sure if I believed that the Opera House was haunted. It was definitely spooky in some parts, and it was the site of a suicide, but I wasn't sure if I believed in an actual ghost inhabiting it. I didn't *not* believe . . . because no one can grow up the daughter of artist Violet O and not have an open mind. But I'd never really come into contact with any ghosts, to my knowledge.

Still, my body had gone into high alert mode at the theater before, with goose-bumps and anxiety spikes and an array of disconcerting symptoms. Until now, I'd written it off as stress-induced and tried to ignore it. What if it was something para-normal instead?

And how *had* Zandra known we'd been looking in the black trunk? Had Malcom really told her, as she claimed? Or had she seen us onstage?

I flipped over to the other side, this time earning a protest from the cat. She made a noise, then jumped over me to curl up in the nook of my stomach on the other side.

Through the window shade, I could see the shadow outline of the few remaining leaves clinging to swaying branches in the gentle wind. It was mesmerizing, and after a while I closed my eyes and began to drift off, only to be jolted awake again when my phone rang soon after.

I shot up in my bed, torn from a dream about Althea Gaines sitting in front of a mirror, making strange gestures. Bella was standing behind her, silently, staring into the glass. It was so vivid I felt as though I'd been there with them.

In a daze, I answered the phone.

"Lila! Get down here." Tolliver shouted. "I need you."

I pulled the phone away from my ear slightly. "Where are you?"

"At the theater. On the double, okay?"

"What's going on —"

But he had already hung up.

I sighed and dressed quickly, zipping up my Stonedale University sweatshirt over a thermal and jeans, scraping my long dark waves into a ponytail. As I grabbed my keys, I told Cady that I'd be back soon, hoping it was true.

I pulled up to the Opera House less than five minutes later. Tolliver met me out front. "I'm sorry to bother you, Petal, but you have to see this for yourself."

He pulled my arm, and we went into the lobby. The spirit wranglers were huddled together, looking at something. When the door slammed shut and caught his attention, Vance waved me over.

"Hi," I said as I joined them.

"Restart it," he said to the guy holding an iPad. "Let Lila see."

After it had been reset, Vance took the iPad and aimed it in my direction. "Night vision," he said curtly.

"Do you have to film at night?"

"Not really," he said. "But it's more dramatic. Plays better."

I watched as the footage began to roll. It was grainy, but there was Vance, his face rendered peculiarly by the night vision camera. Even if there was no ghost captured

160

on film, he looked sufficiently creepy.

"I'm here in the prop room below the stage of the Opera House, where there have been reports of objects moving around. We are about to use the recorder to see if we can capture any voices."

He held up the small rectangular box I'd seen earlier. "The EMF recorder indicates higher electromagnetic activity in this area. As soon as we came into this room, the needle jumped."

Suddenly, there was a loud bang. He jolted, his face registering genuine surprise.

"What was that?"

Off camera, I heard someone yelling, "Over there, over there!" The screen began to shake as the camera operator followed Vance. It was chaotic and jerky, capturing indistinguishable parts of the floor as Vance moved down the hallway and stopped at the corner dressing room.

"Get this!" He gestured wildly to the camera and stepped out of the way to allow us to see the door in the wall to the secret staircase closing, becoming indistinguishable from the rest of the wall. "It's a secret door!" Vance yelled, as he ran over and began pushing so that it would open again. After the third attempt, there was a visible click as the door unlatched.

Vance went through it, the camera followed, and they moved up the spiral staircase. As they emerged, Vance pointed. "Get it!" The shot moved past him to capture an image of a dark figure moving rapidly across the stage.

The camera raced after it but cut soon after.

"We couldn't catch up," Vance explained apologetically.

I looked at Tolliver, who said, "That seems like proof."

"Of what?"

"Malcolm."

Vance was nodding and high-fiving the guys around him.

"But what makes you so sure it wasn't just a person who was faster than you?" I asked.

They all stared at me.

"Didn't you see? It was hovering," Vance said, excitedly. "We got ourselves a floater!"

"Could you replay that part, please?"

They did, but I couldn't tell if the figure was on the floor or above it. It was too dark.

"Trust me. It was a floater," Vance said. "Plus, how about that staircase?"

"Oh. We knew about the staircase," I said. "I'm sorry I forgot to mention it before."

He shrugged. "It's going to make for some great TV."

"Couldn't it be a human? And if so, aren't you guys worried about there being an intruder here, maybe?" I asked.

"Nah. There are more of us than there are of him," Vance laughed. The crew joined in.

"Someone shot our previous director not too long ago," I informed him.

That quieted them down.

"I'm sorry," Vance said. "We didn't know that."

I nodded, fighting the tears welling up in my eyes.

He took stock of my expression, gave my arm a quick squeeze, then steered the crew a few feet away.

I whirled around to go. I just wanted to sit in my car and have a long cry about Jean Claude. I had only known him a short while, but although he was bossy and bellowed a lot, he was talented and passionate and kind-hearted. And I felt his loss.

Grief poked its head up in unexpected ways. I definitely wanted to know who had killed him and why, but I didn't know how to go about finding the answer.

Back at home, I collapsed onto my chenille sofa. Racing over to the Opera House in the middle of the night had shot me into wide-awake mode. Now my brain was buzzing, but my body was moving in slow motion.

I knew I wouldn't be able to fall asleep for awhile. I could clean. I could watch TV. Neither activity was appealing at the moment. Then my conscience kicked in and suggested that I catch up on my grading, and I leaned down to the coffee table and opened the flap of the satchel.

The letters.

I'd completely forgotten I had them. I pulled the bag toward me and scrabbled around until my fingers closed on the packet. Unwinding the red ribbon slowly, I examined them. The paper was old and yellow. The neat cursive writing was the same on all of them. There were six, all sent to Althea Gaines at an address on Oak Street. I arranged them in order of postmark — the first two were a week apart, then there were intervals of several weeks between each of the remaining letters. Setting the first five envelopes on the pillow next to me, I opened the flap of the earliest dated one, carefully removing the sheet of paper inside. Unfolding it, I began scanning the words.

July 7, 1990

Dear Mrs. Gaines,

Thank you for writing. The pleasure was all mine. I was grateful for your inquiries after the performance. It's rare that one meets another who appreciates the dramatic arts with such deep understanding. Of course, your own achievements onstage have far surpassed mine. I hope that we will have an opportunity to meet again soon.

With my best regards,
Camden Drake

It all seemed on the up and up. Polite, professional. I decided to remove the rest of the letters at once and read them in order.

July 15, 1990

Dear Mrs. Gaines,

It was a lovely chat. I hope that we have the chance to further discuss the experiments I am attempting — feebly, I fear — with my latest work. There are not many people in the world who would be willing to sit through an hour-long lecture on the subject, I'm afraid, but thank you for the invitation. If you believe that such an audience exists, I would be honored to prepare something.

With my best regards,
Camden Drake

August 18, 1990

Dear Mrs. Gaines,

I am astonished at the number of Stonedale citizens you were able to drag to my lecture. It is surely due to your organizing talents and not at all due to my own humble area of interest. (Not expertise, as you so kindly called it in your introduction.) May I take you and, if he's available, Mr. Gaines out for dinner at your convenience as a small token of my gratitude?

With my best regards,
Camden Drake

September 22, 1990

Dear Althea,

Has it been a month since our evening together? I can hardly pay attention to the passing of the days. I can hardly pay attention to anything at all. Your face is all I see before me, wherever I look, and

166

I have never been happier. Write me immediately and tell me when we can meet again.

> With deepest affection,
> Camden

October 12, 1990

Dearest A,
I cannot wait much longer. This is preposterous. You must leave him.

> Yours,
> Cam

October 30, 1990

My beloved,
Pack your bags. Tell Malcolm that you're sick and have your understudy go on for you. I'll meet you in your dressing room during the first act. Wait until you see what I'm bringing you — gems for my gem — you are going to shine in New York, in more ways than one.

> With all my love,
> C

I put the last letter down onto the pile and sat back, processing what I'd just read. It was all there — the affair, the plan to run away to New York, and what sounded like some very nice jewelry that he was about to give her.

It was time to put on my scholar hat and see what I could find out about the two of them. I'd been listening to everyone else's accounts for so long, and I wanted to know the facts.

On Monday after class, I went to Pennington library to go through the microfiche. It was going the way of the dinosaur these days, but our campus hadn't yet fully given in to the digital movement, so the town newspapers would still be preserved on film.

I had the date and year of the big fight — Halloween night, 1990 — so I made a stop at the computer to look up the correct call number. Before long, I was seated at a machine, looking at the *Stonedale Scout* from that era.

I scrolled feverishly through the pages until I reached the proper week. The headline for November first screamed "OUTRAGE AT THE OPERA HOUSE!"

The story, written by one Rudy Sharpton, detailed what was known at the time: cast members witnessed Malcolm Gaines discover and confront Camden Drake and Althea Gaines. The two men fought and the police were called. Neither was arrested. Rudy made a point of underlining the adultery aspect. It didn't really seem like it deserved such a lurid headline, but I knew those sold papers.

There wasn't any immediate follow-up to that story, but I kept scrolling until I found, almost twelve months later, an edition that proclaimed "ALTHEA GAINES MISSING." Sharpton again didn't have much to report other than the fact that she was missing. He began by noting that she'd recently put out an album of songs, including a ballad written by Camden, then he rehashed the details of the fight a year earlier, interviewed several witnesses who opined that she had gone to join Camden, who had left for New York after the scandal broke, and that was that. Malcolm, of course, hadn't agreed to speak to the reporter.

Shortly afterwards, "MALCOLM GAINES FOUND DEAD" was the headline. The story described how he'd been found by a member of the cleaning crew and mentioned that he left behind a baby daughter.

Afterwards, it just dropped out of the news. Nothing more appeared about Althea. Nothing about the daughter.

I sat back. That was it?

I resumed scrolling until I had seen every edition in the year following. She had disappeared from the pages of the news the way she had disappeared from the town.

Turning to the fiche for the year before the initial argument, I discovered ads for a variety of plays starring Althea, several articles about Camden Drake and his numerous projects, and an interview with Malcolm about the upcoming season. I felt a rush of empathy: he could never have imagined, when he finalized that lineup, what lay ahead.

Going back to the library computer, I did a quick internet search for Althea Gaines and Camden Drake. There were links leading to the mentions of the scandal, their bios, and pictures of them from various productions at Stonedale. But nothing from New York. They must have changed their names after they left town since theirs had been dragged through the mud. I couldn't blame them.

Moving to let the next patron take my spot, I tried to figure out what to do with the letters. They didn't belong to me, and I didn't know what their value was, but they deserved careful treatment. To whom should I give them? Bella, who had genuine questions about why her parents left her? Clara, who was so deeply invested in the history of the theater? Chip, who seemed to want to own everything connected to the Opera House? The ghost busters would also probably be interested, given that they were foregrounding this very tragedy in their show. And then there was the chancellor, the one who technically had the authority to make decisions about the Opera House.

Definitely needed some caffeine to sort this one out.

CHAPTER 14

After a vat of coffee at Scarlett's Café and a scone to boot, I had narrowed it down to Lex Archer. The detective would give me an impartial take on what to do with the letters — he was the only one I could think of who wouldn't be interested in getting his hands on them himself. As a bonus, I could ask about the murder investigation. In fact, Lex had risen to the top of my list once I realized that asking for his help with the letters gave me the perfect opportunity to try and obtain some information without asking for it directly.

I was curious as to why Lex hadn't already checked in; he knew Jean Claude was my friend. Then again, I wasn't a police officer. And Lex was one of the busiest people I knew. I'd learned that the hard way, after we'd begun to circle around dating a year and a half ago.

Perhaps Lex and I weren't the most obvious fit: when we met during my first semester at Stonedale University, he'd been interrogating me about a crime, which he thought I might have committed. We'd been thrown together during another investigation later that year, and it was clear by then that there was something between us.

And that something made me even more awkward than usual around him. I'd never be one of those elegant women in a love story who pines gracefully and imperceptibly for her man. I'm more the spill-my-drink-on-him and blurt-out-absurdities kind of girl.

He'd asked me out once, but almost immediately had been reassigned to another precinct a few hours north of Denver to work on a serial killer case. He'd been up there ever since. Initially we had talked on the phone occasionally, but he couldn't talk about that case, and I didn't want to burden him with the ins and outs of trying to finish my scholarly book in progress.

Plus, I was already behind on everything else. Teaching was such an all-consuming job. People seemed to think being an English professor means showing up on campus a few hours a week to exchange witty banter with students, like in the movies, but I'd found it to be more like a seven-day-a-week routine, what with the preparation for classes, advising, committee work, research, and grading. There was never enough time in the day to finish it all.

In any case, Lex and I had stopped talking after awhile, and that seemed to be that.

I sighed. No sense in lamenting our missed connection. He'd been back in town for a few months, I'd heard, and he hadn't contacted me. It didn't seem as though he had any interest in getting together.

This was business, however, so I called, apologizing for the short notice and explaining that I needed his assistance. He was surprised but readily agreed, which was a relief. Even if we weren't going to pursue any sort of romance, I wanted us to be able to call each other if we needed to.

I had just enough time for a brisk house cleaning, meaning that I threw everything in the closet and closed the door. Next was menu-planning, which involved rummaging through the cupboards to see what was languishing in there. Since I didn't have time to run to the store, I was thrilled to find a full box of ziti and jar of tomato sauce. Typically, I was more of a warmer-upper than an actual cook, but I could manage pasta. I also tossed a salad, sliced some whole-grain bread, and set the table with barely a minute to spare.

Then used that minute to throw on some lip gloss.

When the doorbell rang, I had a moment of uncertainty about how to greet him. After standing with my hand on the door for a moment, I just decided to let whatever happened happen.

Lex stood on the front step with a bottle of wine in each hand, looking slightly uncomfortable. His dark hair, which he usually wore in a buzz cut, had grown out a bit. It was still short but spikier. I liked it.

"Hello, Professor," he said, smiling.

"Hello, Detective."

I backed up so he could enter.

He handed me the bottles. "I didn't know whether you liked red or white, so I got both."

"Good, because I like both."

He moved into the small bungalow. He wore a dark jacket with his jeans. His biceps looked even more impressive than I remembered. Not that I was looking.

"Do you want red or white?" I walked over to the little galley kitchen and waved him in.

"None for me, thanks. I'm on duty. Milk would be fine, if you got it."

"You're on duty and you're here?"

"My shift starts in an hour." He cast his blue eyes around the kitchen, which was barely big enough for two people. I wondered what he thought of my unfinished to-do lists plastered all over the fridge.

"Oh. Let me feed you quickly, then," I said, reaching for the square white plates I'd stacked on the counter. "Please have a seat at the table over there."

The last time we'd sat at my oak table, he was grilling me about my cousin, who had been arrested. He was probably thinking about that too.

I spooned up some pasta and sauce, then brought the plates out to the dining nook and set them down on the tablecloth. I hadn't displayed any candles because that seemed a bit too romantic given our unclarified situation, but there were fresh flowers in a vase that looked lovely, if I did say so myself.

He didn't say anything, though.

And everything felt wrong.

I wasn't sure what I'd expected the dynamic to be, but it wasn't this. Typically, we had a little spark. Tonight, he seemed distracted. Or bored. Or tired. Or — the breath caught in my throat — suspicious.

I ran back into the kitchen to give myself a second to think, where I realized that I'd forgotten to bring out the parmesan cheese. That was lucky. Now I could pretend it was the reason I'd fled.

My thoughts were racing, but I reassured myself that he wouldn't sit down for dinner if he thought I was a murderer. Heading back to the table, I smiled at Lex.

"So," I said, casually. "How are things going with the Jean Claude case?"

He slowly sprinkled cheese over his pasta and took a big bite.

I waited.

"Funny you should mention that," he said. "I was going to ask you the same thing."

"What do you mean?" I slid into the seat across from him and placed the napkin on my lap.

"Rumor has it that you've been asking around . . ."

I put on a mock affronted look. "Who has been talking about me? Tell me immediately."

He didn't laugh.

Uh oh.

"Just kidding. What do you mean?"

"Clara Worthingham came down to the station yesterday and complained about you."

I froze, fork halfway to my mouth.

"Complained about me? But I haven't —"

"According to her, you've been . . ." he looked up at the ceiling. " 'Snooping,' I think is how she put it."

"Snooping? Who am I, Miss Marple?"

He shrugged and reached again for the parmesan cheese. "Her words, not mine."

"I can't imagine why she thinks that. All I did was —"

"You realize that most of the descriptions of your shenanigans have begun with 'All I did was.' "

"That may be so, but honestly, I just went down to the Historical Society office to ask about the protests. I was trying to keep Tolliver happy and make sure the play could go on. And while I was there, I asked how much she'd spoken to Jean Claude. Nothing much worth mentioning."

"And did something happen at the Opera House?"

"Not that I know of. I mean, I gave her a tour. We found a secret staircase leading from the corner dressing room up to the stage. Did you know that was there?"

I could tell he was surprised, though nothing moved except his eyebrows. "Tell me more."

I walked him through the discovery.

He nodded, chewing slowly. When he was done, he took a long swig of the milk. "This is delicious, thank you. Been a long time since I had," he glanced down at his plate, "noodles."

"Noodles are my specialty."

Wait, *what* did I just say? My face went hot. Maybe he didn't hear it.

"Thanks for telling me about the staircase. We'll check that out." He cleared his throat and put down his glass. "But actually I'm here on official business."

I froze again, thrown completely off balance. Here I'd invited him over for the express purpose of having a conversation about my thing, and I couldn't even get to it because he had his own agenda.

He shifted in his chair a little bit. Good. I was glad to see he was uncomfortable too. "I'm here to ask you, respectfully, to stay out of the Jean Claude Lestronge case."

"Stay out of it? I'm not even in it."

"According to Clara, you're right in the middle of it."

I waved that away. "We just talked. It was nothing."

"Until she came barreling into the station to complain about you and got everyone all riled up."

"I have questions. He was my friend. And I didn't even know what the police were doing, because you didn't tell me anything."

Lex considered this. "It was on the news."

"Good point. But I've been so busy with the play that I haven't had time to keep up. My brain is full of script changes and lighting cues."

"I see." He took another drink of milk.

"Can you at least tell me what's going on? What have you found out?"

"Sorry."

"Even though I just gave you information about how the killer could have gotten out of there so fast?"

He dipped his chin. "And thank you for that."

I stabbed some ziti. "What if I asked *you* some questions? Could you answer them?"

"Give it a try, though you already know I have limitations."

"Why would Clara even think I was snooping unless she had something to hide?"

"I can't answer that."

"And who uses the word 'snooping' anyway these days?"

He shrugged, though I caught a flicker of amusement in his blue eyes. "Do you have something else to add, Professor? Or was that the extent of your question list?"

"Oh, I'm just warming up," I assured him, putting down my fork.

He buttered some bread as he waited for

me to continue.

"Do you have any suspects?"

Lex popped the piece into his mouth and chewed.

"Are you just going to stare at me?"

He stared at me.

"Let's do this: if I'm right, don't do anything. If I'm wrong, shake your head."

He blinked. I took that to mean he was on board.

"Do you have any suspects?" The detective didn't move a muscle.

"Okay, I'm going to do a test of the system. Make sure we're on the same page. Is your given name Lex Luthor?"

He shook his head, never breaking eye contact.

"Thank you. Back to the questions. So is there more than one suspect?"

He moved his head again.

"Just one. Okay. Are they male or —"

Lex rolled his eyes. "This is going to take all night. Lila, I'll just give you the information that we've already given the press, okay? We are working on the case. We have a person of interest. We'll take it from there."

I drummed the table with my fingertips. "Mmm hmm. And the person of interest is . . . ?"

He remained silent. Stubborn, as always,

which I found both maddening and compelling.

"I'm just wondering because we know there are so many potential suspects — everyone working on the play, plus the Historical Society people, not to mention all of his fans. Jean Claude had quite a following. I'm surprised you've whittled it down to just one person already. What's leading you in that direction?"

"I can't tell you anything, Lila. And you shouldn't be doing anything related to the case. I know you've been involved in two already, but you aren't trained, and I . . . I . . ." He looked down at his hands. "Look, I don't want you to get hurt. We haven't even had a chance to go on a proper date yet."

Until that moment, I hadn't been sure that I cared if there was a "we." But now I knew I did.

I smiled at him. "A proper date is hard to accomplish when you run out of town after extending the invitation."

"Yep, that's my *modus operandi.* Easier that way." He looked down, then up through his lashes. If I hadn't been sitting, my knees would have buckled.

"I see."

"But I've been thinking lately that I might

want to try something new. Maybe go through with said date, see what that's like. So how about next weekend?"

"I can't do anything until after the show's over," I said. "We open November first and run for two weeks."

"Just around the corner then."

"Yes. Are you free after that?"

"I could be," he said, fixing those gorgeous blue eyes on mine.

"Wait," I said. "Did you ask me out or did I ask you out? It got kind of confusing there."

"Why does it matter?"

"So I can tell Calista that you asked me on a proper date finally."

"You're already telling people about us?" His cell phone made a sound, and he looked down at a text. "Oh — got to go."

"Can't you stay for a few more minutes?"

"Nope. Sorry ma'am." He tipped an imaginary hat. "Need to make the city streets safe for our citizens again."

We stood up from the table and made our way to the door. Which wasn't hard because it was about three steps away. I wished it were longer because I was reluctant to see him leave. He turned to face me.

"I'm sorry things have been . . ."

I waited while he searched around for the

appropriate word.

"Weird."

That pretty much summed it up.

"It's the job, Lila. Not you."

I felt a rush of relief.

"I understand. I've been overwhelmed with work too."

He moved closer, as though he intended to kiss me. I held my breath. He studied my face for a moment, then grinned. "Thanks for dinner. I can't remember that last time I've had better noodles. They really are your specialty."

Dang, he *had* heard that.

And then he was gone.

CHAPTER 15

As I walked to rehearsal on Wednesday, I realized that I never talked to Lex about the letters. But my mind was still trying to work out what their discovery meant. Had the trunk been placed in the staircase for us to find, and if so, by whom? The ghost himself? Could it be that the production in the Opera House was energizing the spirit, if Malcolm was really present? Or was someone trying to use the legend to get our attention?

I stopped in my tracks next to a plastic skeleton posed cheekily in front of a candy store.

Tolliver was desperate for his play to be a success. Could he be amplifying the ghost presence in order to ensure it? There was that famous saying, though the chancellor would definitely disagree, "No publicity is bad publicity." I wouldn't put it past Tolliver to make sure that word got out.

Also, with Jean Claude out of the way, he could take over as director. But could he have killed him?

As far as I could tell, he had a motive: to see his vision realized. Jean Claude had been making a lot of cuts. I hadn't heard the conversation where Jean Claude informed Tolliver what he'd taken out, but I could only imagine it hadn't gone well.

Still. Would Tolliver kill him for that?

The skeleton seemed more ominous suddenly.

I scooted past it and continued toward the Opera House. Okay, so he had motivation. And as the playwright, he certainly had opportunity to be anywhere in the theater that he needed to be.

But did he have means? I had never seen him with a gun, nor had I heard him talk about one. The police hadn't found anything in the theater as far as I knew–though they hadn't shared much about the case with the public, other than that they were "on it" and, according to Lex, interested in someone.

Something in my gut said that Tolliver wasn't capable of murder. For which I was grateful since I had to spend time in close quarters with him. But perhaps being cautious was a good idea.

When I arrived at the theater, I noted with satisfaction that there were only a few protestors, and they were trudging wearily in a circle. Perhaps they were getting tired of themselves too.

My happiness subsided when I came upon Tolliver and Vance arguing in the lobby.

"You have to get out. This is an artistic space. Where artists work. Your machinery is in the way!" Tolliver fluttered his hands at the cameras.

"But we are out *here,* and your rehearsal is in *there.*" Vance pointed toward the auditorium. "We'll close the door. You won't even know we're working."

"I already know you're working. And simply having that information inside my head is compromising my ability to focus!"

Zandra swept over to Vance. "Malcolm won't perform for you here. He prefers the inner sanctum of the theater." She raised her arms to gesture toward the stage, and the long sleeves of her sheer kimono created a dramatic look. Her acting background was evident.

Vance gave her the side eye, then spoke directly to Tolliver. "We don't need to film inside right now, and we'll be quiet, I promise."

Tolliver, finally accepting that conversation was futile, turned and stormed down the aisle, slamming the door behind him.

The film crew had the shot set up within minutes. Vance was positioned in front of the box office booth, ready to speak on camera when I felt a soft touch on my arm.

"I think Tolly's feeling the pressure," Zandra said.

"It's understandable."

"I just want this play to go well for him. He deserves it."

"How long have you two been together?"

"About a year." She put her hand to her heart. "He's very special to me."

"Oh, I thought you'd been together longer."

"We *have* known each other forever. But our romantic connection didn't blossom until last year, when we both had a little too much punch at the chancellor's Halloween party, and then, well, you know how it goes." She waved the conclusion of that sentence away with her silver-ringed hand. Thank goodness.

The chancellor's annual event required faculty members to attend. Costumes were mandatory. No exceptions. With a chill, I remembered that the party was this weekend, and I hadn't spent a single minute thinking about a costume. I whipped out my cell and typed in a reminder to get something, stat.

"I relish attending that party as ex-faculty," she said, winking at me. "Never imagined that would be the case, but it's true."

"Were you teaching at Stonedale last year, Zandra? Or had you already left?"

"Yes!" She said the word quite loudly. Some of the ghost hunters looked over at us. "I was teaching in the Theater department last year. But it was my find-somewhere-else-to-go year, the one they have to give you after they deny your tenure."

I felt a rush of empathy. "That must have been difficult."

"It was," she nodded. "Every day, I could feel people looking at me. I knew many of them were genuinely sympathetic — I'd cleared the department with no problem, after all, so presumably they wanted me to stay. But still, they all *withdrew,* as if not getting tenure was something they could catch. And the people whom I'd thought were my friends, well, they just drifted away."

"I'm so sorry."

"Thank you." She readjusted the strap of her oversized bag.

"Did you have any sign that there would be an issue?"

"Not at all. I thought I had done everything they asked. Solid teaching evaluations, gobs of committee work, and an appropriate number of acting roles. But someone up the line didn't like my otherworldly ways, I suppose." She examined one of her long, black-lacquered fingernails. "I don't know why I was surprised; I never really did fit in here."

I knew the feeling.

"But," she continued, "it was only when I thought I'd lost everything that I gained focus! My gifts, which had always been there, of course, increased dramatically in potency."

"What do you mean?"

"I knew I was psychic," she said, matter-of-factly. "But," she smiled widely, "last year I became aware that my powers as a medium were much stronger than I'd ever imagined. I attended a séance and during the middle of it, the spirits chose to come through *me* instead of the man leading it. He was absolutely furious, I can tell you," she said, laughing. "Since then, I've put all of my energy into helping the living and the post-living communicate."

"Wow." That was a lot to take in.

190

"It was not an easy transition, though. Believe me, every time we were in the same room, everyone's discomfort at having to deal with my presence was palpable. I made sure to go to the Halloween party because I knew it would make the administrators squirm."

"You're braver than I am," I said with a smile. "What was it like to sit next to the chancellor at the reception?"

"Surreal. But it was an opportunity to remind him to be mindful of his power."

"Seems like you're in a better space now."

"I am. I feel free. It's quite empowering to be able to be myself, without tenure and promotion and judgments hanging over my head."

I could see the upside: professors are evaluated constantly — by students, colleagues, the chair, the dean, and beyond. It could be exhausting.

"Have you continued acting?"

She smiled and smoothed the white streak at the front of her dark tresses. "Numerous roles. Smaller things than I'm used to. But when you get to be a certain age . . ." she trailed off.

"Seems unfair," I said.

"But there are still a few juicy roles to be had. I'm under consideration for the lead in a new production of *Who's Afraid of Virginia Woolf.*"

"Martha? What an excellent part."

She ducked her head. "It's still in the early stages."

"Hope it works out."

"Appreciate the good wishes. Are you going to talk to the spirit squad?" She jerked her head toward the wranglers.

"I think I'll touch base."

"Please let me know if they need any help from me. We're both engaged in the same project, if you think about it. We just use different equipment." She tapped the side of her head.

"Good point. I will."

"Nice talking to you, Lila," she said, giving me a warm smile.

"And to you, Zandra." I smiled back.

She spun around to go to rehearsal, and I went over to where Vance and the crew were working. He was speaking animatedly to the camera. As I drew nearer, I could hear his words.

"If you're ever in Colorado, be sure that you make time to check out the Stonedale Opera House, where a ghost roams the hallways and the line between this world and the next seems very, very thin. Thanks for joining us for another episode of *Spirit*

Wranglers."

He held his position until the red light on the camera went out and the operator gave him the thumbs up. He brushed the hair out of his eyes and grinned at me. "Got it."

The slam of the front door made us both jump.

Chancellor Trawley Wellington strode through, his long wool coat flying out behind him. When he caught sight of me, his eyes narrowed.

"Why am I not surprised? Whenever there's something disagreeable happening, you are right in the middle of it, Dr. Maclean."

As my mother would say, that's a fine how-do-you-do.

"Hello, Chancellor." Really, what else was there to say to such a greeting?

"Explain to me, please, why there's a film crew here?" His eyebrows drew together.

I stared at him. Then I stared at Vance. "You said you had permission from the university."

Vance stuck his hand out. "Hello, Mr. Chancellor."

The chancellor pursed his lips in dissatisfaction at having his title used as a last name. I hurried to perform the necessary introductions.

After the men shook hands, Vance continued merrily on. "We're *Spirit Wranglers,* and we do have written permission."

"Explain that, please."

"We have written permission from your parapsychology department —"

"No such thing," the chancellor murmured.

Vance's eyebrows shot up. "What do you mean, no such thing?"

"We do not *have* a parapsychology department." His voice had risen slightly. "We have one professor in our psychology department with an interest in the paranormal. Who has, apparently, gone rogue."

Vance paled.

"Let me guess: are you speaking of Dr. Gavin Frinkle?"

The ghost buster nodded.

"Well, Dr. Frinkle does not have the authority to *give* permission. He is not the owner of the building. The university is. And we cannot allow our university to be connected with such . . ." he paused, adjusting his wire-rimmed glasses, "nonsense."

The word was delivered with such contempt that Vance took a step backwards. After a moment lost in thought, he rallied. "I can understand your reservations, Chancellor. It's certainly not everyone's cup of

194

tea. But there is no mention of the university, other than the fact that the ghost was a professor —"

The chancellor winced.

"— who got in a fight with another professor who once worked there. Long ago. We don't mention that the building is currently owned by the university."

When the chancellor began to shake his head, Vance rushed on. "This is how we make our living, sir. I would be very grateful if you'd allow us to complete the episode."

The chancellor liked being in the position of allowing things. Also of cancelling things on the people who had displeased him. He tapped his lip with one finger thoughtfully, deciding which way to go.

Then Vance brought it home. "And hey, if you'd like us to promote the school separately, we'd certainly be glad to pay for an advertisement to run during the show. Then it wouldn't be connected with you, but you'd receive some good publicity from it."

Good publicity? That was a winner. I felt the chancellor change his mind even before he agreed and told Vance to send over the paperwork.

If Vance ever wanted a position in politics, he was suited for the job. Many had tried to affect the chancellor's decisions before, and many had failed.

The two of them walked off together, making arrangements.

You never know what a day will bring.

At the end of rehearsal, I asked Tolliver if he'd like to get a drink or some food. I was troubled about the things I'd realized on the way over. Mostly, I wanted to try and cross him off my list of potential suspects.

"Petal, you read my mind. Shall we go to the Gold Rush?" The bar was quite popular for their specials featuring fishbowl-sized glasses of beer. Since it was happy hour, the place would be packed with undergrads.

"How about the Hideout? Perhaps it would be quieter."

He agreed and we walked the few blocks over.

The Hideout was comfortably shabby, relying on low lighting and candles to camouflage the signs of age. But the restaurant was charming in its own way, plus they projected silent black-and-white movies on the back wall nonstop and served free popcorn. Once we'd settled onto the red vinyl seats of the rounded booth and ordered, Tolliver sighed.

"I can't believe it's dress rehearsal tomorrow."

"We made it!"

"Don't say that!" He looked aghast. "We still have so far to go."

"But we're rounding the final . . . uh . . . base, right?"

"You mean we're in the home stretch?" He smiled. "Indeed. Still, let's not say that aloud and jinx it. We theater folk are superstitious, you know."

The waiter brought our drinks — whiskey for him, diet soda for me — and a basket of fresh popcorn. We both took a handful.

"So Tolliver, I've been meaning to ask you. Do you have any thoughts on what happened to Jean Claude?"

He stopped chewing for a moment, his eyes wandering somewhere over my shoulder, then swallowed. "I've gone over and over it in my mind, but I can't imagine a single soul in our company who would want to see him dead." He lowered his voice. "I think it was an outside job."

"Why?"

"Because I can't imagine one of us doing it."

I didn't want to imagine it either, but it was a possibility.

"Unless . . ."

I waited.

"You know that Jean Claude has a reputation." He readjusted his red glasses as he spoke.

"You started to tell me something about that at the reception. What was it?"

He picked up his glass, slammed the whiskey in one shot, and leaned forward. "He's known for ripping apart the playwright's work. Ferociously. He was even chased down the street by an angry dramatist at his last school."

"Really?" He'd been tough on Tolliver's script, but that seemed like part of the job. Perhaps the stories were really about clashing egos.

"Yes." He sat back against the booth, appearing rather pleased with himself for having discharged the gossip. "I don't typically concern myself with that kind of idle talk, you know, but it's difficult to ignore when everyone is repeating it."

"Do you feel that he did that to you?"

Tolliver drummed his fingers on the table as he thought. "I suppose I did, at times. But he isn't the worst I've encountered, let's put it that way."

"Have you ever worked with him before?"

"Many years ago." His eyes shone as he thought back to an apparently happier time.

198

"In New York City, when we were all young and struggling desperately to make it big."

That was news.

"Your mother, Violet, was part of our circle, you know," he said coyly.

I hadn't known. "Really?"

"Oh yes. She's quite a character."

That bit I knew. Try growing up in her shadow.

"Most of us were in love with her, but she was in a whole different league — absolutely bewitching, with that long red curly hair and her striking green eyes. You have her eyes, Petal, though you must get your dark hair from your father."

I fidgeted with a salt shaker. "Did you know my father?"

"No. Who is he?"

I shrugged.

He seemed perplexed, then light dawned. "Oh. I'm sorry. I wish I did."

"Anyway, what did you work on with Jean Claude?"

"We were always trying to put various things together. We failed a lot. None of us knew that we'd eventually reach any sort of status in the world, but we have gotten somewhere, haven't we? Especially Violet. She was always such a talented artist. Do you have any artistic dreams yourself?"

I'd always wanted to write mysteries. But I had never said it out loud.

"There's only room for one artist in our family. Make that two, actually. Calista's a poet."

"She's quite good," he said approvingly. "And I think everyone should pursue their own artistic visions instead of denying them. The world would be a better place if we could just prioritize and appreciate the beauty in each other."

This did not sound like the mantra of a potential killer, but I had to press on.

"Have you ever owned a gun?" Oh, so clunky. I wished I could take it back the instant I said it.

"Petal! You don't actually think that I shot Jean Claude, do you?" He put his hands on either side of his face in distress. "I will admit that there may have been some jealousy there." He reached for his glass, frowning when he discovered it empty. "I'm not going to say that I haven't been recognized at all . . . as you know, I do have my fans. But it was nothing like Jean Claude. He was on a completely different level. The level to which we all aspire."

I nodded.

"But I would *never* kill any living thing." He looked at me sadly.

"I'm sorry." I regretted my directness. I hadn't meant to upset him.

His cellphone binged softly. He looked down at the screen and then jolted upright. "Oh my. Oh my, my, my." His bony hand reached across the table and squeezed mine with surprising force. "Jermaine Banister is coming."

"Who?"

"The *critic*?" At my blank look, he fluttered his hands sideways as if to wipe away my ignorance. "He's very big, very important. I've got a tip here from someone at the *Stonedale Scout* saying that Jermaine intends to do a review of *Puzzled.* Oh, happy day! I'm sorry, but I need to make a call immediately."

With that, he scampered out of the booth and out of the restaurant.

When the waiter returned with his whiskey, I paid for both of us and left. At least I'd learned a little something.

I hoped.

At home, I called my mother and asked about the early years with Jean Claude and Tolliver.

"Darling, it was such a lovely time! We were young and open to everything. We had no money and only our dreams to sustain us . . ." She sighed happily.

I'd heard so many stories about her salad days that I knew I needed to focus the conversation so that she wouldn't begin regaling me with a cascade of memories about the time she went here or there with future celebrity x, y, or z. Once that train left the station, there would be no stopping it.

"What was the relationship between the two of them?"

I heard ice tinkle in a glass. I went into my little kitchen and turned on the kettle to make some tea. Might as well join her in a drink.

"Jean Claude was *toujours* larger than life." She paused. "I can't believe he's gone."

She'd heard about it on the news and had texted to ask if I was okay, though she hadn't specified that Jean Claude was a friend. Now that I knew that, I gave her more details, and we comforted each other as best we could. I promised to keep her updated, then asked about him as a young man.

"He commanded attention — not only because of his size but also because of his energy. He was a passionate, vibrant soul. And once he got working on a creative project, he was wholly committed to ensuring that it was exactly as it should be."

That summed up the man I knew.

"Tolliver, on the other hand, was always worrying about being overlooked, or not measuring up to the others."

That rang true as well.

"He genuinely worshipped Jean Claude, who was fond of him too. They were always together —"

Interesting. I hadn't gotten a super-close-friend vibe from them.

"— while we were living in the Village, long before you were born. Then Jean Claude went back to France for a job and Tolliver moved to California for a while. We moved around so much, trying to find our way."

"I know." At first, we'd lived upstate near my Aunt Rose. Then we'd gone all over the United States while my mother pursued her dream — art colonies, teaching posts, gallery jobs, you name it — until we finally settled in New York City.

"You and Calista were so good at adapting."

Well, that was debatable — we loathed always being the new kids at new schools — but it was a conversation for another day, in any case.

"Did the two of them ever have a disagreement?" I pressed to the heart of my query.

She laughed. "Always."

"About what?"

"Oh, you know. Art. Love. Life. Beauty. Making it. Selling out. And so on. Whatever was the topic of the day. Jean Claude, Tolliver, and our other friends would stay up until all hours of the night, discussing everything from music to politics. But the two of them especially loved to argue." She laughed again. "Make that drink and argue."

"Was there any kind of pattern or long-standing undercurrent of tension?"

The ice cubes clinked in her glass again as my kettle whistled.

"Not that I can remember."

I poured the hot water into a mug and submerged a bag of peppermint tea to steep.

"Was Tolliver jealous of Jean Claude?"

"Why do you ask, darling?"

"We were talking today —"

"Oh right, you're working on his show. How is that going?"

"Um . . ." I stalled, then decided to come clean. She was my mother, after all. "I like working with him, but I'm not sure about the play."

"He's always been pretty out there, but Tolliver's a true visionary. I don't think he's ever really been understood."

"Maybe this audience will get him." I wasn't holding my breath but I hoped so. I told her about some of the challenges we were facing — minus the ghost-related issues — and she reassured me that they all could be overcome.

"Good luck with everything. It will be fabulous." Her confidence was heartening.

We veered into a discussion of her latest endeavor: she was painting a series of portraits of famous authors, though they were faced away from the viewer and recognizable primarily through items they were holding. She was having a difficult time pinning down Emily Dickinson, hemming and hawing between a feather or a candle for her left hand.

"How is Tolliver handling Jean Claude's death?" she asked suddenly.

"It's been a little odd. He doesn't seem overly affected by it. He appears to be more excited about directing his own show."

"Regardless of how he's coming across, he's a man of deep emotion. Perhaps he's trying to keep a stiff upper lip in front of the company. But he's definitely grieving inside."

"If you say so."

"I'd be grateful if you'd please give Tolliver my best? And of course all my love to you and Calista." She blew some kisses over the line.

"Love you too, Mom." I spooned out the tea bag and squeezed it. Steam rose from the fragrant cup.

"And with that, I need to meet some friends soon, darling. Ta ta for now." She disconnected.

I glanced at the clock; it was almost one a.m. there. She had plans to frolic in the big city, and I had a hot date with a mug of tea.

Typical.

CHAPTER 16

On Thursday, I lost track of time while preparing my classes and had to hurry to rehearsal, arriving just before it was about to begin. I did a double take at the large screen onstage. Tolliver came racing up the aisle to meet me, his scarf unwinding itself with each step.

"We have a change in plan," he said breathlessly. "The paranormal guys . . . spirit busters . . . whatever they're called . . . are going to show us a rough cut of the episode."

"Why?"

"The chancellor wants them to. I have no idea why."

I followed him down to our usual chairs and pulled out my notebook. Tolliver had positioned a few cast members at each door, and they directed the arriving company to sit in any row. The auditorium filled quickly.

After a few minutes, Vance materialized in

front of us, brushing his long bangs off to the side. I wondered how many times a day he did that or if he was even aware that he was doing it. Every conversation we'd had to date had been punctuated by a hair swoop.

"Hey guys," he said excitedly to the crowd, thanking them for coming, as if they weren't here for rehearsal in the first place.

"What's all this?" Parker asked, gesturing to the screen.

"You are the first to see our rough cut of the Stonedale episode."

The students cheered.

"I need you to watch closely," Vance said. "If you see yourself, even in the background, we're going to ask you to sign a release form. While we were shooting, we may have inadvertently caught you on film."

The students cheered again, more loudly.

So that's why the chancellor wanted them to screen it for us — to obtain permissions. He always had one eye on the legal ramifications.

"Am I going to get my SAG card for this?" Parker joked.

Vance ignored him and waved at someone in the back. "Roll tape!"

The lights went down and the brick facade of our building appeared onscreen, the gold letters spelling out "Stonedale Opera House" glinting softly in the dim sunlight. There were no protestors. They must have been on lunch break.

The camera zoomed in on Vance emerging through a glass door. He greeted the audience and welcomed them to the show. "We're here in Stonedale, Colorado, a sunny but sleepy college town —"

Not so sleepy, I didn't think.

"— where a strange legend has endured for decades. Locals will tell you about the ghost who roams these halls. There have been noises, sightings, and unexplained phenomena for over twenty-five years after a college professor committed suicide here. You see, he had discovered that his wife," Vance paused and moved closer to the camera, "was in love with someone else."

He continued through the rest of the story as the shots switched to the much darker interior and a quick tour of the lobby. It looked different — probably an effect created by purposeful lighting and angles — and the shadows seemed more menacing than usual. Surely I'd have noticed if it looked like something out of *Nosferatu* every day. Then again, it was a television show. They had viewers to entice.

Soon, Vance and the crew were onstage,

where they demonstrated the various tools they'd be using to ghost bust, as they did on every show. Fans of the series already knew about Spectrometers and Electric Voice Phenomena recorders and other gadgets, but they had to recap for new viewers, and it was interesting to hear them explain how they captured indicators of paranormal activity in measurable ways.

Vance moved stage left to where Jean Claude had been shot — which he used to introduce fluctuations on a small black box in his hand. He took two steps away to show the device registering what he said were regular levels, then went back to the original spot, where the numbers shot upward.

"This," he said excitedly, "is what we call a 'hot zone.' Usually when we get this kind of reading, we can expect to see some additional signs of paranormal activity."

I was thankful that he had decided not to include our dearly departed director in the show. He must have sensed that we were all too raw for that. But it was fascinating to see the readings change there.

The camera pulled back into a wide-angle shot of the very seats in which we were sitting. In a voiceover, Vance told the audience that they'd be looking for lights or other evidence.

The camera rose slowly to capture the area above our heads, then zoomed in. Gradually, four small white balls of light became visible. They swooped and looped in what resembled a waltz. Gasps broke out behind me. I twisted in my seat and looked at the students. Most of them were checking the air over their head in real time, even though the screen was projecting something that had previously been taped. I couldn't help peeking upward as well, where of course I didn't see anything. I turned back around and focused on the screen, where the camera was tracking the movement of the lights.

"Orbs," Vance announced. "Some of the brightest we've ever seen on this show."

The screen displayed a slow-motion replay with the orbs circled in green so that viewers would be sure to see them. It repeated several times as Vance waxed rhapsodic about the quality of the footage.

The episode moved next below stage, capturing the claw marks on the wall and pausing at the corner dressing room where, Vance informed us cheerily, "the readings were off the charts." It was pretty dark beyond the doorjamb — you could just barely make out the rose pattern on the wallpaper inside.

"What happened next," Vance said, "surprised us all."

We stared at the screen.

Suddenly, the door to the room slammed shut, as if someone had been standing behind it and pushed with all their might.

The audience gasped again. Onscreen, Vance raced into the frame, opened the door, and went inside the room. The camera followed, the shot whipping wildly around the room to record the fact that no one else was there.

I knew about the secret staircase, and so did Vance. But was there enough time for someone to use it as an escape after slamming the door, with another person hot on their heels? Or had the door been slammed by an actual spirit?

As if reading my mind, Vance moved to the far wall. "This room has another mystery," he said, pushing on the rose wallpaper to pop open the door. "See this? It leads to a staircase. No one knows why it exists."

That wasn't technically true, but it was much more dramatic than "it was built so that the star of the show could quickly access the stage."

I could hear excited chatter behind me — the students seemed genuinely surprised.

"And you're not going to believe what else

we caught on film," Vance said enthusiastically. Next came the footage of the so-called floater, which pretty much wowed the room. Vance pushed the conclusion that the full-bodied manifestation was Malcolm Gaines himself keeping watch over the theater.

"But there's more to be discovered back downstairs." Vance winked at the camera. They cut to him standing in the prop room.

"There is a play in production here," he said, "so we asked some of the company to tell us about their experiences."

Parker was the first to appear. "This place is freaky. It always feels like hidden eyes are watching. You get used to it, though." He paused dramatically. "You have to."

Next was Rachel. She looked earnestly into the camera, pushing a hank of highlighted hair behind her ear before speaking. "A bunch of us have heard singing, but if you look in the hallway, no one's there." She smiled and shrugged adorably.

The third was Luke Popper, our actor playing Sherlock Holmes. He looked down while he was talking, as if addressing his shoes. "During rehearsal, I had to go into the prop room. No one else was below stage. I heard someone singing, then it turned into a scream. I'll never forget it."

A number of other cast members spoke

about the lights going on and off in their dressing rooms, items appearing in different places than they'd left them, and hearing noises that didn't seem to have an identifiable origin.

Rachel reappeared. "The weirdest thing is walking through the cold pockets. They're everywhere but never in the same place. Oh, except downstairs. That whole below stage area is freezing. Sometimes you can see your breath."

Suddenly, my face loomed above us.

Oh crap.

My hands flew up to cover my face involuntarily, as if attempting to provide a humiliation shield. But I couldn't help peeking.

The whole supposedly off-camera conversation with Vance was included. It had been shot with night vision so that my eyes were dark pools, and I looked like an extra from a horror movie. Sliding down in my chair, I watched through my fingers until the next scene began. It helped. Sort of.

Onscreen, Vance was holding the walkie-talkie-like box I'd seen earlier. "Our final piece of evidence comes from the dressing room we visited earlier. Not only did the door slam, but we also caught some words on our EVP recorder — that stands for

Electronic Voice Phenomena, new ghost hunters."

He began asking questions to the air. The box buzzed with low-level static.

"Who are you?"

"What are you doing here?"

"What do you want to tell us?"

Suddenly the static spiked and a muffled mechanical sound could be heard.

"Did you get that?" Vance asked the camera excitedly. "Let me enhance it." He twisted a dial on the box and played it back. A subtitle appeared on the screen as the voice was magnified and the word became clear: *Beware.*

Ice crept up my spine.

The screen played it back, again, in slow motion.

Beware.

After the screening ended, the students set up for rehearsal. It was going to be a challenge to get the actors to focus after all that excitement, but we'd just have to do our best. Tolliver hadn't made any fuss about the spirit wranglers interrupting his work time, thankfully. Though since the showing was at the chancellor's request, there wasn't anything he could have done about it.

Next to the stage, Vance handed out

release forms to those of us who had appeared in the episode.

I made a beeline for him. "That was gripping, Vance. But you said you weren't taping me."

"I honestly didn't think we were," he said. "But one of the camera guys thought he was supposed to be filming, so he just, you know, did."

That was probably one of their tricks.

"Point is, I don't want to be in the show."

"But the chancellor wants you in it," he retorted, pushing the form at me. "He said having a professor in it lent some credibility."

Now he wanted credibility? For the show he didn't want connected to the university? I couldn't keep track.

"But you didn't even tell me you were filming. I could have been more . . ."

"More what?" He waited, brushing his blond hair to the side. I really wanted to buy him a barrette to take care of that.

A student came up and took a form; he gave her a smile and she practically swooned. When he resumed his attention to the conversation, I grasped the first word I could think of.

"Professorial."

He spoke reassuringly. "You were plenty

professorial."

Untrue.

"Plus, you cover every point we needed covering."

Unintentionally.

I shook my head. "Not comfortable with it, Vance."

He took stock of my expression, realizing I meant it. "Please, Lila. We need your footage. And I need this show to be a hit."

"Your ratings are already huge."

"An even bigger hit, I mean." He bent his head toward me and lowered his volume. "They're thinking of replacing me. Someone up the chain thinks I'm not serious about the work. If I can show them that I am committed to find gripping evidence of paranormal activity, they'll let me stay. Or so says my agent."

I could feel my resolve crumble. I understood job security worries.

"And like I said, the chancellor wants you in it."

Probably so he could use it as evidence against me someday.

"It would do me a solid favor. Help a bro out?" Vance fixed his blue eyes on mine intently.

I read genuine worry there. "Okay."

He blew out a breath. "I appreciate it,

Lila. You have no idea how much."

"No problem." I turned to go, then paused. "Hey, have you ever heard a ghost say 'beware' before?"

"Sure," he said. "But never so clearly or vehemently. You've got a strong force here."

That couldn't be a good sign.

The Friday department meeting was going along as it usually did — a slow crawl through tediously detailed matters dotted by political flare-ups. Spencer Bartholomew, our stalwart department chair who was in the unenviable position of shepherding us along the overcrowded agenda and refereeing the inevitable disputes, sat at the head of the table, about to wrap things up. I was idly admiring the tiny sailboats peppering his navy suspenders when the door to the department library burst open and an unfamiliar man in a black suit strode inside. He was tall and gaunt, with high cheekbones and long wispy gray hair clinging to his skull — his eyes seemed to burn. It was as if the Grim Reaper himself had come to call.

We all froze as he looked around the circle and finally located Tolliver, who shrank down in his seat in response to the man's glare.

"I need to talk to you *now*," the man commanded in a guttural voice, beckoning to the playwright. His teeth seemed unnaturally large, great yellowing blocks that his thin lips had to work hard to accommodate.

He looked familiar somehow, though I couldn't place him.

From a nightmare, maybe.

Or the group of protestors?

Same thing.

"We're in the middle of —" Spencer began.

"Now." The man continued to stare at Tolliver until he gathered up the papers in front of him as if he were about to leave. He paused when Spencer waved his hand in his direction.

"We're about to finish," Spencer said to the intruder. "Please give me a moment, then you and Professor Ingersoll can speak here." He looked at Tolliver. "Is that acceptable to you?"

Tolliver nodded and adjusted the pumpkin-colored scarf around his neck, probably just to have something to do with his hands. All eyes were on him.

The man briefly lowered his head in acknowledgment and took a step back, relinquishing the spotlight.

Nate elbowed me and whispered, "I have a committee meeting after this, but you're not going anywhere, right?"

"Right," I said, out of the corner of my mouth.

"You have to fill me in later." He made a call-me sign out of thumb and pinkie finger and shook it.

"Very subtle," I whispered.

He laughed and returned his attention to the meeting.

Spencer gave us a few additional reminders about upcoming deadlines, then pronounced the meeting adjourned. He stood, removed the charcoal suit coat draped over the back of his chair, and took his time putting it back on.

Faculty members exited quickly, darting curious glances in the man's direction and talking quietly among themselves. Soon, only Spencer, Tolliver, and I were left with the intruder.

The man stomped over and dropped into one of the recently vacated spots across from Tolliver.

Spencer sank back into his chair, ran a hand through his gray hair, and gave him a serious look. "You can't burst into a department meeting like that, Gavin."

So *this* was Dr. Frinkle, the rogue psychology professor we'd been hearing about.

"What else am I supposed to do? This is

an extremely pressing matter, and Ingersoll won't return my calls." He spat the words out and leaned forward, pinning my colleague into his seat with another fiery glare.

Tolliver didn't say a word.

Gavin threw his hands up in exasperation. "See?"

Everyone waited for Tolliver to say something.

Silence.

Gavin clicked his tongue in disgust and looked wildly around the room. When he noticed me sitting there, he demanded to know who I was.

"Lila Maclean. Assistant professor of English and assistant director of *Puzzled*. Thought I'd stay in case you needed me."

He weighed this and decided to let it stand, twisting back toward Tolliver and resuming his white-hot focus.

Spencer assessed the situation and spoke to Tolliver. "Could you please tell me what's happening?"

The playwright narrowed his eyes at Gavin. "He's left at least ten messages *every day,* berating me for not calling him back. If he'd just left one, I would have called him immediately."

Gavin rolled his eyes at that.

"But I will not be bullied. So I choose

silence."

Refusing to reply is the higher education equivalent to sticking one's tongue out at an enemy on the schoolyard.

Spencer turned back to Gavin, who crossed his arms over his chest. After a moment, he spoke angrily. "He wouldn't call me back."

"I believe we've established why," Spencer said.

Tolliver added, "I'm working night and day on the play. I don't have time to deal with this harassment."

Gavin mumbled something.

"What was that?" Tolliver asked.

"Sorry." It may not have been genuine, but it signaled effort, anyway.

"Okay," Spencer said. "Now that we're here, let's try to sort things out. What's going on?"

Gavin sighed. "Tolliver, I need to make sure that you won't continue to give the spirit wranglers such a hard time. They have permission to be there."

"It was the chancellor who didn't want them to go forward, not me, though he's changed his mind for some reason that I can't fathom," Tolliver shot back. "By the by, he wasn't very happy about you giving them permission without the authority to do so, if you hadn't heard that yet."

Gavin smirked, an unpleasant sight involving skin stretching hard to slide over those disturbing teeth. "I know. But the main thing is that he has given his blessing and now you're the one causing the problems."

Tolliver's mouth fell open. "I'm causing problems?"

"I've seen how you treat them during rehearsal."

Tolliver and I stared at each other.

"You've been to rehearsal?" His tone signaled an approaching storm.

"I've been studying the Opera House for seven years," Gavin said. "I'm there constantly."

That was disconcerting news.

"I've never seen you there," Tolliver said, lifting his chin.

"I should expect not. I know how to observe something without intruding upon it. I'm a *scientist.*" Gavin pointed across the table. "Just see that the spirit wranglers have access this week."

Tolliver didn't bother to hide his irritation. "We've been accommodating them the whole time. Yes, they've been underfoot but we managed to work around them, even though it's been very inconvenient. Cords and cameras and people everywhere —"

"They're doing crucial work."

"Crucial work? Are you joking?" Tolliver's face went slightly red. "They're making a television show. We, on the other hand, are creating original art, Gavin. Art! It's important!"

Gavin snorted. "You actually think your little play is *important*?"

Tolliver's face turned bright red and one side of his scarf came unmoored, falling down his chest. He batted it out of the way and opened his mouth to retort, but Gavin spoke first, pointing at Tolliver. "Let me tell you something. We scientists study the workings of the *universe*. While your lot is up on that stage prancing about and warbling happy little songs, I'm trying to answer real questions about potential states of human existence."

Tolliver's chair shot backwards as he stood up and headed for the hallway. He paused at the door and said, "We're done here." Then he threw the end of his scarf over his shoulder and stalked away.

I awarded him big points for dramatic effect.

Spencer gave Gavin a quizzical look. "I still don't understand why you're here. If the chancellor has granted permission and Tolliver is allowing them to complete their work, what do you need?"

"To make sure it happens."

"They already showed us a rough cut," I said.

"They want to add more content and have asked to interview me on location." Gavin scratched his head, resulting in a dry little scritchy sound that made me want to run for the nearest tank of hand sanitizer. "Look, I need the episode to come out as soon as possible. It provides solid evidence that I must reference in my work. I'm going to prove that the Opera House is haunted, and, by extension, that Stonedale needs to have a parapsychology department, which I will chair." He touched the table lightly with his palm. "And if this book isn't completed soon, I won't be promoted to full professor."

Everything clicked into place.

A desperate tone entered his voice. "I received tenure fourteen years ago but they keep refusing my promotion, Spencer. My wife is about to leave me. This is my last chance."

The department chair's face softened. "I understand. And I hope this time you are promoted. But you have to respect the work that other professors are doing simultaneously. If you'd like Tolliver's help, it would be better not to insult him."

Gavin listened intently.

"Perhaps you could offer Tolliver a more robust apology. Would you be willing to do that?"

He didn't move. "I'll think about it."

"That's all I can ask. Thank you, Gavin." Spencer patted the table briskly. "And with that, let's adjourn."

Later, I poked my head into Tolliver's office. It was a madhouse of scripts, textbooks, and play props. His desk rose up in the middle like an island, miraculously clear of clutter. He was typing furiously on his laptop, seemingly unaware of anything other than the words on the screen.

I knocked softly on the door, happy to see that his color was back to normal. He'd had time to cool down and no longer appeared to be teetering on the verge of exploding.

"Lila! My darling, come in."

I looked at the crowded floor and decided to stay put. "I just wanted to check on you. Is everything okay?"

He ripped off his glasses and tossed them on the desktop, then rubbed his eyes with both hands for a minute. Finally, he met my gaze. "Absolutely. Frinkle came by and apologized for denigrating my work. And for harassing me."

"That's good," I said, smiling at him.

"I'm sorry I made a scene." He winced. "But I couldn't take another word. Especially when he began to say that science is more important than art. That I cannot tolerate."

"It's fine," I said. "I understand."

"Some people simply don't comprehend the extraordinary value of exploring and expressing the human condition . . . and how can they dismiss the aesthetic and artistic experience? It's utterly tragic." His eyes appeared to be welling up slightly.

"He just sees the world differently, I guess."

"You can say that again. What did you talk about after I left?"

I filled him in on Gavin's situation.

"Oh, that is a tough one. No wonder he's so close to the edge." He looked back at his computer screen and tapped a key. "Still, no call for slamming another person's discipline, is there, Petal?"

"I'll let you get back to work."

He thanked me for stopping by and returned to his laptop.

As I walked away, I heard him mutter, "Who puts all of his academic eggs in a basket full of ghosts, anyway?"

It sounded like one of the nonsensical lines from his play.

CHAPTER 17

The temperature had dropped noticeably by Saturday morning, but it didn't put a damper on the company. The actors were gearing up for dress rehearsal, darting around like hummingbirds. Everyone was in character, reciting lines or singing scales. It was magical, the way they transformed when the costumes were applied.

I tried not to think about Gavin lurking about unseen as I descended below stage. I'd realized as soon as he told Tolliver he'd been working here that he may have been in the theater on the day Jean Claude died. Could he have been involved? And why had none of us ever seen Gavin around? The collegial thing to do would be to introduce oneself to others sharing the same space. What kind of work required him to stay in the shadows? Or did he stay out of sight because he felt guilty about something?

My train of thought was halted when Parker, aka Oliver, waved frantically to me from the doorway of the corner room he shared with the other main characters. Luke, already in costume as Sherlock Holmes, was looking in the mirror and adjusting his deerstalker cap; Rachel sat in the velvet chair, tying the laces of her Miss Marple shoes.

"I'm nervous." Parker looked it too, extra pale beneath the pancake makeup. Beads of sweat dotted his brow. "What if I forget my lines? What if I fall? I don't know if I can do this. This is only my second play."

"You can do it. You'll be terrific."

"I don't know." He twisted his fingers. "I don't want to let everyone down."

"Listen, stage fright is a real thing. I understand that it's powerful. But once you get on the stage and begin, it will lessen. The anticipation can be the hardest part."

He swallowed hard and his eyes sought mine.

"Take some deep breaths," I advised him.

While he did that, I turned to the other two actors. "How are you doing?"

Luke, giving his cap a pat, said he was fine.

Rachel looked up from her shoe and smiled. "I'm ready. Bring it on."

"Good. Break a leg, everyone." I turned back to Parker and lowered my voice. "My mother is an artist, and she always got nervous before her shows. But eventually she realized that she could only do what she could do. People would like it or not like it, and she couldn't control that. What did matter was being in the moment. Doing the thing. In other words, it's the thought of trying to please the world that creates the nervousness, at least for her. See if you can just focus on the now. Do the thing."

Parker straightened his shoulders. "That helps."

I patted his arm and nodded reassuringly. When he finally gave me a weak smile, I took that as a cue to leave.

Upstairs, I found Tolliver pacing backstage. Looked like Oliver wasn't the only one feeling anxious.

"Hi Tolliver. Are you ready?"

"I don't know. I —" he tilted a little and I reached out to steady him.

"Whoa. Do you want to sit down?"

He waved me off and continued pacing. "No. I need to get into the proper mindset. I keep thinking about the drama critic coming and it throws everything off."

"Well, Banister won't be here today," I said. "So you don't need to worry about the review right now."

Zandra materialized from behind a curtain. "Tolly, come out front. They're getting ready to begin." She smiled at me. "Hi Lila. Isn't this exciting?"

We went to our seats and took out pens to make notes. Tolliver was not going to stop the play for anything, so we'd be here for a good couple of hours.

It still seemed so strange not to have Jean Claude sitting next to me. He used to wave his hands wildly during rehearsal, physically expressing his responses before vocalizing them. I missed having to duck out of the way.

With a sigh, I silenced my cell phone and sat back to watch the show.

We made it past intermission with no major issues. There'd been some lighting cues missed and some minor blocking things to tweak, but overall, it was going smoothly. The actors knew their lines, the dancers were unified for the most part, and the costumes were gorgeous.

We were lucky to have a world-class costume designer overseeing the students' work. Luciana was, like Jean Claude, visiting Stonedale on sabbatical this term. She'd won a Tony for costume design earlier in her career, though she never mentioned it. She hadn't interacted much with the rest of us, preferring to do her work in the studio at the school for the most part. The one time I'd bumped into her downstairs, she'd been deep in conversation with one of the crew members. He told me later she was scared of ghosts and unwilling to spend more than one minute here if she didn't have to.

Onstage, Edgar Allan Poe was supposed to descend from the heavens to offer clarity on the argument.

Sherlock, Miss Marple, and Oliver were in place, waiting for Poe to swing down. He didn't. Again.

There were some unidentifiable metallic sounds.

They all began peeking upward to see what was going on. I could see that they were trying not to break their poses, but they couldn't help themselves.

Then the lights went out.

Tolliver shouted, "What's going on? Wrong, wrong, wrong!"

A loud thump was followed by a scream.

"No, no, we're not doing the party scene now," Tolliver yelled. "What in the heck is happening?"

When the lights went back on, Edgar Allan Poe had fallen — on top of a very surprised Sherlock.

Students swarmed up to Andrew Lu, the actor playing Poe, who was unconscious. Tolliver, Zandra, and I did the same. Luke slid out from under him carefully. "I'm fine," he said in response to a flurry of inquiries, dusting off his deerstalker cap. "Is Andrew okay? What happened?"

Tolliver patted Andrew, who soon began stirring and groaning. After a few minutes, Andrew was back to consciousness enough to tell us that he'd put on the harness and stepped off the exit point above as he was supposed to, but nothing supported him. He said something about being in the wrong harness or the wrong fly space. It didn't make any sense. It was clear at a glance, however, that the rope attached to his harness hadn't simply frayed apart. It had been cut.

Andrew's arm was bent at an odd angle — he grabbed it with his other hand, then bent over in pain.

"Does anything else hurt besides your arm?" I asked.

He shook his head, tears in his eyes.

"If you can stand, we need to get you to the emergency room," Tolliver said. "I want them to check you out from head to toe."

"Should we splint it before you go?" I looked around the group for assistance.

Zandra fashioned one out of a nearby script and Tolliver's purple scarf. It was pretty impressive. She saw me watching and grinned. "Girl Scouts. Lots of first aid lessons."

Todd, a tech crew member and Andrew's roommate, offered to take him to the ER. We thanked Todd, he helped the actor to his feet, and they both left. The cast applauded in a show of support.

"Let's reset," Tolliver said loudly to the cast. "Take ten but then we need to continue."

Out of the corner of his mouth, he said to us, "It's unbelievable. Why do people keep falling?"

"Good question. And who would cut a rope?" I asked.

"It was the ghost," murmured Zandra. "Again."

The rest of the rehearsal was a fiasco. The timing was wrong, people forgot their lines, and the acting was wooden at best. The fall had thrown us off.

By the time we reached the closing number, "Everything Comes Out All Right In

The End," it was clear that everything had *not* come out all right today.

Tolliver told the crew that we'd be reworking the Poe scene. I had hoped he would delete it altogether, but if he would at least reorient the entrance so that it took place on solid ground, perhaps rising from the trap door, that would be better. He also thanked the students and reminded them that our second dress rehearsal would be Monday night. I honestly wasn't sure we were going to pull this play off, but now was not the time for that kind of heartfelt confession. Now was the time for consoling the director, who appeared to be in shambles.

Tolliver sank into his chair, eyes locked onto the stage in an eerie, unblinking stare. Zandra was nowhere to be seen, so I guessed I would have to take this one.

"Are you okay?" I sat next to him, leaning forward so I could see his face.

"It's a disaster." It was strange to hear the words come out of his own mouth, as we'd all been thinking it for weeks. But in this case, my job as assistant director was to say the opposite. So I did.

"It will be fine," I said firmly. "We just need to iron out a few things and then we're ready."

He shifted in his seat and made eye contact. "Do you really think so, Lila?" His hopeful expression made me feel a wee bit guilty for holding back on my real opinion, but I wasn't lying, technically. It would be fine in the sense that we had a play with a beginning, middle, and end. We'd practiced it. A performance could happen.

"I do."

He took a deep breath, then patted the arms of the seat before pulling himself up to a standing position. "All right, then. Thanks, Petal. Onward we go."

CHAPTER 18

I raced home to prepare for the Halloween party. It was happening a few days early this year — the chancellor liked for the shindig to take place on a weekend — and Nate was picking me up in an hour. I hurried through a shower, washing off the theater grime, and dressed in the Medusa costume I'd found at the last minute. It had been slim pickings at the store, but at least she fit the party theme.

I was putting on long silver earrings to match my tunic when the doorbell rang. Nate stood on my front step; his bright blue eyes widened at my wig, which was not only tall, wide, and purple but also featured snakes in various striking positions.

"You look pretty." He cleared his throat. "I mean, fierce. You look pretty fierce." It was one of those moments where the potential for something more was revealed, then wrestled back into the friend zone, which happened sometimes. There was a spark between us, but we both denied it. I still didn't know why and I valued his friendship too much to take a chance on talking about it.

I decided to act like I hadn't noticed anything. "Thank you, kind sir. Please come in."

He stepped inside and gave Cady a gentle pat as she wound around his legs. I got a good look at his costume as he did so.

"Wait, are you a pirate?"

Nate grinned at me. "Yep."

"Isn't the theme great characters in literature?"

"Yes. So if anyone asks, I'm from *Treasure Island.* And don't worry. What are they going to do? Fire me for not following the party rules?"

"I honestly do not know the answer to that question."

He laughed. "I'll take my chances."

We locked up the house and got into his car. The fresh soap scent that always emanated from Nate was present there too.

"How've you been?" he asked, stopping for a light. "Haven't seen much of you in the past few weeks."

"Crazed. The play opens next week, and it's taken up every single moment of my life lately. By the way, I got you a ticket for opening night."

"That's awesome. Can't wait to see the
—"

"Don't say fiasco."

He gasped. "Lila! I was going to say the fruits of your labor."

"No you weren't."

"I was!" He protested loudly for the next few blocks about the importance of trusting your friends who would never slam something you were working on. And how trusting those friends was an integral part of the friendship in the first place. And what kind of friends would they be, anyway, if they didn't support your projects enthusiastically and completely?

When he stopped talking, I looked at him for a long moment. "So *were* you going to say fiasco?"

"Catastrophe, actually."

Yes, I knew him well. "The musical numbers are going to blow your proverbial socks off. They're the best part."

"Well, I look forward to that," he said. "As well as the rest."

"Thank you for saying that, anyway."

"I quite enjoy a good bad play."

"Wow. May we quote you on the posters?"

He chuckled.

When we arrived at Randsworth Hall, it looked like a circus, as it did every year for the party. The building was lit up with spotlights and torches; the lawn was full of performers ranging from jugglers to acrobats to fire-eaters. We admired the spectacle for awhile. Nate dared me to ask the fire-eaters for a turn. I refused.

We made our way inside, where the main floor hallway had been transformed into a party room with walls swathed in orange fabric and strings of fairy lights suspended over the entire area.

As we accepted champagne flutes from a passing tray, we came upon Bella, looking like a misplaced wood nymph. She wore a dark green gown with a bodice of shimmering fabric, and a circlet of flowers graced her hair. We exchanged greetings and she told us she was waiting for someone.

I introduced Nate and we chatted for a few minutes about her costume, which, she explained, was Ophelia.

"I played her once," Bella said. "When I was younger. *Hamlet* is one of my favorites."

"That's a challenging part. How wonderful! I didn't know you acted."

"Since the community theater was shut down, I haven't."

That was interesting. The chancellor had

said Clara and Braxton were the ones to arrange for the funds to dry up. Why would they do that if Bella was part of the productions?

"What happened to the community theater?"

"We ran out of money." Bella looked down and smoothed her skirt.

"Was there no way to raise the —"

"No. We needed too much money."

"I'm so sorry."

"I miss acting. Especially the costumes." She patted her flower crown gently. "Well, all of it, really."

"I hope you can get back to it again in the future."

"Me too." Bella gave me a small smile.

"Which reminds me . . . do you think you could get Clara to call off the protestors?"

She nodded. "I'm working on that. She doesn't tend to listen to me, but I'm not giving up. I'm also keeping her away from the theater while the ghost crew is filming."

"You heard about that?"

"Chip mentioned it," she said. "But I honestly don't think Clara could handle it, so I've been distracting her with other things at work."

"Thank you," I said, perhaps a tad fervently.

We wished her a good evening and claimed seats at an empty table.

"Hello, one and all!" The chancellor's voice was magnified by the sound system. At that volume, cultured and carefully modulated or not, it was still imposing. I looked over at the main stairs where the chancellor stood with both arms out. He moved the microphone back to his mouth to add, "Patsy and I welcome you." He gestured toward a smiling blonde at his side wearing an exquisite flapper costume. He was in a black tuxedo with a top hat, raising his elegance factor, which was already pretty high, yet another notch. They were in full-on Great Gatsby mode

After he instructed us to have a fabulous time and so forth, we were left to our own devices.

Nate looked at me and cocked his head. "Is it too soon to dance?"

"Decidedly so."

"How about another champagne?"

"Maybe one more, thanks." It might help me forget that I was wearing a very short tunic and crazy snake wig in front of all my colleagues.

After Nate left in search of additional libations, I stood up and moved through the tables, intending to find Tolliver to ask how he planned to rework the Edgar Allan Poe entrance. Instead, I spied Braxton, nibbling his way through a plate of cheese and crackers. A shiny white patent-leather purse lay on the table in front of him. He must be on handbag watch for Clara, wherever she was.

Taking the opportunity to speak to him alone, I greeted him warmly.

Braxton's eyes widened and he slapped the plate down. A cheese cube tumbled onto the tablecloth, and he took his time picking it up.

"Sorry about that," I said, smiling. "Didn't mean to scare you."

He popped the cheese into his mouth and chewed fast, his ruddy cheeks moving rapidly up and down. It was almost mesmerizing. After he swallowed, his shoulders relaxed slightly.

"Did you see Bella?"

Braxton's eyes seemed to twinkle at me. "Yes."

"She looks lovely, doesn't she?"

"Yes."

We fell silent. He looked away. The band started playing a jazzy number.

I readjusted my snake wig and attempted to sound casual. "So how long have you been working together on the Opera House project?"

"Oh, I'm not allowed to talk about it," he mumbled.

I nodded.

"But it's been a long time," he added, almost under his breath.

I tried not to show my surprise that he'd continued. "What made you interested in the site in the first place?"

"Can't really say."

"Okay."

"Though it was mostly because Malcolm was our neighbor," he said, stroking his beard.

"What was your relationship with him?"

Braxton ate another cube of cheese. "It was good. Until it wasn't."

"Had he done something wrong?"

He looked away. "I can't talk about it."

I waited for him to go on, but he didn't appear to be offering any addendums this time.

"Bella told me that you and Clara took her in and cared for her. That was very kind of you."

His face lit up. "She was a blessing. Best thing that ever happened to us."

I caught sight of Clara crossing the room to speak to the chancellor nearby and decided to speed things up before she returned. Time to be more direct. "How

245

about Jean Claude? What did you think of him?"

Braxton picked up and inspected a cracker. "I didn't know him. But when people get something stuck in their craw and can't rest until they do something about it . . ."

"Yes?" I urged him on.

"That." He nodded emphatically, as if it were perfectly clear what he was saying. He popped the whole cracker into his mouth and chewed thoroughly.

My mind raced. "Are you talking about Clara?"

He deliberated for a long time, looking around the room to make sure no one was watching before dipping his chin ever so slightly.

A chill ran through me. "You think she was involved in his death?"

He jolted. "Oh no! That's not what I meant at all."

"What did you mean then?"

He fidgeted. "I really couldn't say more than that."

I noticed Chip fast approaching the chancellor. This I definitely wanted to hear. I thanked Braxton for talking to me and excused myself.

"Please keep the information just between

us," he said out of the corner of his mouth. I assured him that I would.

It would be easy since I didn't know what the information was.

I wended my way through the crowd, up to the edge of the chancellor's group. I could feel Braxton follow, then he passed me and moved into his usual position behind his wife, where he stood quietly, clutching her purse.

Clara, outfitted with white feathery wings and a halo, was leaning toward our university leader, her hands clasped in an attitude of prayer. She had a bright smile affixed to her face and was gently pleading. "Chancellor, could you please find it in your heart to consider our offer? We've rounded up a number of grants and donors who are very interested in preserving Stonedale's magnificent history. We can meet your asking price —"

The chancellor looked interested.

"— and then some."

Make that very interested.

"Wait a minute." Chip, clad in another one of his tailored suits, held up his hand as he slid smoothly into the circle. "We already have an agreement."

The chancellor gave him a pointed once-over. Chip wasn't wearing a costume. Those were the rules. Strike one.

"Excuse me, young man, but we're having a private conversation," Clara told him, wagging her finger in his face. "It's rude to interrupt."

Braxton looked somewhat embarrassed, to my surprise.

"But you're trying to interfere with an established deal." Chip informed her, then turned to the chancellor. "We're still good, right, Trawley?"

The chancellor bristled slightly at having his first name invoked. Chip wasn't an academic and probably didn't even know the unspoken rules that governed our interactions within the hierarchy of power, but it was clearly strike two against him.

"It's true that I've made a verbal agreement with Mr. Turner." He used the formal version of his name to reinforce his own desire to be addressed as Chancellor Wellington. "However, we haven't signed anything."

Chip paled. "Like you just said, we have an agreement. You can't back out now!"

Telling the chancellor what he can and can't do? Strike three, ladies and gentlemen.

Just like that, the chancellor swerved. "It has come to my attention that there has been an excessive amount of protesting over the sale of this particular building."

We all knew the protests were about *Puzzled,* not the sale, and we also knew he knew about them before he agreed to sell the place. In fact, he'd probably agreed to sell the place *because* he didn't want to deal with the protests. But the Worthinghams had made a higher offer, and he was annoyed with Chip, so it provided a handy excuse.

He cleared his throat and made the tie-smoothing motion that he favored — only this costume had required a bow tie, so he ended up sliding a palm down his empty shirtfront. He appeared to blanch slightly at the realization and spoke more loudly to regain the upper hand. "I think it in everyone's best interests — citizens of Stonedale particularly — that I review both offers in writing this week before making a decision. You have until Monday night to present them to my office. That seems like the fairest thing I can do in this complicated situation."

"Thank you, Chancellor," Clara gushed, shooting a triumphant look at Chip, who was running a finger around his collar as if it were suddenly too tight.

"One more thing: the picketing stops

now," the chancellor said, fixing Clara with a steely look.

She set her jaw but nodded.

Really wish he would have done that in the beginning, as we'd asked.

He shot me a now-was-that-so-hard? look.

I responded with an it-is-if-you're-not-the-chancellor look, though it was impossible to tell if the message was received.

"If you'll excuse me, I must attend to my guests. Please enjoy your evening." The chancellor abruptly spun around and went over to his wife Patsy, who was speaking with the mayor and assorted deans and department chairs. That was a power circle indeed.

Clara glared at me. "Lila, hasn't anyone told you it's rude to eavesdrop on other people's conversations? You didn't even try to hide it, standing right there for all of us to see."

"I was actually trying to *join* the conversation."

"It did not come across that way," Clara said, smirking at my purple wig. "Nice costume." She grabbed one of Braxton's hands and pulled him away. He looked apologetically over his shoulder as they melted into the crowd.

Wow. She was so not the etiquette expert

she believed herself to be.

"What a piece of work," Chip spat out, watching her walk away. "Can't believe she did that."

I nodded. "She's pretty determined to get her way at all times."

"I never should have come to this place," he said, somewhat glumly.

"What brought you here, anyway?"

"Stayed overnight in Stonedale on a business trip and caught sight of the Opera House while taking a morning jog. I haven't been able to get it out of my head since then."

"It is a lovely building," I agreed.

"It is that. Though I'm talking more about the site itself. We'd of course build something contemporary there —"

By which he meant tear down the Opera House all together.

"— the view is spectacular, and it's close to shops and that pub, The Peak House."

"Did you know that the chancellor owns The Peak House?"

He looked surprised. "No. He didn't mention that."

I wondered if that meant anything. Would the chancellor benefit more from Chip turning the Opera House into an entertainment complex so close to his restaurant? Probably.

"Well, it's not over yet," he said, sounding like he was trying to convince himself. "Since her plan is to offer more money, I will try to sweeten the deal myself." He made a sour face. "Just have to scrape together more cash. Make some calls, do some begging."

"Scrape together? I thought developers had cash to burn. Bought buildings outright. Things like that."

"Most of my money is tied up in other projects," he explained. "This one was more a labor of love. There's just something about this place that speaks to me."

I nodded. "You do understand, though, that the Historical Society feels the same way — that what they're doing is a labor of love? Preserving a piece of Stonedale's history."

He gave a brisk nod. "Think of it this way, though: many people will enjoy the new building. It's hard to be the guy trampling dreams, but it's part of the job. Sometimes you have to do whatever's necessary to achieve your goals. What do you think, Lila?"

I hesitated.

"I'd genuinely like to know."

"The Stonedale Opera House should be restored, not torn down. It's exceptional as well as historically significant."

I paused. Hadn't realized until that moment that I was on the same side as Clara Worthingham.

I was tremendously fond of the place.

Ghosts or no ghosts.

CHAPTER 19

First thing Sunday morning, I was leaning against the Special Collections counter in the library. I'd come on behalf of my book project, centered on Isabella Dare, a mostly unknown but completely fabulous mystery writer. It was a dream to have signed a contract with a university press, but finding time to immerse into the work was difficult. I grabbed hours where I could, but, at this rate, I'd have trouble meeting the deadline.

The thought of not finishing the manuscript on time made my chest ache. Having a book was essential to my tenure bid. I took a deep breath and blew it out slowly.

"May I help you?" A woman with a bright blue bob interrupted my panic spiral. Tattoos snaked up both arms in a floral explosion. Her library nametag said "Eloise."

I handed her the call sheet with the number of the item I needed for a footnote, a manuscript of a detective story written by a woman in the mid-19th century. She went through the door behind the counter that led to storage.

As I waited for her to return, I mused about academics and the expectation that we would cross the "t" and dot the "i" to such an extent as this. No one else, unless they travelled to Pennington library, would ever see this pioneer woman's manuscript.

But there was a pertinent connection to be made, and I was going to make it.

Because that's what scholars did.

We also spent way too much time indoors.

But that was another topic altogether.

I wondered how much time Jean Claude had gotten to spend here.

A wave of melancholy hit me at the thought of my colleague. Now his research, which had brought him across the ocean to Stonedale, would never be completed.

The call sheet book was right in front of me. I pulled it closer and flipped back to the last day I knew he'd been here — he'd mentioned that he was going after rehearsal. There was his familiar signature with the bold looping capital "J." The title next to the call number wasn't related to Damon Runyon as I'd expected but was instead something called *Nocturne, American Style* by Camden Drake.

I froze.

Camden Drake, the professor? Why would Jean Claude be looking at that?

Context? Expansion of his research topic?

Maybe there was more to it.

I quickly grabbed a fresh request sheet from the stack on the other side of the counter and scribbled down the call number and title, then closed the lid on the notebook and slid it back to where it had been.

Just in time too. Eloise burst through the door and set down the pages in front of me with an emphatic little smack, putting a close to her journey. It seemed rough treatment, given that Special Collections housed the old, the delicate, and the rare. Once I'd been yelled at by a zealous librarian for turning a page too quickly.

But Eloise may not have had the same commitment to guardianship. She pushed a pair of gloves to be worn while handling the document across the counter.

"Actually, may I also request this one as well?" I smiled at her apologetically. "I forgot about it."

I could see her sorting through potential retorts in her head, but she landed on a long sigh which, if not in the realm of excellent customer service, was at least not overtly rude.

"I'm sorry."

She nodded and whisked the page from my hand, then disappeared downstairs.

The instant she left, I pulled the notebook back across the counter and went back to the beginning of the semester. I took a picture with my phone of every request Jean Claude had made, so that I could go through them later. It was all Damon Runyon until that puzzling Camden Drake item at the end.

Eloise breezed back in through the door holding a manila folder. She handed it to me without comment and snapped her gum.

"Thank you."

"No prob."

I headed over to a small table and chair by the window. After I'd settled myself, I opened the folder and pulled out the yellowing pages within. The first page looked like any other typed script I'd ever seen. The second also looked legit. But when I flipped to the third page, a smaller page was tucked between them. It had a rough edge on the left — as if it had been ripped from a hardbound book — and was completely handwritten. It was only half-covered with words, the middle of a paragraph apparently.

and then C came to me, just as he said he would, and gave me a necklace, earrings, and bracelet! The diamonds shine like something that fell from heaven. I hid them in the usual place. If M sees them, something terrible will happen. I dream of the day when I can wear them as Mrs. Drake.

I caught my breath. It must be a page from Althea's journal. I stole a glance at Eloise, but she seemed entranced by something on the computer, so I quickly took pictures of the page with my cell phone. Questions tumbled through my mind as I did so. Why had Jean Claude tucked away only one page? Or was Camden the one who had done so decades ago? I didn't have any answers to that, but I had the strongest sense that Althea had hidden her jewelry somewhere in the theater.

And I'd bet someone else thought so too.

I returned the manila folder to the desk, and Eloise helped me locate the rest of Camden Drake's plays, which were preserved in numerous boxes. I spent the better part of the afternoon going through the collection of over fifty pieces ranging from one-acts to fully scored musicals, and found nothing else unusual, though I developed an appreciation for the amount of work he'd done while at Stonedale.

The library also had two boxes of materials relating to Althea Gaines, but there was no journal inside — I'd crossed my fingers that there would be additional ones — just programs and scripts, none of which had any annotations that proved useful.

Finally, I did what I'd gone there to do, found the quote for my footnote, which was admittedly lackluster in comparison.

On my way home, I texted Lex and asked him to meet me at Scarlett's if he was free. Happily, he was.

Once we were ensconced in a booth with hot coffee to fortify us, I described finding the journal page and showed him the pictures I'd taken.

He looked amused. "So now you think there's a buried treasure at the Opera House?"

"Yes," I said, firmly. "Or at Althea's home."

"Really." He stared into his mug, unconvinced.

"And maybe Jean Claude knew about it — or even found it! — and someone killed him for it."

He gave me a long look. "You're not going to stay out of anything, are you?"

I lifted my chin. "I'm helping."

"We don't need your help, Lila. As much as I appreciate the thought."

"Then think of it as me telling a friend about a buried treasure. Totally not related to anything else my friend might be working on."

He threw up his hands. "So what do you propose we do with this information? Scour the place inch by inch?"

"Perfect!"

He laughed. "Althea and Camden left town years ago, Lila. Not exactly relevant to Jean Claude, are they?"

I was a little taken aback by his attitude. "I don't know. Don't you think it would be interesting to have a look around? And since we don't know why someone would kill Jean Claude otherwise, might there be a connection? He's the one who put the journal page into the file, right?"

"Or Camden could have."

"Oh. Right." I was a little deflated to remember that possibility. "Wait, wouldn't it have been noticed by the library staff when they processed his papers? It wasn't noted anywhere as being part of the file. Which means it wasn't there originally." I took a sip of my coffee and held it up in a toast.

"He could have hidden it there later too, after he gave his papers to the university."

My shoulders fell, and I set the mug gently on the table. "Anyway, she said she hid the jewelry in 'the usual place.' It had to be somewhere she spent a lot of time. Like the theater."

"Perhaps 'the usual place' refers to somewhere in her home?"

I stirred some cream into my coffee. "Could you look there too?"

"Nope. The Gaines place burned down, unfortunately. It was suspected that Malcolm set the fire himself."

I stared at him. "Before he committed suicide?"

"That was the general thinking. He was miserable after everything went down. The town really loved his wife, and he didn't have an easy time of things after she disappeared. Especially since he was suddenly a single parent of a daughter that might not be his." He took a large sip. "Poor Bella."

"You already knew Bella is Althea's baby?" I didn't know why I'd thought it was a secret.

"Most people who live in Stonedale do."

I stopped stirring. "Why do you think

261

Althea left?"

"I have no idea."

"What's the general thinking on it?"

"That she ran away to be with Camden."

"And left behind her little daughter?"

"It's been done before."

"Hard to imagine." I felt a surge of sympathy for Bella.

Lex shrugged. "People have their reasons."

I put the spoon down on the napkin next to my mug. "Given the timeline, do you think Bella could be Camden's daughter instead of Malcolm's?"

"It's very possible."

"But that seems like all the more reason for Althea to bring Bella with her," I said.

"Maybe Camden didn't want her."

I gulped. "That's harsh."

"The world can be harsh, Lila." He stared out the window. "Consider that Malcolm burned down his house, left his daughter in a basket on a neighbor's porch, and hung himself."

"True. He snapped, sounds like. It's so tragic."

"Yes, it definitely is."

I was quiet for a moment, processing. "Do you think there might be more to it, though? Maybe someone else burned his house down? Maybe they were looking for the jewelry?"

He ran a hand through his hair and considered this.

"I mean, has anyone ever talked about the jewelry before? Maybe it provides a motive."

"Just you." He smiled at me, his blue eyes steady on mine, then cleared his throat. "How do you know the page was from Althea's journal, anyway?"

"It mentioned both Camden and Malcolm. I mean, it *has* to be hers."

"Perhaps someone else wrote it after the fact."

I shrugged. "It's possible. But it's so specific and . . . wait!" I dug around in my satchel, then pulled out the letters and waved them triumphantly. "In one of these, Camden mentions bringing her some gems. He meant the diamonds."

"What are those?" Lex's eyebrows were drawn together in confusion.

"These are letters that Camden wrote to Althea."

"Yes, but why do *you* have them?" He was sitting perfectly still, but his frustration reached across the table.

"I meant to tell you about them when you were at my house. But I got distracted." I could feel the heat warming my face when I thought about the almost-kissing moment.

"And they . . ."

"Lila," he said sternly. "You should have turned them in immediately."

"To whom?"

"Whoever is in charge of the theater." He tapped his fingers on the table.

"The chancellor? He wouldn't care."

"How do you know? Maybe he knew about the letters and has been searching for them for years. Imagine what will happen when he finds out you kept them."

"I didn't keep them. I just read them. There's still time to . . . Lex, that's not the point. Can we just focus on what they say for a second?" I shook the paper gently.

He took the letters from me and read through them, nodding a little when he reached the one that mentioned the gift.

"You might be right about the jewelry. May I take these?"

"To the station? What about giving them to the chancellor?"

Lex caught my eye. "Were you really going to give them to him, anyway?"

"Yes." I sat up a little straighter.

He stared me down. "Probably."

He waited.

"Eventually, anyway."

"Ha." He folded the letters carefully. "Where did you get them again?"

"They, uh, surfaced at the theater. During rehearsal." That was true. Ish.

He held my eye for a second, then put the letters into his inside coat pocket.

"Please be careful with them," I said.

"Of course."

"Oh and before you take them, may I snap a few pictures?"

He sighed and pulled them out of his pocket again. I captured the images with my phone and handed the pages back.

"They probably should go into the library collection when all of this is over," I said, ever the dutiful scholar.

"Maybe so. We'll take them to the university after we're finished and they can decide what to do with them."

"Does this mean you believe me about the letters being connected to Jean Claude?"

"No. It means I want to take a closer look at them and see if we can establish their authenticity before we begin spinning theories." It was delivered with a meaningful look.

"You don't think it all adds up to something?"

"One step at a time is generally the safer way to go."

"But maybe the letters are the answer to everything!"

"Or maybe the letters are counterfeit."

I shook my head. "I'm not going to let you burst my bubble, Detective. I have a gut feeling about this. Besides, why would someone fake them? It doesn't make any sense."

"Crime doesn't always make sense, Lila."

"But what about innocent until proven guilty? Or the evidence equivalent of that . . . true until proven false?"

He laughed. "I don't think that's a thing."

"Well, maybe it should be."

CHAPTER 20

The next day, I headed to rehearsal after class. We'd spent a great deal of time discussing *The Turn of the Screw*, and the consideration of ghosts and the like was hitting a bit too close to home at the present time. Henry James had certainly posed a relevant question: what are the dangers of interpreting things we cannot fully understand?

As I pulled open the door to the theater, I caught sight of Chip talking to Zandra next to the box office. He gave me a wave. She lifted her head and saw me, said something to him, and they parted. Chip went outside, and she quickly covered the distance between us, her long beaded necklaces clicking against each other as she moved.

"He's hurrying off to a meeting. Are you ready for our final dress rehearsal?"

"Yes. How's Chip?"

"Ecstatic. The chancellor, apparently, has

all but signed on the dotted line. Regardless of how everyone feels about it, he will probably be the new owner soon. For better or for worse."

"But isn't Clara trying to buy it as well?"

"Yes, but she'll never to be able to raise enough money."

"She sounded pretty sure that she could."

"Clara doesn't live in the same world as we do," Zandra said with a laugh. "You know that by now, right?"

"She does seem to have her own point of view."

"Indeed. Now let's put her behind us for the moment and go down to rehearsal." A cloud of her perfume — something musky and oppressively floral — enveloped us as she threaded her arm through mine and pulled me down the aisle. "Tolliver is so excited. He could barely sleep last night."

"I can imagine."

"This is an unbelievable production, don't you agree?"

I was glad she had phrased it that way so I could agree. Unbelievable was the perfect word for it, heavy on the cannot-believe-this-thing-is-being-staged.

We took our usual seats in the front just as Tolliver addressed the company, assembled on the stage. The actors were wearing their costumes, the scenery was in place, and there was an expectant energy in the air.

"Our final dress rehearsal is here! Thank you for your lovely work to date — please clap for yourselves." They did. "Thank you for putting your soul into your performances. And let's give a round of applause to the crew, whose fabulous work behind the scenes has made the world of our play come alive!" The cast applauded and whistled, and the crew members looked gratified.

Tolliver swept his hands up. "And now, my ducklings, it is time to shine. Let us take it from the top. Places, everyone." He clapped twice and made his way down the side stairs toward us. He sank into the chair he favored, which squeaked, then there was silence. The red curtain came down slowly, its gold tassels shining in the lights.

"And go please . . ." Tolliver said quietly into his headset. The stage manager would take over the cues from there.

The theater went dark and the overture began to play as the curtain rose again. A spotlight focused on Oliver standing center stage, reciting random but familiar lines from famous detectives as the other characters filed in. It soon turned into a big number, "Nothing Is Ever As It Seems," with a decidedly carnivalesque feel. There was so much going on that I hardly knew where to look. Actors in multicolored costumes crossed the stage, belting out lyrics, while tap dancers, fire spinners, and acrobats were leaping, twirling, and tumbling. Carts rolled out of the wings and released swarms of balloons. Aerialists spun down from the ceiling on silks and swung in from the sides on hoops. The sea of motion was punctuated by flashes of color and the glitter of sequins. Just when it seemed as though nothing else could possibly be added to the frenzy, a brass band came down the aisle, dividing into two lines that filed up the stairs on both sides, filling up every space on the stage. It was joyful mayhem. When the song came to an end, there was a moment of silence followed by spontaneous cheers from the cast themselves. They knew they'd nailed it.

Tolliver laughed. "I agree with your assessment, but don't applaud for yourselves during performances, okay?"

The rest of the scenes went smoothly and, before long, we'd reached the end. I was surprised to find myself feeling strangely uplifted. Either I was too familiar with the play to be bothered by its absurdities any longer or somehow we had addressed the worst of them and . . . it all sort of worked.

When the lights came up, Tolliver called everyone to the stage again and enthusiastically praised them. "Although it may be unusual for us to take a day off now, right before we open, it's Halloween. That's how the schedule landed, and I think it may sharpen your creative energy! Go enjoy the holiday and come back ready to act your hearts out on Wednesday. Can you do that for me?"

There were sounds of assent around the room. Zandra, who'd gone up to stand next to him, beamed at them.

"Just be sure to give your costume to Luciana before you leave! They are not to be worn for Halloween, ducklings."

After Tolliver said goodbye, the students bustled offstage.

As I stretched my neck to get the kinks out, Zandra glided down the stairs, her chiffon wrap floating out behind her. Her face glowed. "I'm absolutely thrilled, aren't you?"

Luckily, I didn't have to answer because she plowed on ahead.

"He has *outdone* himself. This is his very best play. So cutting edge, don't you think? I think he'll be written up everywhere that *matters.*"

I opened my mouth to reply, but she was off and running again.

"I'm going to go find him and tell him so. He's drifted off somewhere. Then I need to finalize the details for the cast party. I told Tolly I'd take care of everything. There's so much that remains to be done. It has to be fabulous."

She walked right past me, still reciting items on her to-do list. It appeared that we were all a little overwhelmed, with opening night looming.

I took my time gathering up everything that needed to be packed into my satchel and pulled on my coat. I called goodbye to Tolliver, who was nowhere in sight, but maybe he'd hear me.

I switched on the ghost light that had been set onstage by a crew member, as always. "Goodnight, Malcolm," I said. If we did have a ghost, I might as well acknowledge him too. "Thanks for letting us have our play here."

He didn't reply.

In the lobby, I pulled out my script and spent a few minutes jotting ideas for Tolliver on the back page. He'd asked me to email him any final thoughts and I wanted to make notes before I forgot. The company gradually cleared out, and the theater grew quiet.

Then a bloodcurdling scream rent the air.

I whirled around and ran through the empty auditorium, racing toward the cries coming from downstairs. I followed the sounds to the prop room, where Tolliver lay on the floor, directly beneath the open trap door. He wasn't moving. Zandra was bending over him, calling his name, and Parker was standing behind her, looking unsteady.

"Call 911," I said to Parker as I ran to Tolliver. When I knelt next to him, I could see his chest moving and his eyes fluttering. Relief coursed through my body. Zandra burst into tears and shook Tolliver's shoulder.

"The ambulance is on the way," Parker announced. "They're staying on the line if we need anything."

I thanked him and put my hand on Zandra's arm. "Be sure not to shake him too hard. He may have broken something. And he's breathing, so let's just make him comfortable."

She pulled her hand back and wiped her cheek.

I tore off my coat and put it on top of him. I knew there was a chance of him going into shock and that we were supposed to raise his legs as well, but since one of them was in an unnatural position, it seemed better to leave it as is.

"Who could have done this?" Zandra wailed. Her face was contorted, as if more tears were on the way.

"I'm not sure anyone did. Doesn't it seem as though he fell through the trap door? Perhaps he was fiddling with the lock. Did you see or hear him fall?"

"No. I came down to make sure the lights were out and found him like this. Thank goodness I did." She went into another round of sobs.

I took a few deep breaths. It was almost too much to take in. "Where are the mattresses?"

Zandra twisted and pointed to the far wall. "Someone dragged them over there."

The missing mattresses made this situation even more disturbing. We were under strict orders to leave them below the trap door at all times, to keep everyone safe. The entire company knew the rule. Removing them could only have been intentional.

"I can't believe it." She wiped her eyes and bent down to murmur what sounded like comforting words to Tolliver.

I told them we had everything under control, and I tried hard to make it sound convincing.

I almost believed it myself.

An hour later, Zandra and I were in the lobby. The ambulance had taken Tolliver to the hospital. He woke just before they arrived and seemed more irritated than anything else; my guess was that the shock was masking the pain for now, which was a blessing.

Zandra was planning to follow in her car so that they'd have a ride home from the hospital. I offered to come along, but she discouraged me. "I'll take care of him, Lila. It's just a broken leg."

"If it turns out to be more than that, will you call me? And please let me know if there's anything I can do. Anything at all."

"Thank you." She shifted their coats and bags in her arms. "But I will say that I don't think he just fell. I think he was pushed."

"Pushed?"

"This man has done more plays than anyone I know. He wouldn't just fall through the trap door."

"People have accidents."

"I sense that there is more to it, Lila. And, as you know, my otherworldly faculties are sharply attuned." She looked up at the ceiling. "Clearly we are not wanted here anymore. That's the only possible explanation."

Well, not the *only* one.

She reinforced her pronouncement with a dip of her head.

"You're not talking about a person, are you?"

"No."

"You think a ghost pushed him?"

She shrugged. "Stranger things have happened."

"Stranger than a ghost pushing someone through a trap door?"

"Yes." She pressed her lips together.

Now it was my turn to shrug.

CHAPTER 21

I spent Halloween morning grading essays. Although it was always heartening to see evidence of students mastering material, it was difficult work. My eyes were tired and my head had begun pounding slightly, so when my cell phone rang, it was a welcome interruption.

The screen displayed Zandra's name. I pressed the accept button. "Hello?"

She got right to it. "Remember how you offered to help, Lila?"

"Yes. Is Tolliver okay?"

"It's a bad break. He'll be in a cast for awhile."

"I'm so sorry. Is he in a lot of pain?"

"Well, the medicine is taking the edge off and he's resting comfortably right now."

"That's good. Will he be able to make the opening?"

She laughed. "Nothing could keep him away from that. But beforehand, I need your assistance. Are you free tonight?"

I paused. My plans involved handing out candy and getting a good night's sleep before the play opening. "What do you need?"

"I'm going to hold a séance, and I'd like you to be one of the participants. Since you are one of the souls who has had a presence in the Opera House in recent weeks."

"Any number of students —"

"No students. I'm inviting just a few carefully selected individuals. Remember when I said yesterday that I sensed something?"

"Yes."

"Last night, I had a powerful dream. It was Malcolm, telling me he had a message that could only be shared to the group. He even listed the attendees and you were one of them."

Goosebumps broke out on my arms in response to having been hand-picked by a ghost for the guest list. My mind raced to come up with a good excuse.

"You said you were willing to help out, Lila."

She had me there.

"Or was that just lip service?" There was a crisp edge to her voice.

I sighed. "No. I meant it. I'll join you."

"This is very important. I need to know

who has it out for Tolliver. He's a dear man, and he doesn't deserve anyone stalking him. In this realm or the next." Her voice was low and fierce.

Wow. She really thought she could not only clear things up but keep the ghosts in line too? Now I actually wanted to go and see that. "When do you need me?"

"At the Opera House. We'll meet at eleven thirty and begin at midnight. That's the optimal time, of course."

"The witching hour." I'd read enough Gothic texts to know that one.

"It's also the anniversary of the day Malcolm Gaines fought Camden Drake," she said.

That, too.

"Could I bring someone?" I thought Lex should be there.

"No. Only the dream invitees are welcome, I'm sorry."

"Got it. Are the spirit wranglers on the list?" I couldn't bear being filmed again.

"No. Malcolm has said all he needs to say to them."

"Ah."

"You should consider yourself very lucky, Lila. The spirit realm is picky."

So I had that going for me.

Later that afternoon, I was standing in line at the corner market. I'd run out of peppermint tea and biscotti, which were, in my humble opinion, grading essentials. There was a credit card issue with the person checking out ahead of me, and we were at a standstill.

I was half-heartedly eyeing a rack of celebrity magazines when I heard my name and turned around to find Bella smiling at me.

She set a loaf of wheat bread and a container of hummus on the counter.

We exchanged pleasantries, then she surprised me by asking if Zandra had called.

"Yes."

She tilted her head toward me and said, out of the corner of her mouth, "So you're going to the séance?"

"Yes. Are you?"

"I don't really want to participate, but Zandra said it has something to do with my father and, you know . . ." she trailed off, looking uncomfortable.

"You don't have to go if you don't want to," I pointed out.

"I know. But Clara wants me to, and she's

already upset with me, so . . ."

That was interesting. "Why?"

"Because I haven't been able to persuade the chancellor to sell us the theater. And also because I haven't been able to magically produce some long-lost paperwork that proves my father secretly wanted to keep the theater in the family or changed his mind about the bequest to the university. I don't know why she thinks that exists. It doesn't. He disowned my mother and gave the theater to the school."

"Gave? Not sold? So there wasn't any money as a result?"

"Yes. That was the point. He wanted to punish my mother. And, I guess, me."

"I'm sorry, Bella."

"I've never had money so I don't miss it." She laughed, though it sounded somewhat sad.

"I know the feeling," I said.

"Anyway, if you're going to attend, I will too. Though I'm getting tired of Clara bossing me around. Lately I feel compelled to do the opposite of what she wants me to do." She picked at the label on the hummus. "Sorry. I don't know why I'm telling you this."

"It can feel good to vent."

"It does, honestly. And I've just this

minute decided to do something else that will set her teeth on edge."

"Which is?"

"Bring Chip Turner along."

"That might make Clara lose it altogether."

This time, her laugh wasn't sad at all. "I'm turning into a rebel."

It was about time she stood up to Clara. "It will definitely make a point. How well do you know Chip?"

She looked down. And was that a blush?

"Since he approached the Historical Society about eight months ago. I've been the main point of contact since Clara can barely bring herself to speak to him. As for Braxton, well, he doesn't like to talk to anyone, even people he actually likes."

"Has Chip visited Stonedale often?"

"Oh yes. Many times over the past year — ever since he decided to try and buy it."

"What do you think of him?"

Yes, that was definitely a blush.

"I wish he would leave the Opera House alone. Even though I don't have any claim to it, I know it's historically significant. And if we could just find enough funding, we could fix it up and open a museum there or something."

"Have you spent much time with him?"

"Yes." She looked around before taking a step closer and practically whispering. "But don't tell anyone, please. I accepted his dinner invitations at first because I thought I might be able to convince him to buy something else instead of the Opera House. But then . . ." she rolled her finger in a circle.

"It became romantic?"

She nodded, biting her lower lip. "Couldn't help it. He's very charming. And a very good person, despite how he may come across. I know I have to tell Braxton and Clara, but I haven't worked up the nerve yet."

"I understand. Do you think you've managed to persuade him?"

"Maybe. I don't know. I'm still working on it."

My items moved forward on the conveyor belt and the cashier greeted me. After he'd rung me up, I said goodbye to Bella.

She gave me a wave. "See you tonight."

On my way home, I decided to alert Lex to the gathering at the theater. He didn't answer his phone, so I shot him a detailed text and considered my civic duty complete.

After handing out candy to neighborhood children for several hours, I headed over to the theater for Zandra's séance. Many of the homes and stores had gone over the top with festive decor — cauldrons smoldered, oversized monsters crouched on roofs, ghosts fluttered along awnings and porches. The streets were full of partiers in the annual Halloween pub crawl: costumed citizens moved in merry groups and there was a celebratory vibe in the air.

The Opera House looked magnificent from the sidewalk. The chandelier hanging in the lobby was visible through the large arched window that graced the facade. Perhaps because of the fanciful spell cast by Halloween, it was easy to imagine a well-dressed crowd, in days of yore, all top hats and gowns, descending from their carriages to enjoy a performance. Or, perhaps, a less-elegantly-clad throng of townspeople clamoring for a seat at a vaudeville show.

I pushed open the door and entered the lobby. Zandra immediately swooped over. "Oh good, you're here! You're the last one." She pulled me toward the theater. "We're on the stage."

I followed her to the stage, where a circular table with a white cloth was set up over the trap door. Bella, Clara, Braxton, and Tolliver were already seated. I greeted them and gave Tolliver a little hug before claiming the chair next to him.

"How are you?"

He looked down at his cast ruefully. "It's a bit painful, but the doctors assure me I'll heal with proper rest and therapy."

"What happened?"

"Someone pushed me." His forehead creased as he thought. "I just opened the trap door to make sure it was working properly for the scene we changed — you know, the one that now has Poe arising from the grave instead of flying down from above? — and as soon as it was all the way open, I felt a shove."

"Did you hear anything? Any footsteps? Or catch sight of anyone?"

"No. Not a sound. I know it sounds crazy but I'm positive there was no one else on the stage. It was empty. Except . . . we do have a ghost here. I mean, that's been proven."

I didn't know about the proven part. "It's certainly been repeated as a possibility."

He rearranged the skull-patterned scarf around his neck. "Well, I don't know how else to explain it. I'm an open-minded man. And even Sherlock Holmes recognized that sometimes the truth can seem improbable."

"I'm sorry you were hurt."

"Thank you, Petal."

Zandra approached us. The white streak in the front of her hair was stunning against the all-black ensemble she wore. She was carrying a clear crystal ball, which she set carefully on a small metal stand in the middle of the table.

"This is my amplifier," she explained, removing her black gloves and placing them on her lap. "It allows me to more easily connect with the other realm. Something to keep in mind is that occasionally, the connection will happen on multiple frequencies."

"Meaning?" Clara demanded in a clipped tone.

"Meaning that there are times when the spirits who come through are still very much a part of this world. Not on the other side."

"You mean they're alive?" Clara said, snorting.

Zandra spoke evenly. "That's exactly what I mean. Sometimes when people are asleep, for example, they are able to make connections. They may think they're just having a dream. But if I can connect with their spirit, and if they have a message, they may come through."

"Are you saying that when I go to sleep and have a dream, I may be participating in

286

a séance *without my knowledge?*" Clara's voice squeaked a little in her outrage.

"Or something like that," Zandra confirmed, flashing a smile at her. I had the feeling she was enjoying staying calm while Clara's frustration increased.

"Now," Zandra said, going around the table and making eye contact with everyone individually, "we begin. Please clear your minds of everything and take several deep breaths."

We all did as she instructed.

"In a little while, I will ask you to take each other's hands so that we form a circle. It is imperative that you do not break the circle for any reason. Do you understand?"

We agreed, except for Clara, who sputtered a little. "I'm an upright woman. I'm not sure about this sort of hocus-pocus."

Zandra smiled at her. "This isn't witch-craft. This is providing a channel for spirits to speak to me. Or through me. It's pulling aside the veil, ever so briefly. Making a connection to another realm that is already here but not visible to everyone. But if you're uncomfortable —"

The lobby door flew open and we all jumped.

"Sorry, sorry." The man moved quickly down the aisle. "It's just me, Chip."

"What's he doing here?" Clara hissed.

"He wasn't on the guest list," Zandra added.

"I invited him," Bella said firmly. "He has a right to know what's going on in this property. And if he goes, I go."

"Bella! Why, you've . . . you've betrayed us!" Clara shot Bella a furious glare.

"No, Clara." Bella leaned forward and spoke earnestly. "I'm trying to get him to see how important this place is. To all of us and to generations to come."

Clara remained silent, shaking with anger.

"I've been trying to tell him that for months now. And we . . . we . . ." she faltered, casting a glance at Chip, who had just stepped onto the stage.

"We fell in love," he said, moving behind Bella's chair and putting his hand on her shoulder.

"What?" Clara gasped. "You think you're in *love*?" She turned to Braxton, whose face reflected her shock, and stood up abruptly. Her chair shot backwards and crashed to the ground. "Come on, Brax. We're leaving immediately. And Bella," she shook her finger across the table, "do *not* bother coming back to work. You're fired, you ungrateful, wretched child. After all we've done for you."

"Wait," Zandra said. "Why is this an issue? Bella just told you that she's trying to convince Chip to save the Opera House, not tear it down. She didn't betray you."

"She did," Clara retorted. "By having anything to do with that man."

Zandra addressed the table. "I'm going to speak to Clara for a few minutes. Please don't go anywhere. We'll be back."

She went over and put her arm through Clara's. I thought Clara was going to shake her off, but, to my surprise, she allowed herself to be led backstage.

The rest of us sat silently for a moment, then Braxton looked back and forth between Bella and Chip. "Is he a good man, Bel?" Chip was standing right there, but at the same time, it was said so simply and with such affection that the awkwardness was outweighed by the obvious depth of feeling.

Bella said, "He is, Braxton. He really is."

Braxton nodded, then looked at Chip for a long while before speaking directly to him. "If you have her heart, you must treasure it."

Chip nodded vehemently. "I will."

"If you don't, I'll find you." Braxton fixed him with an intense look. I had no doubt that he was capable of far more than I'd previously imagined.

Chip froze. "I understand." He looked down at Bella and tilted his head slightly, urging her to say something.

"He asked me to marry him last night," Bella said. "We're engaged."

Braxton drew his eyebrows together and considered this for a long moment. "If you're truly happy, dearest, then I'm happy for you too."

By the time Clara and Zandra returned, we were all — except Tolliver — standing around them in a circle, having jumped up to hug and congratulate them.

"What's this?" Clara demanded. I don't know what Zandra said to her, but it seemed to have set her on a kinder path. Upon hearing the engagement news, she only allowed herself a small scowl, then pressed her lips together, tugged her jacket down, and grimly congratulated them.

The etiquette expertise served her well in that instance. For once.

Zandra gushed over the betrothed for several minutes before asking us to sit so we could proceed with the séance.

Oh yes. That's why we were here in the first place.

CHAPTER 22

We all took our seats and Zandra performed a quick blessing ritual, lighting several white candles arranged around the crystal ball. The reflection of the flames in the glass was mesmerizing.

"Now," she said, "please join hands and no matter what you see or hear, do *not* break the circle. One never knows what form the communication will come in. Sometimes they speak and I translate for them. Other times, well, they speak right through me. But don't be afraid, whether I'm translating or channeling."

Tolliver took my hand on the left and Zandra took mine on the right. Both were tighter than I would have liked, but I let my hands rest in theirs and tried not to wince.

"Take several deep breaths, please." Zandra closed her eyes and inhaled and exhaled, loudly.

We followed her lead.

"Dear spirits," she said, in a conversational tone, "we are here to listen. Please come forward. This is your chance to make yourself heard."

It was silent for several minutes. The candles flickered slightly and Zandra squeezed my hand. "Someone's here," she breathed.

A sense of anticipation rose but we remained silent.

I watched Zandra, who seemed to be watching something behind Bella's head, directly across the table from her. She smiled. "He's here. I see you, Malcolm. What do you want to say?" She nodded. "Yes, I hear you."

I cast a glance around the table. All eyes were fixed on Zandra.

"He says that we are welcome here —"

"I knew it," Clara pronounced, looking satisfied. "He is happy that we're trying to preserve his home."

"— as long as we are —" She paused and squinted for awhile, then nodded decisively. "— as long as we are *respectful*. Thank you, Malcolm."

A loud thump came from below us, and we all jumped.

Zandra's expression changed. "Someone else is here too."

292

The crystal ball glowed and one of the candles went out.

My heart began to beat a little faster.

Suddenly Zandra sat up straighter. She hummed something.

Bella's mouth fell open. "It's Althea's song — the one Camden wrote for her that was recorded."

Zandra's humming grew louder and more insistent. Her face seemed to undergo a reassembling of features, resulting in a softer shape. She blinked her eyes coquettishly and curved her lips up. "I'm here," she said quietly.

Clara and Braxton exchanged a look that I couldn't read.

"No one can hear me," she continued. "Why?"

"I hear you," Bella said earnestly. "Mother."

Zandra froze, then turned her face across the table in Bella's direction, though she was looking above her.

"It's me, Bella. Your daughter." Tears glistened in her eyes.

Zandra's gaze landed upon Bella and turned sorrowful. "My angel. Know that you are loved. I had to leave, and I am sorry, but you belong here."

"Why did you leave me?" Bella asked,

leaning forward, staring at Zandra.

"Be strong. Seek what you deserve." Zandra closed her eyes and began humming again.

"Please, who is my father?" Bella pleaded. "Can you just tell me that?"

"This is nonsense," Clara pronounced, though her voice quavered. "And not very convincing at that. Bella, don't fall for this."

Zandra's features reassembled themselves into a hard, angry mask. The words came out in a low growl. "Why did you have to come here? Everything was fine until you came along. She was mine. MINE!"

There was a loud double rap, like someone pounding on wood.

Clara squeaked and Chip yelped. The room seemed to be growing hazy.

"Where did that noise come from?" Chip demanded.

Zandra's voice changed again, her face contorting into an anguished expression we hadn't seen before. "Stop, stop!" she commanded, in a low baritone. "For the love of God!"

"Is it Malcolm again?" Clara asked, her voice small, like a child.

"It's Camden," Bella breathed.

"No!" Zandra's voice slid back into a growl again and began to rise until she was shouting. "YOU ARE NOT WELCOME HERE —"

The rapping grew steadily louder.

Bella cried out, as if in pain. "Are they fighting?"

"Is he talking to us?" Clara gasped. "How dare he tell us we're not welcome!"

"How many people are talking? I don't understand what's happening." Chip's voice was higher than usual.

All at once, a rush of wind seemed to circle the table, and the crystal ball glowed even brighter.

"ENOUGH!" Zandra roared, then her head lolled forward over her chest, her dark hair covering her face.

Everything went completely still. It felt as though we were all waiting for someone else to say something.

I finally caught Tolliver's eye. "Should we stop?"

He shook his head. "Let it play out."

We sat silently until Zandra's head raised again. Her eyes were glittering. This time, her voice was gruff. "And don't you forget about *me.*"

Bella and I locked eyes.

Zandra mumbled something, then repeated it more loudly. *"Bonjour."*

Clara gasped again. "He's here too?"

Zandra's eyebrows drew together and she seemed to grow in stature as she glared at Clara. "*Mais oui.* And there is nothing you can do to shut me down *now,* Madame."

Clara's mouth flopped open and closed, but no words came out.

"We miss you, Jean Claude." I plunged forward, even though I wasn't sure if it was acceptable to ask people about their own demise. "Can you tell us who killed you?"

The laugh that came out of Zandra's throat was harsh and disturbing. It seemed to be all around us somehow. When the lights flickered, she inhaled sharply, and released my hand. The laughter stopped immediately.

She raised her arm slowly, pointed a finger at Clara, and screamed. "It was *you,* Clara! You shot Jean Claude!"

The older woman started slightly, then raised both of her palms in the air as though Zandra was aiming an actual gun at her. "I did not! That's absurd."

A loud clunk came from beneath the table.

We all leaned down to see what it was, pawing at the tablecloth. A silver gun with a pink handle lay on the floor.

"My pistol!" Clara screeched, reaching for it.

"Don't touch it," I said. "It needs to be

checked for fingerprints. It may be the weapon that was used on Jean Claude."

"That's what the ghosts are saying too," Zandra said, glaring at Clara.

We straightened up and looked around the table at each other suspiciously.

"How did it get there?" Bella asked.

"Spirits can move objects," Zandra said. "They're offering evidence."

"You're serious?" Chip stared at her.

Zandra continued as if he hadn't spoken. "And when the police get ahold of this, Clara will be proven guilty beyond a shadow of a doubt."

"How dare you!" Clara's face was growing increasingly redder.

"Don't try to deny it," Zandra spit at her. "The spirits don't lie!"

Tolliver blinked rapidly. "How is this even —"

"Not now, Tolly." Zandra pulled out her cell phone and started dialing. "I'm calling the police."

"No need. We're already here." I recognized Lex's voice. He was coming toward the stage with several other officers. They must have snuck in at some point during the séance.

I stood up and went to meet him, as the officers made their way over to the group.

"Thanks for sending that text, Lila," he said. "I'm glad I didn't miss this."

"It would have been hard to describe in a way that did it any justice," I said, smiling at him. He gave me a quick side hug, which I appreciated since I was still a little unnerved.

Also because it was a hug from Lex.

"Are you going to take Clara in?"

"Well, there needs to be slightly more evidence than, um . . ." he grinned at me, "a ghost's accusation before that happens, but we'll question her thoroughly for starters."

I grinned back, then remembered. "There's a gun too, though."

"We can take it from here," he said. "By which I mean, *please* let us take it from here."

"I hear you, Detective."

"Is there anything else you think I should know about her?" Lex pulled out his trusty black notepad and flipped to an empty page.

"You probably know more than I do. Clara's been adamant that the theater stays in the hands of the Historical Society. And as the person who raised Bella, she feels it is her right somehow. Or her duty."

"Mmm hmm. What about Clara's relationship with Chip Turner?"

That was an abrupt shift.

"I don't know Chip very well, but he certainly has made it clear that he wants to get his hands on this property too."

"Why?"

I cocked my head, shooting Lex a c'mon-now look.

"What?"

"You already know why. You're a very good detective, or so I've heard."

"How kind." He winked and held his pen over the page. "Now humor me."

"Okay, he has said —"

"To you?"

"In front of me."

Lex jotted something.

"He wants to tear down the Opera House and turn it into a state-of-the-art performance complex where plays can be staged without —"

"Without fear of damaging this historical site. Got it."

I raised an eyebrow. "The whole tearing-down of the historical site is pretty damaging, wouldn't you say?"

He had the grace to look abashed.

I resumed my earlier tack. "I was *going* to say where plays can be staged without interference from the Historical Society, which presides over the activities here with an iron fist, to say the least."

"And the Historical Society is unhappy with that idea."

"Of course."

"Anything else?"

"His narrative has also gotten people's dander up. He keeps saying he wants to bring culture to Stonedale, as if we don't have a long artistic tradition here, thank you very much."

His lips quirked.

"What?" I demanded.

"Sounds like you're defending our little town."

I paused. "I guess I am."

"Well, you've lived here long enough to be considered a Stonedalian."

"A what now?"

"Stonedalian. That's what we call ourselves."

"Seriously? Not Stonedale-ite? Or Stonedale-r?"

"Nope. And happily because those are pretty awful."

"I don't know that they're *that* much worse."

"Oh, they are," he said, flipping the page over. "Okay, back to the matter at hand. Is there anything else I should know about Chip or Clara?"

"He and Bella are engaged."

His pen scribbled away. "That's new."

"Yes. And a bit of a surprise to Clara and Braxton, who are diametrically opposed to anything Chip-related. Clara outright said that she feels betrayed."

"Got it. Anything else?"

When I said no, he shut the notepad and tucked it back into his pocket. "That's helpful. Thanks, Lila."

"Do I need to stay any longer?"

"No. It's late. I'll call you tomorrow, okay?"

I nodded and watched him walk away.

Bella greeted him as she came down the stairs, then joined me in the aisle. "Wow. That was something, wasn't it?"

"I know, right?"

She smiled, which surprised me, considering that her guardian had just been descended upon by police. But the source of her happiness became immediately clear. "It really felt as though I was talking to my mother. There was this burst of love that went right through me."

"Wow."

"I know it sounds odd. But I felt her presence. I swear." Her smile faltered. "Though I can't believe Jean Claude accused Clara of killing him. There's no way she's a killer."

301

"Well, maybe it wasn't Jean Claude. Maybe it was just Zandra," I suggested.

"That's true. It wasn't clear there at the end, was it?"

"No, it wasn't."

She turned back to the stage, observing the activity. Two police had sat down at the table and were talking to Clara and Braxton. Two more were on the stage, chatting with Zandra and Tolliver. Lex was examining the crystal ball on the table, which wasn't glowing at all now.

Chip was nowhere to be seen.

Bella touched my arm softly. "Want to join me? I just need to sit down for a minute."

"Sure."

We sank into the shabby red seats and sat in comfortable silence. The discussions onstage concluded and, eventually, we were the only ones left in the quiet theater.

"Do you think the ghosts really did return Clara's pistol?"

I gave her a look.

"I know, it sounds absurd. But did you see anyone carrying a gun when we got there?"

"No," I admitted.

She thought for a moment. "And we were all holding hands in the circle the whole time, right?"

302

"True."

"So wouldn't we have noticed if one of us let go?"

She had a point.

"Plus the alternative is that one of us is guilty, and I don't even know how to begin processing that," she said. "I trust every single person who was here."

I didn't know whom I trusted anymore. Including Bella, even though she had never given me a reason not to trust her. As far as I knew.

I snapped my fingers. "We should check out the table." I pointed to the stage. "Maybe it's rigged."

She gave me a small smile. "I'm so tired. I'll wait here."

I trudged up the stairs and crawled under the table. I felt around every corner of it, but there was nothing unusual — no flaps, doors, or bumpy spots where a secret compartment might be housed. Using the flashlight on my phone, I scrutinized it again until I was sure.

Dejected, I returned to Bella.

"It was a good idea," she said to comfort me.

"Thanks. And now I think I'll call it a night."

"I appreciate your sleuthing efforts, anyway."

"You're very kind. And congratulations again on your engagement, Bella. I hope this doesn't put a damper on things."

"Thank you. I appreciate that. And I hope you believe that Clara is innocent. I know that with every fiber of my being."

I hoped she was right.

The pistol seemed to suggest otherwise, though.

CHAPTER 23

Lex called the next morning, as promised. Clara had been questioned and although they didn't feel they had enough to charge her for anything, they weren't forgetting about her, either. Fingerprint results would take awhile but even if her prints *were* on the pistol, it wouldn't prove anything because it was her gun.

I pointed out that perhaps it was her plan all along to claim the gun was stolen, use it as a weapon, make it appear in public, then insist she was being framed.

In which case she was kind of an evil genius.

Lex said he appreciated my theory but didn't think she was capable of that.

I said it was always the ones you didn't think were capable who were the most capable.

He said I read too many mysteries.

I said there is no such thing as too many

mysteries.

And that was the end of that conversation.

After we said goodbye, I mused over various possibilities as I washed my coffee cup. One thing I knew for sure: both Clara and Chip wanted to get control of the Opera House.

But how would shooting Jean Claude accomplish that?

As I rinsed the mug and set it upside down on the rack next to the sink, it occurred to me that perhaps he was not the primary target but someone who got in the way.

Or maybe he was chosen because he was so famous and his death would receive a lot of attention.

Creating a sense of peril might be useful for Chip. If he could generate enough negative publicity that made people not want to go to the theater, it might lower its value. Then the chancellor could be more easily persuaded to dump the property. We all knew that bad publicity was one of his least favorite things.

Yet the same could be true for Clara. If she generated enough negative publicity, perhaps Chip wouldn't want to buy the property in the first place.

And of course Tolliver had something at stake as well: the success of his play, which would be helped by publicity. Then again, he wouldn't throw himself through a trap door and suffer a broken leg in order to sell tickets . . . would he?

I dried my hands on a flowered towel and folded it, pushing my speculations further.

Bella was engaged to Chip, so she might be in on whatever he was up to.

Zandra was Tolliver's companion, so she might be in on his plan.

And Braxton was married to Clara. He'd do whatever she wanted, no question, though somehow it was difficult to think of him as actively guilty. He was more like a casualty swept up in the tsunami of her relentless determination.

Then there was Gavin Frinkle. He was all about the hype, hoping the *Spirit Wranglers* episode would promote the theater, provide support for his forthcoming book, and pave the way for a parapsychology department.

The actors would also benefit from having participated in a production at a well-known site.

So would the wranglers, come to think of it.

Did *everyone* have a motive for shining a spotlight on the theater?

I hung the towel across the bar and froze as a realization struck me: if murdering Jean Claude was indeed intended to draw attention, we were all still very much in danger.

After class, I dropped off an exam to be copied. Glynnis Klein, who ran the front office, told me that she was coming to the opening performance. She wore a dotted A-line dress paired with a bright fuzzy cardigan; the sweater clip had a tiny row of cats across the front. She always found the best things during her vintage store pilgrimages.

"Thank you, Glynnis. I'm glad."

"So am I," she said. "The students are so excited. I can't wait to see them onstage. Plus, I gather that the plotline is very . . . unique." She pushed up her cat-eye glasses and winked at me. "Tolliver's artistic vision has captured the imagination of more than a few faculty members as well. I'd describe the general mood as anticipatory."

"You've heard them discussing it?"

"You'd be surprised what they say when they're picking up their mail." She gestured to the row of wooden boxes perpendicular to the front office door. The divider created the sense that you were in a room of sorts and faculty were a bit more outspoken than they might otherwise be accordingly. I'd heard a few choice commentaries from the other side more than once.

"It's nice that they're supporting him by going," she went on.

I didn't want to tarnish her shiny view by explaining that a few people were likely going for the opposite reason, to have something to snark about privately — some colleagues had a habit of putting others down to make themselves feel better. So I didn't. "I'm very happy that you'll be joining us."

"I know that helping out with the play has taken up quite a bit of your time." She smiled at me. "It's kind of you. And I hope you know that the students really like working with you."

I blushed. "That's nice to hear. I enjoy working with them too." Which was always true. Some of the faculty could be challenging, but there was no need to advertise that all over town. In general, I was fond of my colleagues, and the speed bumps we hit from time to time were usually temporary. So far, anyway.

"Did you need anything else?"

"No." I thanked her for the forthcoming copies and for coming to the play. "If you like, I could give you a tour backstage. It's a lovely old theater. There might be some vintage costumes tucked away somewhere."

She beamed. "I'd adore that. Thanks, Lila. I wouldn't want to intrude on opening night, but I will take you up on it another time." She gave a cheery wave and began typing on her computer keyboard at light speed. Not for the first time, I sent a little thank you to the universe for bringing her to our department.

When I arrived at the theater, everything was in chaos. Luciana was wheeling a cart full of gloves around, urging cast members to hurry. Someone was pounding on one of the backdrops, and Tolliver was clomping around the stage on his crutches, shouting instructions at several crew members who were adjusting the furniture angles.

I said hello and he paused long enough to ask me to check the mattresses. I agreed and headed below stage. As always, the temperature drop hit me with a vengeance, and I pulled my velvet coat closed.

Students were running about in various states of costume. A row of actors were applying makeup at a long mirror in one of the side rooms. At the end of the hall, I knocked on the door of the corner dressing room. Parker was pacing back and forth. His face was pale and there were beads of perspiration on his forehead. He was wringing his hands anxiously.

"Are you okay?"

His grimace in return suggested otherwise. His eyes remained focused on his own image.

I smiled encouragingly. "You've got this. Just stay in the moment."

He gave me a thumbs-up sign and I left him to his pacing, continuing on to the prop room to make sure everything was in order. The room was empty but the lights were on. I was relieved to see that the mattresses were lined up properly beneath the trap door. The rolling steps that Andrew would use to emerge as Poe were also at the ready. I eyeballed the trap door to confirm that the lock was in place. In doing so, I flashed back to the thump we'd heard at the séance. Our table had been set up directly over the trap door, so pretty much anything could have been struck against the wood to create the sound. The only problem was: everyone in attendance had been sitting around the table, as far as I knew. Had it been a true signal from the beyond? Or had Zandra teamed up with someone to create the sound effects? If so, who?

Or had she simply stomped on the wood? I couldn't imagine how. I'd been holding her hand and it didn't feel as though she'd moved in any way.

It was all very confusing. Was she capable of truly channeling spirits? I didn't know where I stood on the matter. I hadn't seen any ghosts, but that didn't mean I was going to say they didn't exist. Plus, if Zandra wasn't an authentic medium, why would she pose as one?

Too many questions and not enough answers.

The sound of students running upstairs brought me back to the business at hand. I cast one more glance around the prop room, then went up to join them.

The audience was far more responsive than I ever could have dreamed. They laughed and gasped in all the right places, and by the time the curtain went down for intermission, it seemed that the play was on the way to being a triumph.

Backstage, I congratulated the actors and crew gathered there. They were giddy with adrenaline. Tolliver was presiding, leaning on his crutches, a huge smile on his face as he listened to the animated students. Zandra was fluttering around him, saying something I couldn't hear. I had almost reached him when I noticed Chip and Bella approaching from the other side, Clara and Braxton trailing behind them. We all reached Tolliver at the same time and praised the first act.

"Thank you, darlings," he said, readjusting his position so that he was facing the circle we formed around him. "I am delighted that the audience is recognizing positive aspects in the work."

Zandra clicked her tongue. "It's more than recognizing, Tolly. They love it! You're a success!"

"Please don't say another word," Tolliver said, "It's bad luck to forecast the reception."

She made a dismissive gesture and looked at the rest of us. "I told you he was a genius."

"I'm enjoying it," Chip said. "And I have news." He glanced at Bella, who appeared apprehensive about what he was going to say next.

"I'm sorry —" she said to Clara, who stood perfectly still.

Chip cut her off. "Chancellor Wellington has agreed to sell the theater to me. The papers have been drawn up, and we can close tomorrow."

Clara gasped, her hand going up to her pearls.

Braxton steadied her with a hand on either side of her back.

Clara took one step toward Chip, trembling with fury. "You are a heartless, horrible man."

"Now hold on there a minute —" he began.

"I will not!" I wouldn't have been surprised if she took a swing at him. She had the air of a cobra about to strike.

Zandra swiveled her gaze back and forth between them. "When will you break ground?"

Chip rubbed his chin. "I admit, I've been stubborn about making my entertainment complex idea a reality. But Bella has been talking to me for months about preserving the theater instead, and there's so much more to consider than I had initially realized. Besides, this theater rightly belongs to her, as the descendent of Malcolm and Althea Gaines —"

"Or Camden Drake and Althea Gaines," Zandra interjected. When we all stared at her, she laughed. "Well, you know it's a strong possibility. Let's not pretend otherwise."

"In any case," Chip proceeded, with a pointed look at Zandra, "Althea is her mother and she owned the theater with

Malcolm. So by rights, it should have gone to Bella and would have, if Malcolm hadn't given it away."

He looked down at Bella, who blushed and returned his gaze, eyes shining.

"We're going to be married, and I don't know if I could live with myself if I tore down her family inheritance. I know Bella would rather that we do everything we can to preserve it."

Clara twisted her pearls. "Are you saying that you're *not* going to destroy our beloved Opera House?"

He put his palms up in a wait-please gesture. "I'm not saying anything definitive yet. I have investors, and I'll need to do some strenuous tap dancing — maybe even some hardcore faction-building — with them in order to pull this off. Bella and I need to discuss this further as well. It doesn't make sense to carry the cost of repairing the theater if we can't make a profit when all is said and done. That's just good business."

"But we might be able to save it," Bella said quietly. She addressed Clara and Braxton. "We like the idea of developing an arts center, widening the range of ways to use the Opera House, and we want to hear your ideas too. You've done so much for me, and

I told Chip that you know more than anyone how to take care of this place."

Clara clamped her mouth shut, but Braxton winked at Bella.

"At this point, all I know is that I'll be acquiring the theater. We close tomorrow, so this will be the last night the Historical Society and university agreement holds. I feel it only fair to let you know that."

"You mean we won't be able to keep an eye on things anymore?" Clara asked, her eyes narrowed.

"Well, you'll be able to do that from afar," he said. "Through Bella."

"That's an enormous mistake," Clara snapped. "Colossal."

Chip turned to Tolliver. "You'll be able to finish the run of the play, of course."

"Thank you, Chip. And now I need to get back to it, if you'll excuse me." He aimed his crutches to the side and moved out of the group. Zandra, after a moment, followed him. He paused and said, over his shoulder, "I'll be interested to see what happens next, and I hope you'll consider staging my future work here."

"Typical," said Clara. "He's already sucking up."

Chip laughed. "Well, either way, I hope there will be many more performances to come. Perhaps fixing up the theater so that it isn't in danger of crumbling into pieces will still allow us to bring more culture to Stonedale."

"You *have* to stop saying that," Clara retorted. "We have culture here already."

"Aw, you know what I mean." Chip flashed a big smile. Clara didn't return it.

The actors and crew were bustling around us. It was almost time for the second act to begin.

"Let's take our seats, shall we?" I gestured to the house and everyone left without a fuss.

"We're leaving," I heard Clara say to Braxton.

He didn't reply but patted her arm as they walked toward the door that led to the hallway.

Poor Braxton. He was about to get an earful.

The curtain rose and the play went on. Again, it was flowing smoothly.

Tolliver had asked me to watch from the back of the house, to keep an eye on sound. In a theater this old, there were sometimes acoustical issues. As I moved up the aisle, I was delighted to see Lex leaning against the wall near the lobby. A slow smile spread across his face as I approached. That set my heart a-thumping, but I did my best to look nonchalant as I slid into the space next to him.

"Hello, Detective," I whispered.

"Things seem to be going well, Professor."

I crossed my fingers for luck, and we watched the play continue. At first everything seemed fine, but during a quieter scene, I heard a strange tinny sound.

I took a few steps toward the left, where it seemed to originate, and strained to listen. After another few lines of dialogue onstage, there it was again.

I murmured to Lex that I'd be right back. He nodded.

Moving as quickly as I could, I went out into the lobby, back through the hallway parallel to the auditorium, and down the stairs that led below stage. The sound rang out again, much louder. I could tell it came from the corner dressing room.

I hurried down the hallway and threw open the door.

Clara was near the mirror supervising Braxton, who was on his knees, pounding with a hammer at the bottom of the long crack in the wall that blossomed upward from the floor. The same one Clara had been scrutinizing during the tour. Small chunks of rubble lay around him.

"What are you doing?" I cried.

"Go away, Lila!" Clara came at me with her fingers bent forward like claws.

I pushed her away. She stumbled backwards and sat down heavily on the floor next to the velvet chair.

"This is family business!" she spat.

I ignored her. "Braxton, stop!" He paused and looked dismayed as I went over toward him. I could hear Clara scrambling to get up, and I repeated his name, holding my hand out for the hammer. He handed it up to me with an air of defeat, his face reddening.

"Hit her, Brax!" Clara shrieked.

Once the hammer was safely in my palm, I whirled to face her. "Did you seriously tell him *to hit me*? What are you thinking?"

She glared at me defiantly, her face drawn and tight. "Lila, this has nothing to do with you. Just go away."

"Tell me what's going on," I commanded. "Now." I was so angry she'd told Braxton to hit me that my social niceties had gone out the window.

"I'd like to know too," I heard from behind me. Lex had followed me. Thank goodness.

Clara walked over to Braxton and helped him up. The two of them faced us and clasped hands, not saying a word. For a second, they reminded me of the twins from *The Shining.*

I shook my head to refocus.

"What are you looking for?" Lex asked calmly.

Clara and Braxton turned their heads to exchange glances.

"You might as well say," Lex told them. "You'll be charged with vandalism at the very least. The other charges will depend upon how much you cooperate."

I didn't know if that was really the case, but it sounded fitting.

Clara flapped her hand at the detective. "Oh, all right."

We all waited for her to explain.

She removed the ever-present crinkled-up tissue from her sleeve and patted her forehead with it. Then she smoothed her clothes for a bit. Apparently she wasn't going to talk until she was good and ready.

Lex didn't say anything.

Braxton shuffled his feet a little.

"It's the jewelry." I blurted out, waving the hammer. "Right? Althea's jewelry?"

A flash of annoyance crossed Clara's face.

Well, if she wanted to be the one to say it

first, she should have said it. She had plenty of time.

Lex watched Clara closely until she admitted that I was right.

"Why do you think it's here?" I pressed.

"Because she wrote in her journal that she hid it in the usual place," Clara said, lifting her chin defiantly. "And we've looked everywhere else."

I couldn't help but shoot a slightly triumphant look at Lex. Clara was confirming what we'd read in the page I had found. It was authentic.

"You don't think that would be in her home?"

"No. I've read the journal so many times I've nearly memorized it. She never mentions her house, which makes sense since she practically lived here at the theater."

I wanted to know everything. "Where did you get ahold of the journal originally?"

"It was on the velvet chair there right after she left town. But this," she said exasperatedly, "is family business. That jewelry belongs to us. We're just trying to get what we deserve."

Lex took a turn. "Why do you say that?"

"Because Althea owes it to us. For raising her child. It wasn't easy, you know. Or free."

Wow.

She continued. "We're going to sell the jewelry and use the money to help us buy the theater."

Lex didn't comment on her plan. "Does Bella know what Althea wrote?"

"No. We never let her read it. We felt it best to keep her away from anything related to her mother. That hussy."

"*Really,* Clara." I didn't bother to disguise my revulsion.

"Well, this is all her fault. She had no morals whatsoever."

"Says the woman trying to rob her."

Clara sputtered at that and readjusted her hat.

"Were you just going to smash the whole wall down?" Lex inquired coolly.

I was horrified to see tears run down Clara's face, dragging along black streaks of mascara like leaks from an oil can. "If we had to. Detective Archer, if we just had the money, we could fix it . . . and everything else. Don't you think it pains me to make a single mark on this beautiful place? I've devoted my life to saving it!"

Lex ignored her tears. "Why did you decide to hunt for it now, during the play? Surely there are less public times to hammer."

"After tonight, we won't be allowed access. Chip just told us that." She pulled the tissue from inside her sleeve again and dabbed at her eyes. "And everyone's up there watching the play now, so this seemed like our best chance."

"Well, I'm going to ask you to come down to the station," Lex said. "No big surprise there, I'm sure."

Clara's shoulders sagged. She gestured toward the wall and began to weep. "Look what we did, Braxton."

He patted her arm, looking miserable as well and sighing deeply.

She cried loudly for a moment, then held up a finger. "I will take responsibility for the wall. But let me be perfectly clear: we didn't have anything to do with that dreadful shooting."

Lex pulled out his cell phone and pressed something.

She waved until she caught his eye. "Please don't parade us out in front of everyone, Detective Archer."

"I'll do my best," he said, talking to someone on the line, already making arrangements.

CHAPTER 24

The throbbing beat of the music stretched an entire block up the street. As I approached Tolliver's Victorian house near campus, I wondered how his neighbors were feeling about the cast party. It was very late and it was very loud.

Everyone inside the house appeared to be having an excellent time, anyway. The first floor was filled with dancing bodies and animated conversations. There was a general spirit of joyfulness. The cast deserved it after all their hard work.

With some precise moves between dancers, I made my way to the kitchen where Zandra, Tolliver, Chip, and Bella were gathered around a large white granite island. The kitchen was more modern than the rest of the house, which had antique furniture and carpets that had seen better days.

At that thought, something tickled the

back of my mind, but I couldn't quite grasp it.

"Champagne?" Zandra held up a half-empty bottle. "We're toasting Tolliver."

"Sure," I said.

She poured some of the yellow bubbling liquid into a slim flute and handed it to me.

"Follow me, kids," she said, charging toward the front of the house.

I waited until everyone else had gone and followed Tolliver. He had evidently mastered the crutches because he moved along at a fantastic pace.

She waved at the DJ across the room, making a patting motion with her hand, until he turned the music down. There were some protests, but once the group saw Tolliver, indignation was replaced with applause.

The clapping sound swelled until it seemed as though it would bring the house down. Cries of "huzzah" and "bravo" could be heard, and some of the crew stomped their feet and whistled.

Tolliver leaned on one crutch and held up the other in acknowledgment.

"Thank you, all. You are so dear. But the congratulations should go to you." He spoke for several minutes, praising the actors and crew members by name. At the end, he also gave me a shout out.

No matter what else people said about him, they would have to admit that he was a gracious director.

At the end of his speech, he thanked the company and said he was excited about our remaining performances.

Just as he wrapped things up, cell phones around the room began to go off. Someone yelled, "It's up! Jermaine Banister's review is posted. Let me through!"

With everything that was going on, I'd completely forgotten about the critic coming to see the play. I hoped that Tolliver's euphoria wasn't about to be crushed.

The crowd parted and Parker appeared before Tolliver. He was holding his cell phone in one hand and scanning it feverishly. He used his finger to scroll up.

"What does it say?" Tolliver stood perfectly still. A play of emotions crossed his face, ending with a resolutely stoic expression. "Just tell us."

"He *loved* it!" Parker pumped his fist in the air and the crowd cheered. Once they'd calmed down sufficiently, he went on. "Banister said it's the most original show he's seen in years. Oh, and that you have a *brilliant* mind."

Tolliver swallowed hard as Zandra threw

her arms around him.

"And he said we all did a great job too," Parker informed the cast. "Except for when I tripped coming on stage that time." He shrugged and flashed a grin. "My bad. Hey, at least I didn't fall on my face!"

The music was turned back up and the throng of people went back to their celebrating with renewed vigor.

My head began to pound. The emotional rollercoaster I'd been on today was sinking in.

I followed everyone back into the kitchen and listened for a few moments as they discussed the review. Tolliver leaned against the counter and let his crutches rest on either side of him.

"Congratulations, Tolliver," I said, walking over to give him a hug. "You did it."

He hugged me back, then held my shoulders with both hands as he looked into my eyes. "With your help. I couldn't have done it without you, Lila."

"Pshaw," I said as he let go.

"Truly. Thank you." He put his hands back on the counter and smiled at me.

Zandra swept in and stood between us, jumping up and down a little. "Isn't this so exciting? What a night. More of this to come, I hope."

Chip, standing on the other side of Tolliver, tilted his head slightly. "What do you
mean?"

"I mean," Zandra said, "that whatever Tolliver writes could be produced by you. That
we" — she swirled her champagne glass
around the circle — "make a spectacular
team! That there is more ahead for us."

Chip looked slightly pained. "Zandra, you
know that whatever direction we go in with
the Opera House, there will be a selection
process for each season. I can't promise
anything."

She gave him a steely glare. "But —"

"I can't promise anything."

"What are you talking about?" Bella, who
had just come from the other room, asked.

"Nothing," Zandra said, staring intently
at Chip.

"Is everything okay?" She looked back and
forth between them.

Chip didn't break eye contact either.
"Zandra suggested that the new arts center
could produce more of Tolliver's plays. I'm
telling her that I can't make any promises."

"Got it," Zandra said curtly.

Bella reached out and touched Zandra's
arm. "We don't know what's happening yet.
But you and Tolliver will receive full consideration whatever direction we choose."

Zandra slowly dragged her eyes away from Chip and focused on Bella. "Thank you, Bella. We appreciate your . . . consideration." She spat the last word out, as if it were supremely distasteful. It was clear that she felt Tolliver was being treated poorly.

Bella lowered her eyes, perhaps to regroup from Zandra's obvious hostility, then glanced at Chip, her lips curving up as they always did lately when she looked at him, before addressing her. "I'm sorry if that didn't come out right. I mean in all sincerity that you and Tolliver — and Clara and Braxton — are very important in terms of our vision for the Opera House. We absolutely want your input as you go forward. And you will be at the top of our list with future productions."

Zandra seemed somewhat appeased. She inclined her head slowly toward Bella. "Thank you for saying that."

The mention of Clara and Braxton had brought me back to the dressing room incident. I told the group about what had happened.

Bella paled and clutched at Chip. "Are you serious? I can't believe it."

"I'm completely serious."

"They just . . . bashed the wall in?" She shook her head a little as if to refuse the truth, then pulled out her cell phone. "That doesn't sound like them at all. I need to call Clara."

"I think they're probably still talking to Detective Archer," I said softly.

"Still," she said. "I need to try."

She walked to the other end of the kitchen and put the phone to her ear.

"There's treasure in the Opera House? I can't believe it." Chip looked at Zandra and laughed. "Gosh, I wonder why the spirits didn't tell you. You'd think they would have picked up their Batphones and given you first dibs."

She gave him a dirty look. "Shut up, Chip."

He backed away, hands up in mock surrender.

"Now now, ducklings," Tolliver said. "Tonight we must celebrate! Let's go join the others."

After awhile, I said my goodbyes and went out into the cool, fresh air.

CHAPTER 25

I woke the next morning to sunshine streaming in through a crack in the curtain. I'd had a longer dream about Althea and Bella in the dressing room, and it lingered tantalizingly, but the more I tried to assemble the fragments into a cohesive narrative, the faster they slipped away from me. All I could remember was what I'd dreamt before: mother and daughter looking into the mirror, Althea moving her hands in gestures I didn't comprehend.

Cady was curled up beside me, and when I petted her, she began purring. The peaceful start was exactly what I needed after the intensity of yesterday. I stretched and checked the alarm clock, which read almost nine a.m. I was usually wide awake at six, so that was a surprise.

Luckily, I didn't have classes today — just a long day of grading before tonight's performance — so I could take things slow.

The coffee was brewing, and I was just putting bread in the toaster when my cell phone chirped. I pulled it out of my robe pocket and squinted at the screen, then answered.

"Hi Bella," I said. "How are you?"

We chatted for a bit about Clara and Braxton. She thanked me for letting her know about what had happened and filled me in on their mindset when they returned home, which was both humiliated and outraged, apparently.

"They're very angry with me," she said sadly.

"Why?"

"Because they feel like I'm taking the Opera House away from them. No matter how many times I tell them that they'll still be able to be a part of things, they don't believe me. They've been in charge for so long that it feels like they're being rejected or replaced or something."

"They'll come around," I said. "Or I hope they will."

She was silent for a moment.

"Thank you, Lila. I feel like you're the only one who is giving Chip a chance, and that means so much to me."

I had my suspicions about Chip too but she was right that I hadn't expressed them overtly. Which was kind of like giving him a chance.

"I just want you to be safe." This was a weird conversation. I felt very . . . maternal.

"Again, thank you."

"Sure."

"Okay. See you at the meeting."

"What meeting?"

"The one Tolliver called. Didn't you get his text?"

"Hold on." I put her on speaker and opened up my messages. "Nope, nothing here."

"It's in an hour at the Opera House," she said. "I don't know what it's about. But I'm sure you're supposed to be there."

"See you then." I scrolled through my messages again after we hung up. Definitely not there. But I'd just head over. I left my script there last night anyway. I think I set it down in the dressing room when I'd been so surprised to find the Worthinghams removing the wall.

Still couldn't believe they did that.

I fed Cady, showered and dressed, and walked quickly to the Opera House. The lobby was empty, so I went into the auditorium. It too was devoid of others — dark and quiet except for the ghost light up on the stage. Perhaps everyone was downstairs.

I was a little late and they may have decided to go measure the damage to the dressing room.

Suddenly, I heard a scream and a banging sound. I ran down the aisle, up the stage steps, and down the stairs toward the lower level. The only light on was at the end of the hallway, in the large dressing room.

I burst into the room and found Zandra sitting calmly in the chair in front of the mirror, flipping through the notebook that held my copy of the script.

"What happened? Are you okay?"

She looked up. "Yes, fine. Why? What are you doing here, Lila?"

I looked around the room. "I thought I heard someone scream."

"Oh," she laughed. "That was me. I'm so sorry — didn't mean to scare you."

"What about the banging?"

Zandra blushed. "This is embarrassing. I tripped on the chair leg and it made me so mad that I screamed and then pounded the table top."

"Are you okay? You aren't hurt, are you?"

"No, thank you. I just saw red for a second. I'm feeling much better now. It actually helped to vent some of the frustration that has been building up. It's been an emotional couple of weeks, you know?"

"Definitely. Where's Bella? I thought she was coming to the meeting."

"She cancelled," she said, flipping another page and squinting to decipher my margin comments.

"Is that my script?" I already knew it was.

"Oh, is it?" She closed it and looked at the front cover, which had my name written on it. "So it is." She held out the notebook toward me. "Here you go."

"Thank you." I put the notebook on the table. "What's the meeting about?"

"Tolliver had an idea. But, as I said, she cancelled. Why are you here?"

"Bella thought everyone was invited."

"Did you get an invitation?" She was looking down at one of her fingernails and examining the polish.

"No, but —"

"If you were wanted here, you would have been invited too, don't you think?" She gave me a level look, then refocused on her fingernail polish.

Message received.

"Not to exclude you or anything. Tolliver just wanted to speak to her privately."

"Got it."

"But since you're here," she continued, standing and walking over to the hole Braxton had made with the hammer, "would you please help me look into this wall?"

"What?"

She clicked on the flashlight app of her phone and held it out. "Hold this for me, would you?" She got down on her hands and knees and peered inside the hole. I angled the light for her the best I could.

"Do you see anything?" I moved the light slightly from side to side.

"No," she said. She straightened out one of her arms and felt around, grimacing slightly, then pulled it back and dusted off her sleeve. "Nothing's in there."

I was torn between disappointment and relief. It would have been exciting to find the diamonds, but it didn't seem right that Zandra was poking around the theater without Bella.

"We should probably wait for Bella to do any more searching," I said, handing back her phone.

"Good idea," she said. "We can talk to her at the performance tonight."

"Are you done? I'll walk you out," I said.

She stared at me for a moment. I had the feeling she was grasping for a reason to refuse my offer but couldn't come up with anything.

When we reached the lobby, I realized something. "Where's Tolliver? You said he wanted to talk to Bella."

Was she squirming a little or was that my imagination? "He was on the way over, but when she cancelled, I called and told him not to bother. It's such a hassle for him to move around with the crutches and all."

"So why were you here without him?" It wasn't adding up.

She looked down for a long while, then met my eyes. "Okay, I confess. I wanted to look in that hole."

Fair enough. I was curious too.

"You would have given anything you found to Bella, though, right?"

"Absolutely." She laughed. "C'mon, Lila. I just wanted to play pirate and search for gold. Not steal anything." Her phone rang. She set her giant bag down on the carpet and shuffled through it until she found her cell, which she held up triumphantly. "Mind if I take this? It's Tolly."

I watched as she went through the door into the auditorium. Clearly she wanted some privacy. I wasn't leaving her alone in the Opera House though. Who knows what she would do to the wall if I left her unsupervised?

The funny thing was that she seemed as determined not to leave me behind as I was determined not to leave her behind. I wondered if she thought I was treasure-hunting too. Probably.

I leaned against the wall and looked up at the elegant chandelier. Then my gaze fell on the man standing at the far end of the lobby, faced away from me. He had a dark suit and excessively long arms. It was the same person who'd been watching the dancers and disappeared from sight almost instantly.

The mere sight of him gave me the creeps.

I entertained the possibility that it was our resident ghost.

I scurried across the lobby, trying to be quiet so he wouldn't disappear through a wall or something. When I got close enough, I tapped him on the shoulder. It was solid, not ectoplasmic, thank goodness.

He let out a yell loud enough to wake the dead and spun around.

I yelled too.

"Dr. Maclean," he said, breathing heavily. "Give me a second." He put his hand on his chest and calmed his breathing. "You scared me."

I'd recognize those enormous teeth anywhere. "Dr. Frinkle! I'm so sorry I startled you."

"I didn't see you coming. But why did *you* yell?" He cocked an eyebrow and made a rumbling sound that I realized after a second was a laugh. "You thought I was a ghost, didn't you?"

"No," I lied.

"Wouldn't be the first time someone has taken me for Malcolm Gaines here. I've long thought that it might be the suit."

I thought it might be the creepiness.

He grinned, an unsettling sight. "I'm meeting the spirit wranglers to shoot something for the promos. They should be here soon."

"We have a performance tonight," I reminded him.

"Don't worry. We'll be done long before then," he said.

I smiled at him. "Thank you. And please tell Vance hello from me."

Zandra re-emerged and scooped up her bag, tossing her phone inside. She stopped short at the sight of Gavin.

"Do you two know each other?" I asked.

He nodded, but she shook her head.

"I've seen *you* around," he said to her.

She blanched.

Quickly, I introduced them.

"Hello." Zandra turned to me. "I'm going to meet Tolliver at Scarlett's. Would you like to join us?" She paused and addressed Gavin haltingly. "You're welcome as well."

He declined, tipped an imaginary hat, and

wandered off.

"Good luck with everything," I called after him.

He waved without looking back.

She looked at me expectantly.

"Thanks for the offer, but I have some work to do. I'm heading that way, though. Shall we walk together?"

We left the theater and walked silently for a bit.

Zandra finally spoke. "So why was Gavin there? I hope never to encounter him again." She shivered. "How do you know him?"

I explained his Opera House research, ending with my embarrassment at thinking I was seeing a ghost in the lobby.

She laughed. "Malcolm is *much* more attractive than that."

"What do you see when you see him?"

"He looks like he does in the picture hanging on the lobby wall. More or less."

"Nice. Do you think the students who believe they're seeing Malcolm are just seeing Gavin? He has been studying the Opera House for seven years, so I'm sure he found the staircase."

"The Worthinghams didn't know about it, did they? They've been here even longer. I didn't know about it either until you all discovered it."

"That's true. Though if Gavin has been working while we rehearsed, as he said, and he *did* use the staircase, it would provide an explanation for the full-body manifestation rumor."

"But Lila," Zandra said earnestly, "Malcolm really *is* there. I've seen him."

"Oh, right." Forgot who I was talking to for a minute.

Soon, Scarlett's familiar awning swam into view, and we said goodbye. The bells on the door jingled as she went inside and although the fragrant burst of coffee and fresh bread almost tempted me to join them, I made myself keep going.

A few minutes past the café, I realized that I had left my script back at the Opera House. Again.

I paused to weigh the pros and cons of returning now. It would be there waiting for me later, after all. And I wasn't eager to run into Gavin again. Especially since the talk about the staircase was making me wonder more if he could have been involved in the murder? I bet he did know about the staircase, and even used it to stay unobtrusive. I'd have to talk to Lex about him as soon as possible.

However, if Zandra went back and read my script, there were a few comments I'd prefer she not share with Tolliver. The image of her flipping through my script earlier that morning popped back into my mind. She hadn't mentioned any of my margin notes, but she'd definitely had a strange energy. It seemed purposefully casual, with an air of anticipation, almost as if she was expecting me to call her out for reading my script.

Something clicked.

But it wasn't about the script. It was about what she'd done *before* reading my script.

If my hunch was right, there was no time to lose.

I whirled around and ran toward the theater.

After racing downstairs, I flew down the dark hallway to the dressing room and reached around the doorframe to switch the light on.

Just then, I heard a low moan.

All the hairs on my neck rose.

I dropped down and crawled to the hole in the wall. Whipping my cell phone out of my pocket, I tapped the flashlight icon and aimed the beam into the hole. Nothing.

The moan came again, growing louder. It was behind me.

Leaving my phone, I scrambled over to the door of the secret staircase. No matter how hard I pressed, it wouldn't unlatch, but inside, there was some kind of movement.

I knew it.

"Bella!" I called. "Is that you?"

I stood up and put my ear to the door. There was another moan.

"Hang on. I'm going to find something to open this."

I ran to the prop room and searched around, making a mess of the neatly hung tools in the workshop, flailing around until I found a crowbar. Racing back to the dressing room, I slid my fingers along the wall until I felt a slight vertical line just big enough for me to insert the end of the crowbar. I pulled on it with all my might, trying to remember that physics lecture where my professor talked about angles and leverage, attempting different tactics until something gave way and the door finally sprang open.

Bella was curled up in a ball on the lowest step, weeping in the dark. I went inside and touched her arm. "You're safe," I repeated until she calmed down.

I helped her stand slowly and move out into the dressing room. She stopped and blinked in the bright light. I led her over to the velvet chair near the table. Bella sank down into it, grabbing a tissue to wipe the tears from her eyes.

I leaned against the wall, watching her closely. "What happened?"

She took a deep breath and let it out slowly. "I couldn't open the door."

"Who put you in there?"

"I was in the dressing room talking to Zandra. She hit me with something" — she pointed to a nasty-looking bump on her forehead — "and I must have passed out."

"Are you okay?"

"It hurts," she said, uncertainly. "I just want to sit here for a minute to see if it makes the dizziness go away."

"Okay. Does the staircase open on the upper level or is it jammed there too?"

"I don't know. I just woke up, pressed on the lower door, and panicked. Didn't even think of going up the stairs. My head hurt so much, I couldn't think straight."

I stood up and inspected the panel more closely. There was a bent nail sticking out right above where I'd shoved in the crowbar.

"Well, I think I know why she hit you." I watched Bella's face.

"Why?" She appeared completely confused.

"If last night is any indication, she wants Chip to build the entertainment complex he originally proposed. And he was heading that way until you two got engaged. I don't know if she attacked you to try and stop you from selling, or to punish you for getting in the way."

"Maybe both? She was saying some strange things about Chip. I couldn't follow it all."

"Or perhaps she thought if you were incapacitated, the closing wouldn't take place?"

"It already happened. We went in early this morning and signed all the paperwork." She winced and touched the bump on her head.

"Good. But we need to get you looked at right now," I said.

"I'm fine," she protested. "I just need to rest."

"We're going to the doctor, Bella. I insist."

We spent the next few hours at the emergency room. She was thoroughly checked out and her tests came back fine. She did not appear to have a concussion, surprisingly, though she would need monitoring.

Chip came to pick her up. He was effusively grateful. He hovered over Bella and helped her very gently, as if she were made of glass, discussing his plan for concussion patrol all the while. They gave me a ride home, where I threw all thoughts of working out the window. I had to rest up for the events ahead, so I curled up on the sofa with Cady and streamed an old noir film on TV.

I'd spent much of my ER waiting time on the phone with Lex. He was unhappy to learn about the latest turn of events and said he'd be paying Zandra a call immediately. I had asked him to hold off just a bit. I wanted to try and get her to admit to me privately what she'd done. We needed to find out whether it had been a rogue move or a plot involving someone else. And I hoped to be able to find out what her end game was.

He was resistant at first, but eventually I had been able to convince him that it was advantageous, listing the reasons over and over again. Promising another round of noodles if we were successful may or may not have been the clincher. Probably not, though it did make him chuckle.

He called back later, having obtained the required approvals, and we strategized further. We'd finalized the plan and agreed to meet in the lobby before tonight's performance at the Opera House.

It wasn't quite a date but it was invigorating nonetheless.

CHAPTER 26

After making all the necessary preparations outside with Lex, I went into the lobby. Tolliver stood by the box office, where students were selling tickets at a rapid clip.

I sidled up and said hello.

"Lila, guess what?" He pointed toward the window, through which I could see a long line. "We're almost sold out!"

"That's exciting." I lowered my voice. "Hey, did you call a meeting this morning?"

He looked confused. "No. I was at the doctor, getting a cast adjustment. My other one was too tight and my leg was swelling up."

"I'm sorry to hear that."

"Why?"

"Just curious. Is Zandra here?"

"Yes." He craned his neck a bit. "She was a minute ago, anyway. But why are you asking about a meeting? Did I miss something?"

"No," I soothed him. "Someone said you'd called for one in a text. I must have misunderstood."

"How strange." He shook his head. "I didn't text anyone today." He pulled out his phone and tapped on the screen. "See?"

There was nothing in his message list.

Well, that didn't really prove anything. He could have deleted them.

Or Zandra could have. After she used his phone to text Bella.

"Thanks, Tolliver." I smiled at him. "Do you need some help getting down the aisle?"

He waved that away.

"Let me know if you change your mind, please. I'm going to go check on the cast."

"See you soon, Petal." He turned to watch the box office sales again.

I observed him, then sighed. It was difficult to talk to anyone, wondering if they were in league with Zandra. Hopefully we'd find out the truth soon enough.

Lex caught my eye from the opposite end of the lobby, and I went over. We made a few final arrangements and I was off on my mission, waving perkily at Nate, Calista, and Francisco, who had just come into the lobby. I was happy to see them there but would have to wait until later to catch up.

I wandered through the theater and stage,

but didn't find her, so I went downstairs, where Zandra was fussing around in the prop room. It should have made me nervous that she might be arming herself — the workshop was loaded with numerous dangerous tools — but it only made me angry.

"I need to talk to you," I said. "Could you please come to the corner dressing room?"

She didn't miss a beat. "Sure. Everything okay?"

I didn't know how she could act so blasé. We both knew what she did.

It was chilling.

"Everything's fine," I said. "I just wanted to talk to you alone, get some advice on something."

"Happy to help." She followed me into the dressing room.

The actors had agreed via text to have their makeup applied elsewhere. Parker had confided to me privately that the new hole in the wall freaked him out, so he was glad to do it.

When we were inside, I took the velvet chair in front of the mirror and turned to face the staircase. She dropped her bag on the table and stood in front of me.

"How can I be of service?" She looked at me expectantly.

I cut right to it. "What happened this

morning?"

"What do you mean?"

"I mean, when I found you here, you acted as if you didn't have a care in the world. Right after you hit Bella and shoved her into the staircase."

She laughed. "What? That's ridiculous. I didn't do that."

"I know it was you, Zandra. You're the only one who could have texted her from Tolliver's phone. I already asked him, and he said he didn't call a meeting."

Her eyes widened slightly.

"So what's going on? Just tell me, please."

Zandra looked away for long time, as if she was deciding something, then turned back. "Okay, fine. I needed her out of the way for a little while."

"So you could stop the sale of the Opera House?"

She surveyed me grimly. "If you must know, that's what I had hoped."

"But she'd already closed on it before-hand."

"So I heard," she said sourly.

"What were you hoping to do?"

"I just wanted a chance to talk to Chip. He'd promised me —" she stopped abruptly and clamped her mouth shut.

"What did he promise you?"

"It doesn't matter," she said. "It's all over."

"Why is it all over? Bella said you'll be part of everything related to the Opera —"

"That little slut!" Zandra said bitterly. "He was *mine*."

"Wait, you and Chip were a thing?"

"Yes. When he first came to town, he took me out to dinner. He told me that he'd seen me perform in Tolliver's last play and thought I was magnificent." She lifted her head and preened. "I was, actually."

"And . . ." I rolled my hand to invite her to finish the story.

"He said he was going to stage a production just for me."

"Who's Afraid of Virginia Woolf?"

"You remember. Well done." She brushed back her hair. "But it was more than that. We were going to be together."

I bit my lips to hide a smile. "You and Chip? I thought you loved Tolliver."

"I did. I mean, I do. In a way. But Chip is my soulmate."

"Does *he* know that?" I winced. I didn't mean to blurt that out, especially in such an incredulous tone.

She didn't seem to be bothered by it. "Trust me. When we started working on the play, he would have fallen for me. All my directors do."

"But Chip isn't a director."

"He was a director before and would have been again. I had plans for him. And honestly, it may not be too late." She reached toward her bag, as if she were going to leave.

I needed her to keep talking, so I dialed my tone down a few notches. "What about Tolliver? Do you think he would just move out of the way for Chip?" I mentally crossed my fingers for the next lie. "I could see how you and Chip would make a great couple."

Zandra stopped moving and glowed at that. "Thank you. And don't worry. I have plans for Tolliver too."

"Plans he would like?"

"He'll be taken care of."

"Do you mean 'taken care of' as in having a new job or as in swimming with the fishes?" I said it lightly.

She didn't say anything.

"Kidding, of course."

"Very funny, Lila."

I softened my tone again, aiming for confidant mode. "Just between us, why *did* you push Tolliver through the trap door?"

Zandra narrowed her eyes. "Who said I did that?"

"No one. I'm just assuming."

She sighed. "I already told you, Lila, the night it happened. It was Malcolm."

"You did say that."

"It's true." Zandra lifted her chin defiantly. "Ghosts can do all kinds of things."

"But you also said you needed Tolliver out of the way, so —"

"Tolliver's not dead," she said flatly.

The unspoken *yet* hung in the air between us.

I wanted to cajole a confession out of her, but it was hard not to shriek in her cruel face.

She shrugged. "Don't say I never did anything for him. I gave him this play, after all. And it's going to be a success."

"I'm sure he's grateful."

"For more than you know."

I tilted my head and raised my eyebrows, trying to radiate confusion.

"Honey, I *got* him this director gig."

"Meaning . . ." I trailed off intentionally and held my breath.

She hesitated but I could see that she wanted to brag. Somehow I summoned up the ability to smile at her encouragingly. "You can tell me. Do you mean —"

She smirked. "Yes, okay? I killed Jean Claude."

I made a big production of gasping, even though she'd finally said exactly what I'd hoped she'd say.

353

She took it as a gasp of admiration and a smile stretched across her face. "You have no idea how *good* it feels to say that out loud. Yes, he needed to be out of the way so that Tolly could take over as director." She mimicked one of his signature hand gestures. "Though I did have a moment of panic when Jean Claude tried to tell you all during the séance. I had to pull myself out of the depths of the trance in order to nip that in the bud."

"How did you ever pull it off?" I attempted to infuse admiration into the words, though I was gritting my teeth.

"It wasn't even that hard," she said gleefully. "Just had to create a reason to get him into the wings during the party scene by rigging the catwalk to break. Then it was just a matter of timing my real shot to coincide with the blank one. I'd seen the rehearsal of that scene so many times that I had it down." She stretched her arms up and laced her hands behind her head, the picture of relaxation. "You have to admit, it's partly Jean Claude's fault. If he wasn't such a perfectionist, I wouldn't have had a chance to perfect my timing."

Rage was spiraling up from deep within, and I struggled to sound calm. "And you ran down the secret staircase afterwards."

"Yes." The smugness on her face was intolerable.

"Was anyone else helping you? That was a lot to pull off."

"No," she said. "It was all me."

"How did you drop the gun on the floor at the séance?"

"It was resting on my thighs the whole time. My legs were bent, so it was flat enough. After I pointed at Clara, I just straightened them and let the pistol tumble down the slide."

"You were trying to frame her?"

"Isn't it obvious?" She frowned and let her arms fall to her sides. "Though *that* could have gone better. No one took it seriously until she was caught hammering away at the wall last night." After a moment, she brightened. "Still, she's a suspect now and she did that to herself, so . . . we'll see how it goes."

It was hard not to address her blaming of everyone else, but I managed to press on. "So let me see if I have this right: you broke into the Historical Society office twice — first, you stole the journal, then you went back and stole the gun."

"Correct. Jean Claude was becoming a nuisance. He had found the journal, which had fallen from my bag somehow at rehearsal. He didn't know whose it was and thought it had been abandoned, so he tore out the page about the jewelry because he wanted to use it somehow in a future play."

"He didn't know that it was Althea's?"

"Not at first. I saw him looking at the page scrap at rehearsal one day and confronted him. That was my mistake. Once he knew it was real, he made me tell him the whole legend. Then he said he would give the page back if I'd let him help look for the jewelry."

"Did you tell him you'd stolen the journal from the Historical Society?"

"No. I never said where it came from. I just told him about the scandal."

That warmed my heart a bit, to hear that Jean Claude was telling the truth about not knowing who Clara was when we'd first seen the protestors. It sounded as though he'd simply been engaged by the dramatic aspects of the story as an artist, then was intrigued by the idea of finding treasure. I was glad to hear he wasn't scheming with Zandra.

Something else occurred to me. "Clara's going to have a conniption about the page being torn out."

She tilted her head. "You're right. How marvelous."

"So then what happened?"

"I refused to let him help, of course. He didn't even want the diamonds themselves — just the adventure of finding them. Or maybe he was planning to steal them from me later."

"He wasn't a thief."

Zandra made a *tsk, tsk* sound. "Doesn't matter. He had no idea who he was dealing with." She reached down into her bag and removed a pair of gloves, which she pulled on quickly before plunging one hand back into the depths. "And neither do you."

She raised her arm, which held a stainless steel knitting needle. "Feeling lucky, Lila?"

Adrenaline coursed through my veins and it was difficult to think straight. "What about bad karma?"

She affected a small pout. "I think that ship has definitely sailed. Don't worry — I sharpened up the end of this needle in the workshop. It should go in quite smoothly."

Her oppressive perfume was filling the warm room. My stomach clenched. Then the scent of something else washed over me — was it roses?

I stood up abruptly, then wished I hadn't. Swaying, I grabbed on to the back of the chair to steady myself. "Zandra, you don't have to do this."

"Sorry." She smiled. "But I only told you

357

about Jean Claude because I know what's going to happen next. And not just because I'm psychic." She laughed.

I thought about making a break for it or yelling for help, but she would definitely run at me. I didn't have anything to defend myself and if she stuck that point into my neck, it would be over fast. My entire body was drenched in sweat, and I had begun to tremble, but somehow I kept my voice steady. "I promise I won't say anything. You don't need to stab me."

"No, you won't say anything. I'm going to make sure of that, trust me. We just need to wait for the music . . . in case you scream."

The overture began to play directly above us as she said that. She was right. No one would hear anything.

She gripped the needle with both hands and took a step toward me. "Say goodbye, Lila."

Just then, the staircase door flew open, pushing her forward to the ground, and police officers swarmed into the room. She dropped the needle as she fell.

Lex came directly over and wrapped his arms around me. I gladly breathed in his spicy scent. "Are you okay?"

I nodded but stayed right there, shaking. After a minute, he moved his head down to look into my eyes. "We got it all," he said. "On tape. Well done."

"What took you so long?" I edged away from him.

He let go of me and rubbed his chin. "Sorry about that — it escalated faster than we thought it would. We couldn't tell what was going on at the end until you said the word 'stab.'"

"I'll be sure to yell out the method of my impending demise sooner next time."

He grinned.

I slid out of my jacket, ripped off the bulletproof vest he'd insisted I wear, and shoved it at Lex.

He dropped it on the ground beside him.

Then he kissed me. Right in front of everyone.

It was so worth the wait.

CHAPTER 27

Once the adrenaline had subsided and the last officer had gone through the lobby door, I asked Lex if he would come with me back downstairs.

He handed me one of the bottled waters he was carrying. "Aren't you ready to go?"

"Soon, but there's something I think we should check out. And it's going to sound a little odd, but bear with me."

"You certainly do keep things interesting, Lila Maclean." His voice was low and teasing.

Ignoring his undeniably alluring tone for the time being, I recounted the odd dream I'd had about Althea sitting in front of the mirror. The whole time I'd waited for Lex and the police officers to process the scene, I couldn't get it out of my mind.

"Haven't you spent enough time in that dressing room today?"

"Yes, but I need to look. I can't explain it."

"Let's go, then."

I led the way, shivering as always at the icy blast at the bottom of the stairs. Once we were at the dressing room door, Lex gestured for me to go in first.

"What's next, Professor? You're in charge of this investigation."

I moved to the antique table, patting the top of it lightly. "Althea and Bella were here, looking into the mirror. Althea was seated in the chair, dressed in black but covered in diamonds — she had stones sewn all over her clothing. Bella was standing behind her, wearing white from head to toe. She didn't have any jewelry on. But Althea did something with her hands, a sort of twist of the wrists. Instantly, all of the jewelry appeared on Bella. Her clothes sparkled so much, it was almost blinding."

"And then?"

"And then I woke up."

He blinked, clearly expecting more of an explanation.

I blushed. "Don't you ever have dreams that you feel are vitally important?"

"No," he said, lifting up his bottled water. "After I wake up, I mostly just have breakfast and get on with my day."

"Well," I said, "my mother has always stressed that we need to take them very seriously. Both of us have had dreams about things that came true later. She says we have a bit of a sixth sense."

He took a sip of his drink and regarded me curiously. "Example, please?"

I thought back. "Once I lost a ring and dreamt I found it under my bed. And the next morning, it was actually there."

His lip twitched. "Could have been your memory in action."

"I guess so. But it's happened many times. And my mother gets half of her ideas for her art from dreams."

He leaned against the rose wallpaper. "Dreams can be a source of inspiration for many people."

"Although you sound kind of patronizing right now," I gave him a warning look, "I'm going to let it slide because I want to focus on the dream. Do you think that's what it meant, that Althea wants her jewelry to go to Bella?"

"Perhaps," he said, taking another sip. "But why wouldn't she just send them to her in the mail, if she wanted her to have them?"

"She could have left them here on purpose. Clara and Braxton certainly thought they were here. She wrote in the journal that she hid them, right? So maybe it was intentional."

"But wouldn't she have taken them with her?"

"Maybe she was worried that they'd be stolen or lost if she brought them. Maybe she was going to come back for them later. Maybe she left town so fast she didn't have a chance to pack. Or maybe she wanted to leave them for Bella to find? Who knows?"

Lex looked skeptical.

"And you're a detective, after all. Maybe you'll be able to help me find something everyone else missed."

He gave a brisk nod. "Fair enough. So what happens now?"

"We look for a secret hiding place." I slid my hand slowly over the wood of the antique table, moving inch by inch across the back, underneath, and along each leg. I pulled the shallow drawer out of the top and checked it for a false bottom but didn't find anything.

I moved closer to the mirror, ran my fingers across the ornately scrolled frame, and tilted the bottom edge away from the wall. "Can you help me take this down? I want to look behind it."

"To see if there's a safe?" He perked up.

"Exactly."

Together, we lifted the mirror completely off of the wall. Nothing there either.

Lex re-hung the mirror while I flopped down on the velvet chair. Where else could she have hidden them?

"Let's do the light next," I said.

We went to the corner and gave the light a thorough going-over. All that showed us was it hadn't been dusted in a long time.

I closed my eyes and thought back to my dream.

"Wait," I exclaimed and turned the velvet chair carefully upside down. The bottom was recessed and open — no place to secure any secret compartments there — but I felt around the sides of the frame just in case. Althea's wrist-twisting motion flashed in front of my eyes, and I tested the fat wooden chair legs, one by one. They were all rock solid until I hit the fourth one, which turned. I held my breath as I unscrewed the leg and pulled it from the frame.

Lex knelt down next to me.

I examined the leg carefully, noticing a thin line of separation halfway down. I compared it to the other legs, which did not have the same mark.

"I think it opens here," I said to him. I turned the two pieces in separate directions, twisting with all my strength. Nothing.

"Is it stuck? It's been a long time since it's been opened, I bet," said Lex. "Keep trying."

Eventually, it gave way and I was able to separate the two parts. I set the top half down and looked inside. A blue velvet bag was visible.

"Look!" I cried, sliding the bag out and pulling apart the gathered neck carefully. I reached inside and touched something cold and metallic. What emerged in my hand was a ball of jewelry. I gasped and began untangling. There was a thick gold necklace with an egg-shaped center diamond set in an ornate pendant as well as numerous smaller diamonds at two-inch intervals all the way around the chain, a wide hammered gold bracelet with eight almond-sized diamonds embedded in a circle pattern, and a pair of large diamond drop earrings.

"Gorgeous. These must be worth a fortune, Lex."

"How did Camden ever get the money for these? Not on a professor's salary," he said. "No offense."

"None taken." I stared at the jewelry on the ground in front of us. "We need to get these to Bella immediately."

He took some pictures with his phone,

and we carefully wrapped the items back up, using some plastic we borrowed from the prop room to keep them separated in the blue bag.

"I wish Bella had been here," I said. "But I didn't want to bring her on a wild-goose chase if my dream had turned out to be nothing."

"You mean sometimes they *don't* turn out to be true?" He grinned.

"I have a very respectable ratio," I said, elbowing him.

"She'll be grateful to have them," Lex said. "And if Bella decides to sell them, she'll be set for life."

"Would you like some more, Lila?" Bella inquired, holding a pot decorated with violets over my cup. She had invited Lex and me to the Historical Society for tea. Almost two weeks had passed since the play — somewhat shockingly deemed a success by all who reviewed it — had closed.

"Yes, please."

She poured the steaming liquid into the delicate cup and settled back on the velvet settee. I said no to her offer of sugar and milk and took a sip.

"How's your head, Bella?" I asked.

She touched the bruise on her forehead,

which had faded to an almost-imperceptible light blue. "I've been thinking about it. Just idly, really." Bella set her jaw. "I'm not going to let her take up too much space in my brain. But she didn't care if I died, and that's kind of hard to process. She even nailed the door shut after she hit me and shoved me in the stairwell!"

"She did. I heard the banging after you screamed. Though I didn't know it was you screaming."

"I was already out by then. Went down hard, like someone had shot me with a tranquilizer gun. I didn't wake up until you'd come back. Thank you for coming back, Lila."

"The top of the staircase had also been nailed shut. She must have done it earlier," Lex informed us. "She planned it all."

Chip plunked his cup onto the saucer, sloshing tea onto the elegant coffee table, and winced. "Oops, sorry Bel. I'm so not a tea guy."

She laughed and mopped up the spill with a lace napkin. "Don't worry, honey."

He picked up one of the dainty cucumber sandwiches from his plate and took a bite. His mouth twisted in displeasure, but he said nothing.

She watched him fondly. "It's an acquired taste."

"Well," he said, brushing crumbs from his hands, "I'll work on it."

Bella faced us and said, "Anyway, we have news."

"Did you get married?" I guessed.

"No, but that's on the agenda," Chip said, beaming at his fiancée. "This spring."

"How exciting," I said.

Bella clasped her hands together. "We found my parents. I mean, we found Althea and Camden."

"Online?" I asked, elated. "Did they change their names?"

She shook her head. "I'm sorry to say that they aren't alive. They were still in the Opera House."

"What?" Lex and I both said at the same time.

"Remember how you said something, Lila, about how the secret stairwell must have been added on later? That stuck with me for some reason. Plus, the floor was higher than in the dressing room, which didn't make any sense. We did some research and there was no permit pulled for the addition of a staircase."

"So I got my crew to dig up a little bit of

the floor," Chip interjected. "Experimentally."

"— and they found them. In two different layers of concrete. Their skeletons. I mean, we're having the tests done to confirm it, but who else could it be?"

"I'm so sorry," I said.

"Thank you. I am too. I had hoped against hope that they might be living on a beach somewhere, but at least we know."

"When did this happen?" Lex asked, frowning. "I didn't hear anything about it."

"This morning," Chip said. "Right before you got here, we received the call from my foreman. They probably called the police while you were driving over. I'm sure you'll be brought in soon."

Lex rearranged himself on the chair but, to his credit, did not immediately pull out his cell phone. I knew he'd be checking it the second we walked outside.

"For the record, I will never again claim Malcolm as my father," she said. "Would you?"

"I certainly wouldn't," Chip stated.

"It all fits together," Bella said. "Malcolm must have killed my mother sometime after I was born. Why would he do that unless she told him I wasn't his?"

"Residual anger about the affair?" Lex offered. "Revenge?"

Bella looked thoughtful. "Honestly, I think he murdered Camden the night he found them together in the dressing room. He built the secret room in order to hide the body. She probably thought Camden had gone to New York without her. Then after I was born, he murdered my mother and put her in there too, in a new layer of concrete." Her eyes welled up with tears. "I can't imagine how horrible everything was for her."

"I'm so sorry," I said, reaching across the table to squeeze her hand.

"Thank you," she murmured. "It's helped, though, that I've finally had a chance to read the journal. Clara would never let anyone touch it. She kept it in a locked glass case. But inside, there was page after page about how much my mother loved me even before I was born, and pages more afterwards describing our first months together. She never would have left me behind after all."

We smiled at each other.

"And, oh, I also read there that the jewelry had been handed down for generations in the Drake family. That's how Camden could afford them."

"Aha! Mystery solved," said Lex.

"I want to thank you again for finding the jewelry. And saving me from that stairwell," Bella said. "And leading me toward knowing what happened to my parents. Honestly, I owe you a nonstop stream of thank yous. Everything seems so inadequate."

I shook my head. "There's no need. I'm just glad you're okay."

She leapt up from the settee. "I really need to hug you both."

As she bestowed her hug, the scent of roses washed over me.

"What's that perfume? It's lovely."

"It's tea rose." Bella's face lit up. "My mother's signature scent. I read that in her journal."

"This is going to sound crazy," I said slowly, "but I swear I could smell roses in the dressing room the night Zandra confessed."

Bella's face grew solemn. "That doesn't sound crazy at all. I smelled it in the staircase when I awoke too."

"It was very strong. Came in like a wave," I said, remembering.

"Yes! I think my mother was there, trying to protect us."

"Um. Couldn't Zandra have been the one wearing it?" Lex raised an eyebrow. "She was in both places."

"No," Bella and I said simultaneously.

"Zandra's perfume was something altogether different," she said. "It was musky and dark and heavy. Nothing like tea rose."

"Exactly," I said. "Trust us on this, Lex."

He put both hands up, acquiescing.

Bella said, "I love that you were led to the room by a dream."

"Lila has a sixth sense," Lex said. "Or so she says."

"My mother is the one who says it runs in the family," I told Bella, ignoring Lex. I knew he had a difficult time accepting things that he couldn't explain.

Even though my dream *had* led us right to the jewelry.

Ahem.

I took another drink and set my cup down gently into the saucer. "How are Clara and Braxton?"

"They're fine. I mean, they're humiliated. They've retreated to their mountain home," Bella said. "And they apologized. Clara was the one behind all of the horrible behavior, but Braxton enabled her."

Beside me, I could feel Lex nodding.

"I knew Clara was worried about money. She'd never had to worry in her life, nor had Braxton. But they'd put so much money into trying to preserve the Opera

House over the past decade and, well, the coffers were getting low. Braxton wanted to sell the mountain house — in fact, they may be making arrangements to do that right now — but Clara wouldn't hear of it. It had been in her family for years. Both of them come from wealthy backgrounds but don't have any relatives who will help."

Chip gave her an encouraging smile.

"She was going to sell the diamonds if she found them. She thought she needed the money."

"That's what she told us the night they tried to knock down the wall," I said.

"But they're your mother's jewels," Chip said. "I can't believe she would try to steal them."

Bella sat up straighter. "You might not understand, but I *am* going to sell the jewelry and give some of the money to Clara and Braxton. They need my help."

I could tell she'd made up her mind.

"We'll have replicas of the jewelry made to display in the theater, but we need some of the money to move forward anyway, so the proceeds will also benefit the Opera House."

"Turns out the center diamond, the one shaped like an egg, is famous. It's worth millions." Chip winked.

"Congratulations," I said to Bella. "That's fantastic!"

"Thank you again for your help. I can hardly believe how much everything has changed." She looked down at her hands. "I just wish Clara and Braxton weren't feeling so horrible."

Chip started. "But they acted horribly, so . . ."

"Are you going to press charges?" Lex asked.

"For making a hole in the wall? No." Bella twisted the napkin as she spoke. "They took me in when I was a baby. I can forgive a desperate act."

"But —" Chip began.

"Please don't try to change my mind. I know Clara didn't seem overtly kind. And yes, she was very controlling. But she cared for me all of these years. And she watched out for me. In her way."

"In fact, we're going to find some way for them to be part of the Opera House operations after we've restored it," Chip said. "It's the least we can do. They really have fought for it for so many years."

I could hardly believe the way he was talking. He'd come in as a developer and had been transformed into a preserver. No one should ever underestimate Bella's powers of persuasion.

"But we want them to understand that it's better for the community to have a live, active site than something that's off-limits to practically everyone." Bella smiled. "We want it to be an inclusive place for all."

Chip regarded her fondly. "That's right. And tell them what the society did."

She blushed. "He means that I've been voted in as president of the Historical Society as well, so we'll be unified with them while we perform the work."

We congratulated her.

"What's the first thing you're going to do as president?" I bet the society was thrilled about her taking over.

"We'll go through the process to request that the Stonedale Opera House be added to the National Register of Historic Places."

"Clara didn't do that?"

"She said it gave too much power to the government," Bella said. "I don't think she understood what it meant. You know Clara. Once she makes her mind up, that's her reality."

"What's going to happen with Zandra?" Chip asked Lex. "I hope she is locked up without a key."

"She'll soon have her hands full with the trial. Our justice system in Stonedale moves quickly. Small town and all."

"I bet the papers will love following that story closely," Chip said. "She's larger than life. Oh, and Lila, I heard she told you that she was part of the entertainment complex plan. I just want you to know that she was one hundred percent delusional. I never made any kind of agreement with her whatsoever."

I nodded. "She thought you were going to feature her in a play. Does that sound like something she could have gotten from any conversation you had?"

He shook his head. "I mean, once we talked about roles for women of a certain age, but I certainly didn't promise her anything. I didn't even know what form the entertainment complex might take yet."

Bella tapped him on the shoulder. "And *were* you romantically involved?" She had a mischievous look in her eyes.

"I'm a one-woman man. You know that." He kissed her on the cheek.

"She was absolutely obsessed with him," Bella said to me. "When we were in the dressing room, she told me that he was her soulmate. And that I was insane if I thought he loved me instead of her."

"She's the one who was crazy," Chip pronounced, pulling Bella in for a hug.

"Sabotaging everything and attacking people."

"Did she admit to pushing Tolliver through the trap door?" I asked Lex.

"No," he said. "But who else could have done it?"

"The ghost of Malcolm?" Chip said. "He was a mean old dude."

"Why? To register his disapproval of the play?" I grinned at him.

Bella laughed. "Maybe. More likely, though, it was Zandra. What do you think, Lila?"

"She said she needed Tolliver out of the way so Chip could be her new director. But when I asked her point blank if she had pushed him, she claimed it was Malcolm."

"That's her story and she's sticking to it," Lex said. "But she took responsibility for just about everything else."

"Cutting the rope on the harness?" I asked. Poor Andrew.

"That one she did admit."

"Hey, do you think she was a real psychic or medium or whatever it was she claimed to be?" Bella asked.

I considered this. "Well, you did say it felt like you'd spoken to your mother . . ."

"That's true. And her crystal ball actually glowed," she said.

377

"Well, scratch that part as proof. The crystal ball glowed because of batteries," Lex said. "Programmable light. You can buy one yourself online."

"Zandra was a fake," Chip said. "That thumping sound below us at the séance was made by her own feet."

"I was sitting right next to her, though," I protested. "She didn't move. Not one inch. I'd have felt it if she did."

"Maybe she had already hypnotized you so you didn't feel it," Chip suggested.

"I don't think that's how it works, honey," Bella said.

"And she did move her leg somehow to drop the pistol on the floor," Lex said.

I twisted to face him. "Are you challenging my movement-detecting abilities?"

He shrugged. "Just saying."

"Zandra could have slid her leg down very slowly to allow the gun to fall, but you cannot make a thump without big movement. Thus, the loud noise remains unexplainable." I flashed him a triumphant look.

"So you're blaming ghosts for that?" He raised an eyebrow.

"I don't know, Lex. How do we explain all of the things that happened? Like the incredibly cold spots? Or the singing? Or the orbs?"

"And what about that gust of wind that came in and swirled all around us at the séance?" Bella was right. That didn't seem like something Zandra could have manufactured without using fans blasting from the wings. We would have seen and heard those.

"I was in the back of the auditorium, and I didn't see any wind," Lex said.

"Oh man, it was definitely there," Chip said. "I forgot about that. Like a storm just swept right through the room . . . and kind of through you at the same time. Super strange. But it's all good. Part of the experience, and we'll be able to advertise it, anyway."

"Wait, so you think it's haunted for real?" I asked, not knowing which way I wanted them to answer.

"Yes," said Bella.

"And we're not only going to keep it that way, we're going to celebrate it," Chip said. "My investors have agreed that preserving the historical site is worthwhile. We'll keep the original structure but reinforce everything, refinish the good parts inside, and bring in some state-of-the-art elements that will allow us to hold productions there — safely — for years to come. We've already convinced the mayor to reinstate the budget for the community theater."

"How?" I asked.

"He's going to be given a private box after the remodel. Plus, we told him Clara would be leaving him alone about the budget and so forth in the future. We'll make that a condition of our work agreement with her."

"That'll be worth its weight in gold," Lex muttered, winking at me.

Chip reached for another sandwich and stared down at it. "These cucumber things are better than I thought, by the way. I think I'm acquiring the taste."

"That was fast." Bella giggled.

"Hey, we can serve them at the theater for special events and call them Gaineswiches." He waved the sandwich in the air. "Or ghostwiches."

Bella beamed at him, then leaned forward to address us. "I'm going to open a museum area and a gift shop so that people can learn about the site's history and take home mementos. And we'll give tours."

"We will promote the Opera House outside of Stonedale as well," Chip said. "See if we can get some folks from New York to consider us a viable place for theater workshops."

"Wow," I said. "Very impressive plan. I wish you the best of luck with everything."

"We hope you'll do more than that," Bella

said, making eye contact with me. "We want to produce a play based on a mystery you've written."

I froze. "But I haven't written a mystery."

"Someday you will," she said confidently. "You're not the only one with a sixth sense, you know."

We were dangerously close to discussing a dream I'd never told anyone. I played it casual. "Well, I'd better get started writing a mystery then."

She smiled. "When you finish, please bring it to us."

"Don't worry," Lex said, taking my hand. "I'll remind her."

That sounded promising.

AUTHOR'S NOTE

Colorado has a number of beautiful opera houses still standing, and the idea for this book was sparked by a fascinating tour of the Tabor Opera House in Leadville. Soon afterwards, I was delighted to learn that the Tivoli Turnhalle, part of the student union on the campus where I teach, was originally an opera house as well.

The visits of Oscar Wilde, Harry Houdini, John Philip Sousa, P.T. Barnum, and others contributed to the rich history of places such as the Tabor and the Central City Opera House. For fictional purposes, I retrospectively "added" Stonedale Opera House as a stop on their tours.

ABOUT THE AUTHOR

Cynthia Kuhn writes the Lila Maclean Academic Mystery Series: *The Semester of Our Discontent,* an Agatha Award recipient (Best First Novel); *The Art of Vanishing,* a Lefty Award nominee (Best Humorous Mystery); and *The Spirit in Question.* She is professor of English at MSU Denver, president of Sisters in Crime-Colorado, and member of Mystery Writers of America, International Thriller Writers, and Rocky Mountain Fiction Writers. For more information, please visit cynthiakuhn.net.

The employees of Thorndike Press hope you have enjoyed this Large Print book. All our Thorndike, Wheeler, and Kennebec Large Print titles are designed for easy reading, and all our books are made to last. Other Thorndike Press Large Print books are available at your library, through selected bookstores, or directly from us.

For information about titles, please call:
    (800) 223-1244

or visit our website at:
    gale.com/thorndike

To share your comments, please write:
    Publisher
    Thorndike Press
    10 Water St., Suite 310
    Waterville, ME 04901